TIMELESS *Regency* COLLECTION

A *Seaside* Summer

TIMELESS *Regency* COLLECTION

A *Seaside* Summer

JOSI S. KILPACK
MARTHA KEYES
HEATHER B. MOORE

Mirror Press

Copyright © 2021 Mirror Press
Paperback edition
All rights reserved

No part of this book may be reproduced in any form whatsoever without prior written permission of the publisher, except in the case of brief passages embodied in critical reviews and articles. These novels are works of fiction. The characters, names, incidents, places, and dialog are products of the authors' imaginations and are not to be construed as real.

Interior Design by Cora Johnson
Edited by Joanne Lui, Meghan Hoesch, and Lisa Shepherd
Cover design by Rachael Anderson
Cover Photo Credit: Martha Keyes

Published by Mirror Press, LLC

A Seaside Summer is part of the Timeless Romance Anthology® brand which is a registered trademark of Mirror Press, LLC

ISBN: 978-1-952611-18-6

Timeless Regency Collections

Autumn Masquerade
A Midwinter Ball
Spring in Hyde Park
Summer House Party
A Country Christmas
A Season in London
Falling for a Duke
A Night in Grosvenor Square
Road to Gretna Green
Wedding Wagers
An Evening at Almack's
A Week in Brighton
To Love a Governess
Widows of Somerset
A Christmas Promise
A Seaside Summer
The Inns of Devonshire

Timeless Victorian Collections

Summer Holiday
A Grand Tour
The Orient Express
The Queen's Ball
A Note of Change
A Gentlewoman Scholar

The New Countess

Josi S. Kilpack

Chapter One

DIANE LIFTED HER FACE toward the summer sun, closed her eyes, and breathed in the warm, salty air of the ocean breeze. She held her breath while listening to the orchestra of sea birds, crashing waves, and laughing children.

This.

This was what had carried her through the uncomfortable fall, the cold winter, and busy spring of her new life as the Countess of Avery. This was the payoff of managing new households, attending every party on the earl's arm, and sitting across from the man who was still little more than a stranger to her.

This.

The sea. Open country. Freedom!

She pushed her bonnet from her head, letting it hang down her back. Now that London Society was not watching how she would perform her role as countess, it did not matter that her fair cheeks had become a bit browner or her brown hair had become a bit fairer. Three weeks in the country and she felt like Diane again.

"Mama!"

Diane blinked her eyes open, remembering in an instant that she was watching the children. She turned her head

The New Countess

quickly to count wind-blown heads—one, two, three—and exhaled the panic that came so easily to a mother. She put her hand on her rounded belly and fixed her eyes on Benjamin—the child who had called to her—and hurried in his direction while confirming that Alston and Tabby were a safe distance from the water. Some days they played in the surf or swam in a cove some distance farther down the beach—today they were simply exploring.

There were few things that did not excite nine-year-old Benjamin, and upon reaching him, she gathered her skirts up to her knees so that they would not drag in the sand and crouched beside the tide pool, oohing and aahing over the tiny crab he had found.

"It is trapped," he said, holding a stick but not poking at his discovery, though she was certain he was tempted. "Should I put it back in the sea?"

"No, it is safest right here until the tide comes in."

"Can I take it home?"

"No, my darling. It would not be happy in a people-house."

He frowned, puckering his eyebrows as he looked back at the crab he could not keep.

"Shall we show the others?" she asked, hoping that the thrill of sharing his discovery would overshadow his disappointment.

When Alston and Tabby joined them, Tabby stretched her arms toward Diane, who lifted the child onto her knee and held her around the waist while pointing to the crab. The little girl shrieked, part fear and part delight, as she pressed into Diane's shoulder.

Tabby's mother—the former Countess of Avery—had died when Tabby was born. Trying to make up for the little girl's loss had been the easiest part of the marriage for Diane. Tabby had proved as eager to be loved as Diane had been to love her. The boys had been excited to have a new sister, and Tabby had quickly fallen into place with them too.

Diane brushed Tabby's wild curls behind the girl's ear and thought of Tabby's father—Michael Richard Sterling, the Earl of Avery; Diane's *husband*.

She repeated the word in her mind: husband. Hus-band. Hub-sand.

Ten months had passed and it was not any easier to say it in her mind than it was for the boys to say Tabby's full name—Tabitha.

The boys began to argue over the stick Benjamin had put down, and Diane determined it was time to return to the holiday cottage they would call home for another six blessed weeks. She rose to her feet with Tabby still in her arms, tottering a moment as she shifted Tabby to one hip.

"Are you all right, Mama?" Benjamin asked as he took hold of her arm and looked up at her with his father's soft brown eyes. Jacob, her first husband, had been gone nearly three years now—he and the former countess had died within months of one another. Back then Diane had only known the Earl of Avery from a distance—they had never been introduced. Diane had met Margaret, the former Countess of Avery, a few times before she had married the earl. Margaret had been young, smart, and had a lovely laugh that made everyone smile.

Now Diane was married to Margaret's husband and raising Margaret's daughter.

"I am lucky to have you here to keep me steady," she said to Benjamin. Now balanced, she placed her free hand on her belly responsible for the unsteadiness and watched Benjamin run to catch up with Alston.

That she had delivered two healthy boys was part of what had attracted the earl's attention when he'd determined he needed a wife. That Diane's father and Jacob had had parliamentary connections, and she had proven an excellent hostess for both, had been another credit.

Tabby squirmed and Diane released her, watching her run after her new brothers on her short, three-year-old legs. Diane was nearly six months along now and would not be able to lift Tabby for much longer.

The seafaring group took their time on the path that led away from the beach, up to the cliffs, and through the woods, exclaiming over birds and leaves and things that scampered into the foliage ahead of them.

They came out of the woods behind the stables, and after giving each child a chance to pet the horses, Diane ushered them toward the house. She was getting tired—as was to be expected at this point in pregnancy—and would be glad to turn the children over to Nanny so she could lay down for an hour or so. She would enjoy a simple dinner with the children in the evening, then read by the light of the oil lamp for as long as she liked. In the morning, she would sleep late, enjoy breakfast in bed as had become her habit here, and perhaps visit the local vicar and his wife who had left a basket the day before—currant tarts and a fresh loaf of bread. Or maybe she would put off the visit a few days, or simply thank them at church on Sunday. She was the master of her schedule here, or lack of schedule, and took full advantage of that gift.

Once inside, the children scampered up the wooden staircase for the promised biscuits awaiting them in the nursery. Diane let out a satisfied breath as she undid the ribbons of her bonnet that still hung down her back.

She turned to hang the bonnet on one of the hooks beside the door and froze, bonnet extended, eyes fixed upon a man's hat hanging on a peg.

A man's hat that had not been there when she had left some hours earlier.

A man's hat she recognized but did not expect to see here.

Chapter Two

DIANE WAS STILL PROCESSING the possible implications of *this* hat being in *this* foyer when she heard footfalls behind her. She turned in time to see the earl come out of the parlor, a newspaper in his hands.

She kept her surprise and, dare she admit it, disappointment from showing on her face as she moved her eyes to the floor and sunk into a shallow curtsy.

"My lord," she said.

He bowed his head in return. "Lady Avery."

She returned to standing but did not look him in the eye for fear he would see more than she wanted him to see. "I had understood that you would be returning to Bentmore House once you had finished your affairs in London."

"I did return to Bentmore, but there was a small fire in the servants' quarters that prevented my staying. I hope you do not mind if I join you here until the repairs are complete."

"Certainly not," she said evenly, still looking at the floor between them. "Was anyone hurt in the fire?"

"No, thank goodness. The damage is nothing that cannot be fixed."

"That is good," Diane said, relieved.

"Yes," he said simply.

An awkward silence—like so many other awkward silences they had shared—stretched between them as they both seemed to wait for the other to speak.

Diane finally gave in. "H-How long shall you be in residence, my Lord?"

"A fortnight, I think. I had hoped my arrival would be a good surprise."

She looked up and met his dark blue eyes as she considered carefully what to say in response. In the life they had shared these last months, she had sat across from him at dinner, attended parties on his arm, and thrilled a little when he tapped on the door that connected their rooms. But she did not ask what he did with his time, solicit his opinion on her activities, or know anything about him that any other person of society did not already know. Except, perhaps, that his hands were gentle in the dark. She did not *dislike* this man who was her husband, but the consideration afforded him would change what she had been enjoying here in the cottage.

"It *is* a good surprise, is it not, Lady Avery?"

Diane brought out her London smile—the polite, perfectly acceptable smile that she'd thought she could store away all summer. "Of course, Lord Avery. Of course, it is a good surprise."

Chapter Three

"I APOLOGIZE FOR THE dinner, my lord," she said after they had eaten in silence for a few minutes—like so many other dinners they had shared at Bentmore House. In London they had gone out nearly every night, thus avoiding the awkward meals shared by just the two of them. At least they were awkward for Diane; the earl seemed quite comfortable with the formality. The children had eaten in the nursery without her, and she hated that she'd traded out their lively and comfortable company for the earl's companionship, which consisted of him talking about mutual friends and her saying "I see" and "How lovely" and "Isn't that interesting".

For most of the time she'd been in London—March through June—the children had stayed at Bentmore House in Reddich. She and the earl were so busy with the engagements of the Season and parliamentary session that it had not made sense to take the children away from their routines and the wide-open spaces of the country estate. Here in the cottage, Diane had enjoyed spoiling them with the time and attention she'd missed during those months in London. She hated losing even one night of their new routine, yet this would be the first of many now that the earl was here.

The New Countess

"It is fine, you did not know I was coming," he said, lifting another spoonful of mutton stew to his mouth.

"I hired a woman from the village to do the cooking and told her that we would be content with plain meals she could cook at her own home and bring here," Diane explained, wondering if the earl had ever eaten mutton stew in his life. He'd hired a chef from France several years ago, and every meal was an event at both Bentmore and the London house, as the chef came with them to Town. It was a wonder that the earl was still such a slender man for how much he enjoyed the cream sauces and pastries Phillipe was so proficient in preparing. "I shall, of course, speak with her about new menus now that you are here."

"That will be very good, thank you."

Any hope that he would agree to simplified meals went down her throat with the next bite of soda bread. Could the local woman she'd hired make such fine meals the earl was used to? Certainly she would not be able to compete with Phillipe's skill, but could she even do a four-course meal? Was there a different alternative? The kitchen here was small, with a tiny cooking stove and open hearth.

"If I had known that you were coming," Diane continued, unable to keep from defending herself and perhaps making a subtle comment about his unexpected arrival, "I would have planned differently."

"It is fine, Lady Avery, do not worry yourself." He waved a hand through the air, which Diane interpreted as his belief the changes she had to make were simple ones. "Such is the risk of surprising one's family, right?"

She looked at him to try and determine if he were making a joke, her spoon hovering above her bowl. He had nice eyes—dark blue—set into an oval face. His nose was a bit large but not so much as to be ill-suited. His dark hair had the slightest hint of gray at the temples, though he was only thirty-five years old—only a few years older than herself. That he was an attractive man was tempered by the knowledge that she'd have accepted his proposal even if he were old, portly, and had hair growing out of his ears.

Jacob had not left her well cared for, and she'd needed security and purpose when the earl had come calling. There had never been any question as to whether or not she would accept his offer of marriage.

"Yes, I suppose that is a risk," she confirmed in an even tone. "If I had known, I'd have made sure to accommodate you in a manner you are used to."

He laughed and it made her back stiffen, though he did not seem to notice. "That would be quite impossible here in Southwood," he said, waving his hand about the roughly plastered walls and split wood doorframes. He was right, of course. It was impossible for a simple holiday cottage to accommodate the elegant meals and three dozen servants of Bentmore House with its eighteen bedrooms, four parlors, ballroom, and full floor of servants' quarters.

His derision, however, triggered her defenses. She had loved this cottage from the first moment she'd heard word of it from his mother. When Diane had stepped inside it nearly a month ago, she'd been completely seduced. Small, but cozy; simple, but perfect. Not that she did not enjoy the grandeur of the Bentmore estate or the London house, but she loved this too for all that it was and all that it was not.

"I am sure you could return to London. The staff would keep the house open for you, and they are well-versed in how to accommodate your preferences."

"I considered that," he said, as he broke off a piece of the bread. "But, if I am honest, I have had my fill of London. Fresh air and time with my family sounded rather nice."

She looked up at his starched collar, lace cuffs, and perfectly tied cravat. Though not a dandy, Lord Avery cut a fine figure in London—he had even been featured among the best dressed of parliament in one of the gossip rags. He looked as out of place in this room as Benjamin's crab would have been. In the months since their marriage, he'd stayed very busy with estate management, parliamentary duties, and shoring up his connections. What would he do here in Southwood for two weeks? She did not imagine for a moment that he would enjoy long walks to the seashore or looking for bugs with the children.

Diane turned back to her meal, which continued in silence. When she finished eating, she stood, and he followed suit—always a man of the finest manners.

"I shall see you in the parlor, then, Lady Avery?"

She clenched her teeth together, giving up on the plan to tuck the children in with a story or two, then read her current novel of choice until her eyes began to close of their own volition. Everything would be different now, and it was difficult not to feel irritated. But it was not helpful to be irritated. She was Countess Avery, wife to an earl, and therefore responsible for his comfort and happiness. He had essentially said as much when he'd proposed marriage one year ago. *"I have the means to care for you and your children in a manner of comfort and security. Your connections in London, hostess experience, and ability to produce fine, healthy children makes our marriage ideal for me as well."*

Hardly the stuff of romance, but then again Diane had been a wife before and already knew that romance was far more fantasy than reality. They were partners—she had her duties and he had his.

Two weeks, she told herself as her London smile came into place once more. She could do anything for two weeks.

"Of course, my lord. Let me check on the children, and then I shall join you."

Chapter Four

DIANE AWAKENED THE NEXT morning to the sound of the earl whistling. It was a habit of his she had accepted long before now, but in London she arose at the same time he did most days, and in Bentmore House the stone walls between their large bedroom suites prevented her from being able to hear it much at all. In the tiny cottage, there was no avoiding it.

She rolled onto her side and put a pillow over her ears, then rolled to her other side, easily tracking his movements out of the room and down the creaking stairs. He was likely going for his morning ride, a habit he kept when they were in Bentmore and missed in London. She closed her eyes, thinking she could sleep again, only to realize she could hear the low timbre of his voice as he spoke to Mrs. Steadman in the breakfast room beneath her. Were the walls and floors made of paper?

By the time the house returned to silence, she was fully awake and decided to get ready for the day, choosing one of her nicer dresses instead of the simple, wide-cut ones she found more comfortable. She also took extra time on her hair to better look the part of a countess. She'd been wearing her hair down most days at the cottage.

She'd given her lady's maid leave to visit family in south

The New Countess

Sussex for the duration of her stay in Southwood, liking the idea of caring for herself all by herself. Should Diane fetch her back, or would it be more efficient to hire someone from the village to assist her for the duration of the earl's visit? She would need to ask Mrs. Steadman her thoughts on the matter. And about the cook, and a dozen other details the earl's arrival had changed.

Since she had not been able to share dinner with the children, Diane joined them for breakfast—sausages and toast—at the short table set up in the nursery. They had shared dinner together in the dining room each evening until last night but took their other meals here.

They talked over what to do with their day, as was their custom every morning, and decided to walk into town for pastries they would take with them to the cliffs. They were on their way down the stairs when the front door opened, and the earl came inside. Diane had *almost* forgotten he was here.

"Papa!" Tabby said as she hurried down the stairs and jumped toward him from the third step. Diane's heart skipped a beat when she thought he might not catch her, but he snatched her out of the air and spun her in a circle before placing her back on the floor. Diane had never seen him show such quick reflexes. The boys maintained their rather stiff postures, which they always adopted in the earl's company, as they finished descending to the main level, one on either side of her.

"Good morning, Benjamin. Good morning, Alston," the earl said as he tried to pry Tabby's grip from his legs where she had attached herself. It seemed the seaside had untaught her all manners of conduct, but then she was only three years old.

"Good morning, Lord Avery," the boys said in such perfect unison that Diane wondered if Nanny had been making them practice.

The earl nodded at them both. "I wondered if either of you would like to do some riding today?"

Benjamin's eyes went wide, and he looked at Diane. "Could we, Mama?"

Alston looked equally excited at the idea but said nothing.

"There are no riding horses fit for boys their size," Diane said. "Only the carriage horses and they are much too big for them."

"I asked Mrs. Steadman if there might be some we could hire, and a farmer brought them over just now as I was finishing my ride." He pointed a thumb over his shoulder, which was not in the direction of the stables. "One is an older mare, and the other a gelding the farmer used for all his children when they were learning to ride. Tabby shall mostly watch for this lesson."

It was not yet ten o'clock, and he had already hired out for horses?

"I want to wide howses," Tabby whined, her face between the earl's knees.

Diane stepped forward and successfully untwined Tabby from the earl's legs. She held the child's hand tightly and stepped back while the earl straightened his waistcoat and nodded his thanks.

"I am afraid the boys do not have much experience riding." Besides, they were going to get pastries from town and have a picnic at the cliffs.

"I believe that riding is the only remedy for that," the earl said.

His face stayed completely stoic for a few seconds, until one side of his mouth twitched. Was he being humorous? She could not read him at all. She looked at her boys again, both wide-eyed with anticipation, and accepted that she would not be taking the children to town. The earl had made the decision and the arrangements. It was her role to support him.

She smiled tightly. "They would enjoy the lesson very much. I shall help Nanny find them appropriate clothes."

While the boys got their first riding lesson, Diane met with Mrs. Steadman, changing the overall running of the household. The earl's valet had taken the maid's room, which had been empty because Mrs. Steadman had been able to look after Diane and the children fine on her own. Until now. Mrs. Steadman would now find a maid to come in and help with the household chores during the day and act as Diane's lady's maid when needed—Mrs. Steadman would primarily manage the staff and the household. First thing on Diane's list was working out the menus with the cook and finding a full set of dishes—the cottage set was incomplete—and stocking the wine cellar with the earl's favorite vintages. The meeting took all morning.

The children had luncheon in the nursery when the riding lesson came to an end. Diane and the earl ate cold ham and crisp cucumbers from opposite sides of the table. She asked how the riding lesson had gone. He talked about Alston being particularly attentive and how Benjamin had tried to get his horse to run without success—proof that the earl had hired the right mounts.

"Did they never ride when you were living with your brother?" the earl asked. "They have no experience with horses at all."

Diane's thoughts only darkened further to go back in time to the damp cottage on her brother's estate she'd moved into after Jacob's death. It had been small and remote, a full four miles from the village. On Sundays they went to the main house to enjoy dinner with her brother and his family, but other than that they were alone all the time. It had been a horrible time, and it was good for Diane to remember how improved all their lives had become because of the earl.

"No, my lord," she said simply, buttering a slice of bread and mourning that, beginning tomorrow, even lunch would be a full meal. She would miss the simplicity, as would her stomach, which did not do so well with rich and hearty foods when she was pregnant.

"That is unfortunate," the earl said. "It is such beautiful country there."

"Yes, my lord."

She stopped shaking her knee in agitation when she realized it was shaking the table, then asked after his mother, who had been at the London house when she and the children had departed. Diane had liked his mother from the start, especially in regard to the way the woman doted on the boys. Diane's own parents were gone, and she loved that the boys had a grandmother to spoil them.

The earl updated her on his mother's plans for the summer—a month in Newport and then a stay with a cousin in Bath where she would take the waters in hopes of preparing her constitution for winter. She would return to Bentmore in time for Diane's confinement. It was understood that the baby would be born at the family estate, as was tradition. If it were a boy, the entire estate would be his one day, and every earl since the first had been born at Bentmore House. If Diane had her way, she'd stay in the cottage and deliver here. It would be lovely to use the local midwife—who she'd met upon her arrival here—and enjoy getting to know this new child away from the duties of being Countess Avery. But, as with most things, she deferred to the earl and his expectations.

Once they finished their meal, Diane headed to the nursery in hopes of rallying the children for an afternoon excursion to the beach only to find Tabby napping and the boys playing with the horse figurines Nanny had found for them upon arrival, which they had not been the least bit attentive to before now.

"Can we take the horses to the garden?" Benjamin asked after several minutes.

"Do you mean the real horses or the play horses?" she asked.

The boys thought this a grand joke and had a good laugh until reassuring her they meant the play horses. Since Nanny needed to stay close for Tabby, Diane fetched her novel from her room and accompanied the boys to the garden, hoping they would tire of the game that consisted of galloping their toys over every rock and bench and bush. Instead, they found sticks to build stables and pulled up grass to serve as hay. It was rather adorable even though Diane would have preferred an excursion.

Diane fell asleep reading in one of the garden chairs and awoke with a crick in her neck just in time to change for dinner, though she had not brought any dresses truly suitable for evening. The earl would expect her to do her best, however. If she sent a request to Bentmore to have a trunk shipped to her, would it arrive in enough time to do any good?

The evening played out just as the first had, save that the meal was three courses and included lemon cake. Once in the parlor, Diane made progress on the stitching she did not care for one bit while the earl read up on William the Conqueror. She had not spent a single evening stitching since her arrival. Now it seemed she would finish this cushion and be able to start on a new one while Nanny readied the children for bed, told them stories, and kissed their sweet foreheads goodnight.

The next morning, Diane screamed into her pillow when the earl started up his whistling before the sun had begun to rise. Once again, she could not sleep even after he'd left for his morning ride, and so she got up early and spent more time than she wanted to on her toilet. The only comfort she took amid her frustration was that surely the children would want to go to the beach today after having missed it yesterday.

The earl was waiting for them in the foyer when they came down the stairs again and offered riding lessons, which the boys were even more excited to do now that they felt like experts. The boys were much more comfortable with the earl today compared to yesterday, which should've pleased her. *He is their father now,* she told herself, and yet she couldn't stop feeling as though something had been taken away from her when they ran through the door like two shots from a gun. The earl smiled at her as Tabby ran after them. Diane stood where she was, her pasted smile tacked up at both corners of her mouth. When the door shut behind him, she let the smile fall and glared at the door.

"Ma'am?"

Diane turned to Mrs. Steadman, who held out two letters. "These came this morning."

The letters were addressed to Lord and Lady Avery. She took them into the parlor and sighed when she opened and read the notes—dinner invitations. One for Thursday evening and another for the following Wednesday. Diane leaned back in her chair and closed her eyes. She'd had a few morning visits from local gentlewomen since her arrival and dinner at the vicarage once but had enjoyed the overall lack of social engagements. Now that a Peer of the Realm was in residence, that would change. She allowed herself two minutes to whine and complain in her mind, then she straightened her spine and set about her duties to respond to the invitations—*of course, they we would love to attend, thank you so much.*

Chapter Five

THE EARL WAS DELIGHTED to hear of the invitations.

"Lord Mannington and I were in school together, you know," he explained as he cut into his pigeon. There had been a creamy soup and a plate of fish with lemon butter before this course, and there would be pudding when they finished, thanks to the new menus Diane had reviewed with Mrs. Steadman this morning. It was fortunate that the cook she'd hired had a wide repertoire and the time to accommodate the change. "Have you met Lady Mannington?"

"She visited me the first week I was here."

"I understand she is exceptionally intellectual; did you sense that?"

"She did speak of a science journal she had read," Diane commented. "I did not find her too much of a scholar, however."

"Perhaps she managed it so as not to make you uncomfortable."

What did he mean by that?

"We should host a dinner party while I am in Southwood."

Diane snapped her chin up to look at him. "Here?"

"It has been some time since I have been here, not since before . . ." His voice trailed off, and she knew that he was about to say before the death of Margaret. Or perhaps it was before he'd even met Margaret. They had been married just over a year.

The earl cleared his throat. "I believe there are eight families, though I do not think we could fit them all. Perhaps four at a time."

Diane swallowed. "Two dinner parties, then, to accommodate all eight families."

The earl considered that, then nodded. "Yes, two dinner parties should do it. It will be an excellent opportunity for you to meet some of the other gentry. I am surprised you have not been out and about more in the time you've been here."

"Certainly," she said, taking one more bite though she could not taste it. Two dinner parties! He filled the rest of the meal with descriptions of the families he knew. Diane paid careful attention since it would be her responsibility to retain the information in order to create the right evening and seating arrangement for each guest.

She spent the time in the parlor that night writing out lists and menus while the earl continued his reading. More than once she was tempted to throw her pencil at him, but she did not give in.

"Diane?"

She looked up from the writing desk to see the earl looking at her. She had to consciously relax her grip on the pencil as she lifted her eyebrows in an expression of accommodation.

"I asked how you are feeling," he said.

Had he?

For an instant she thought he was asking after her mood, then realized he likely meant the pregnancy. She was much rounder than she'd been when she'd left London last month. Once at the cottage, she'd gladly traded the pinching gowns that hid her condition better for the soft, comfortable ones she'd worn during her prior pregnancies that left no questions in the mind of anyone who saw her. "I feel very well," she assured him.

"No, um, discomfort or difficulty?"

Of course, there was discomfort and difficulty, but it would be inappropriate for her to discuss such things. "No, my lord."

"You seem to be handling the pregnancy very . . . capably."

"Yes, my lord, I have done this before."

He smiled as though she'd made a joke—had she made a joke? "I take great comfort in your confidence that all is well."

She felt her tension soften, remembering that Margaret had not survived Tabitha's birth. Diane had heard from the staff that after Margaret's death, the earl had not left Bentmore for six full months—Tabby had been born early. "All is well, my lord, I assure you."

"And if it weren't, you would tell me, wouldn't you? You would ask for a doctor."

"I would ask for a midwife, my lord, not a doctor. I met the local midwife upon my arrival so that if I needed anything, she would already know me. She professed me healthy in every way. The baby too. If anything felt out of place, I would be certain to address it, I assure you."

She watched him visibly relax and had an entirely new thought come to mind. "Is that why you came, my lord? To ensure that I was well?"

He looked away but she saw his cheeks pink the slightest amount, which seemed to confirm her suspicions. "It was one reason," he said.

She did not see the vulnerable side of the earl very often. "I hope that you are convinced that I am hale and healthy and happy. You have no need to worry."

His eyes found hers again. "You are happy?"

His attention was uncomfortable, but she could not precisely say why. "Yes, my lord, I love it here at the seaside. My grandfather lived near Brighton, and each summer when I was young, my family would travel there. It is the place of my happiest memories, and creating those memories with my own children is a great joy to me."

"I am glad to hear it," he said, nodding and looking toward the fireplace. "We came here a few times when I was young but did not stay very long. Most of my childhood memories are of the nursery in Bentmore House and the procession of nannies hired to raise me up." He cleared his throat, perhaps to rid his tone of the regret she'd heard there. "I am very glad that you genuinely enjoy the children so much. It is a gift I hope each of them never take for granted."

"As they are children, I am sure they will take it for granted," Diane said with gentle teasing, "but one day, when they are grown, they will better understand it and hopefully enjoy their children in much the same way. I am very grateful to provide such a life for my—our—children, which I would not have been able to do without your generosity."

He looked back at his book, seemingly uncomfortable with her praise. "Yes, well, it seems to be working out well for all parties, then."

She was disappointed to feel the softness leave the room. Still, she held tight to the exchange. It had been a step . . . though toward what she did not know.

Chapter Six

THE EARL DECIDED TO call on Lord Mannington the next day, and Diane hurried to usher the children out of the house before he returned so as not to have her plans waylaid with riding lessons. The children wanted to swim today, and Diane was so excited to go to the beach that she did not pose a single argument. They went to the part of the beach where an inlet created a pool only a few feet deep, and the children stripped to their underthings while Diane removed her outer dress, careful to lay all the clothing in the sun so it would be warmed and ready for them when they finished. Then, in her knee-length shift, she joined the children in the water and picked up where they had left off from the last lesson—putting their heads all the way under the water. She'd been taught to swim in much the same way in Brighton and felt the tension melt away in the summer sun as they laughed and played. When Diane knew the children would be hungry soon, she ushered them out of the water, and they all laid upon the large quilt she'd brought for just this reason—to let the sun dry them before they put their clothes back on and headed back to the cottage for lunch.

This, Diane thought, hands on her belly as her child also settled down within her. Tabby lay beside her, and Benjamin and Alston were laying on their stomachs, drawing in the wet sand past the edge of the quilt with rocks. It was very difficult for them to be still for long, but they were trying and she was grateful. The thin linen of her shift would dry quickly, but she was in no hurry. This was exactly the medicine she'd needed.

Sun.

Sand.

Her children.

The lapping of waves upon the shore.

Her muscles relaxed.

Her breathing slowed.

This.

Exactly this.

"There you are!"

Diane sat up so quickly that she felt dizzy as the sun blinded her and the sleepy summer afternoon snapped away.

"I have been looking for you—oh."

Diane was on her feet now, facing the earl who stood several paces away. Tabby scampered off the blanket to run to her father, but the earl's eyes were fixed on Diane, her bare feet and legs to her knees and her thin linen shift still damp, which meant it clung to her overly curvaceous body. She crossed her arms over her chest as her cheeks heated to have such direct attention. He had not knocked on her door since she'd announced her pregnancy, had not seen the changes it had made to her body. She hurried toward her dress—a simple frock that she quickly slipped over her head and tied into place at both sides, keeping her back to him as she dressed herself.

Tabby was babbling in the background while Diane put herself back together and ran her fingers through her hair, chiding herself for not having considered this possibility. Ladies did not swim, nor strip to their shifts, nor lay in the sun like a beached whale.

"Benjamin! Alston!" she called as she turned, too embarrassed to apologize—she could not stomach drawing any attention to what had happened. "Time to go, come here and dress."

They whined but obeyed and soon enough the party—though they looked like a gaggle of hoodlums—was rounded up. The earl had been quiet as she marshalled the children, holding Tabby against his shoulder where she looked very sleepy as they began the walk back to the house.

"So, um, how was your visit with Lord Mannington?" she asked, running her hands through her hair again, hoping it was not too terribly knotted.

"Very good, thank you."

They walked a few more steps in silence. "You were swimming."

"Yes, my lord." She braced herself for a reprimand—even a gentle one.

"Have you gone swimming before today?"

"A few times. It is a very remote cove, I have never seen anyone else in the vicinity. I assure you it is quite private."

"I found you easily enough."

Diane said nothing but crossed swimming off her list of appropriate activities she could participate in while the earl was here. She felt very foolish for having done it at all. If she had considered that he would come looking for them, she would not have.

The boys found something of interest along the path, and the earl increased his strides in order to catch up while Diane shortened hers. She was still embarrassed but also annoyed. She had swam every summer as a girl and wanted her children to have the same opportunity, even if it was not seen as generally acceptable amid the noble classes. It was fun; did that not count for anything?

Because her shift had not been completely dry when she put on her dress, her dress was now taking on the dampness, causing it to bunch and stick in uncomfortable places. She tried to walk as normally as possible and hide the fact that she was adjusting her clothing with almost every step.

Mrs. Steadman always had a bath prepared so that she and the children could wash the seawater away when they returned from the beach. Upon entering the cottage, the housekeeper ushered the children toward the kitchen where the washtub was set up.

"Lady Avery," the earl said from the foyer as she began to follow after them.

Diane smiled at Nanny, allowing her to finish the herding, and turned to face her husband, chin lifted.

"Are you sure that swimming is wise given your present, um, condition?"

Diane took a breath to keep from showing her annoyance; she did not want contention. "I shall avoid it in the future, my lord."

"I am not telling you what to do and what not to do. I just . . . I know that things can be delicate, with the pregnancy, and I am simply concerned. For you, of course, and for the child."

Mixed emotions moved through Diane's chest. She remembered the softness of his questions about her condition the other night. At the same time, she had assured him she was fine and she was. She did not want to be managed by his fear, but neither did she want to discount his concerns. "A healthy woman with a healthy child is not as delicate as you might think, my lord. It is good for me to walk, be out of doors, and active; it is part of why I came here. I do not take chances with any of my children." She put both of her hands on her belly to emphasize how protective she was of their baby not yet born.

"I only think, I mean, there is risk in being in the water and managing the children on your own. If something happened..."

"As I told you the other night, I have done this before. Both of my pregnancies with my sons were just like this one. I do not get ill, I do not have difficulties carrying or delivering the babies. I know my body and I know my limits."

"Did you swim while supervising three children when you were pregnant with the boys?"

She clenched her jaw and looked at the floor, giving up the argument. "No, my lord."

He was silent. "I do not wish to be a dictator, Lady Avery. I am only concerned for the welfare of my family."

"I understand," she said, though her teeth were clenched tightly.

"Thank you," he said, shifting awkwardly on his feet. "And, um, did you remember that we have dinner with Mr. and Mrs. Cuthright tonight? We are to be there at six o'clock."

Diane took another steadying breath. In fact, she had forgotten. "I shall be ready, my lord."

"Thank you, Lady Avery."

They continued standing in the foyer, facing one another but saying nothing.

"Will that be all, my lord?" She finally looked up at him but was unable to give even a fake smile.

He held her eyes, looking uncomfortable—as he should. "Yes, Lady Avery, that is all."

Chapter Seven

DINNER AT THE CUTHRIGHTS went well, and Diane smiled all the right smiles and said all the right words as she was introduced to the gentry of Southwood. Her worst fears were realized when a few of the guests said they would be sending invitations to have Lord and Lady Avery to dinner while the earl was in town.

The next day, Diane received the expected morning visits while the earl took the children riding. Again. When the visits were finished, she conferred with Mrs. Steadman, responded to new invitations, and finalized the plans for the dinner parties she would be hosting. She interviewed the maid Mrs. Steadman had hired and approved more elaborate menus.

The next day played out similarly, though she spent time with Tabby in the nursery and napped in the afternoon before getting ready for yet another dinner, which led to more visits the next day and additional invitations. She had socialized and played her part as Countess yet had barely seen her children over the course of the last few days. The only solace she could find was that in another week, the earl would be gone and she would have a few weeks to be alone with the children again.

At dinner that night the earl announced that he would like to take the boys fishing the next day.

"Fishing?" Diane asked, setting down her knife and fork. "They have never gone fishing."

"Then I should say it's about time," he said with a smile.

Was he insulting her? Pointing out that they were missing some of the coming-of-age activities of boyhood, like knowing how to ride?

"Their father died when they were very young; Alston was barely older than Tabby is now. There was little opportunity for them to learn to fish."

He looked up at her, his smile fading quickly. "I was not trying to be rude. Forgive me if I was."

She looked at her plate—filled with beef Wellington and burgundy potatoes, thanks to her resetting of the menus—and took a breath in order to keep from letting all her frustrations spill out. She picked up her fork and knife in order to cut a bite of potato.

"I am sure they would love to go fishing," she said in an even tone as she cut another bite.

The next morning, Diane woke up to the sounds of the earl whistling even earlier than usual—outside her curtains, the sky was barely gray. She put a pillow over her ears and squeezed her eyes shut, but she could not fall back asleep. She heard the children in the hall, and Mrs. Steadman fussing over them in the foyer below. Half a dozen times she considered going out to see the children off; each time she talked herself out of it, not wanting the earl to see her undone and in her night dress.

She waited until the house was quiet for half an hour before ringing for her breakfast tray, then lingered over her meal as long as possible before getting out of bed and readying herself for the day.

It was eleven o'clock when she finished the meeting with Mrs. Steadman, and the party had still not returned—how long did it take to catch a fish? If morning were best for fishing, why weren't they back already? She had hoped they could still go to the beach, but she only had a few hours to make that happen.

She tried to read while she waited but could not concentrate, so she headed to the nursery where she expected to find Tabby. Except Tabby was not there. Nanny explained she'd gone fishing with the others.

"He took all three children?" Diane asked, feeling alarmed. The man had no experience managing so many children by himself; they would be near water! She hadn't expected for a moment that the earl would take a three-year-old girl fishing.

"Surely he took a groom with him."

Nanny shrugged—of course, she would not know.

"Do you know where they went?" Diane asked, panic rising as she imagined Benjamin getting a hook in his finger while Tabby waded into the water unattended, the earl trying not to get his coat dirty.

"Brown's Pond, I think."

Diane thanked her—Brown's Pond was located nearer to town, and Diane had taken the children there a few times to look for frogs and throw rocks in the water, which was so still compared to the crashing waves of the sea they encountered at the beach.

Diane changed into her walking shoes, grabbed her bonnet off the hook, and hurried toward the fishing expedition. A quick check with the stables confirmed that the earl had not taken a groomsman to help. She took the trail into the woods, expecting to encounter the pond around every turn on the path that went on and on and on—had it always been this far or was her anxiety making it seem farther? When she noticed how hard she was breathing, she slowed her pace but felt no reduction of worry.

Ten minutes later she stopped when she heard the sound of voices. Children's voices. She took another step and heard the lower rumble of another voice—the earl?

She moved forward quietly, then stopped when Benjamin's unmistakable laugh rang through the trees. She began walking again in the direction of the voices, then caught a flash of blue through the trees along the side of the path. Slowly and quietly, she stepped forward and peered through the trees into a small clearing where she saw Benjamin and Alston laying on their backs in a patch of sunlight. She looked to one side and found the earl . . . laying on his stomach in the grass, propped up on his elbows, with Tabby sitting astride his back and dropping torn grass into his hair. Tabby's blue dress accounted for the flash of color that had caught Diane's eye.

The earl had taken off his coat and waistcoat, and the boys had their shoes and stockings off like regular hoodlums—what if they got thorns in their feet?

Tabby looked a complete disaster, with a muddy hem and hair a wild compilation of curls. But they were all smiling. The earl laughed at something Alston said, which made Tabby bounce upon his back. Tabby shrieked with delight and the boys laughed. Benjamin threw a rock at a tree and the group cheered when he hit it, startling Diane so much she stumbled backward onto the path. She hurried back the way she had come until pausing to once again catch her breath and review the circumstances. Why was she running away from them? Why had she not announced herself?

The reason was easy enough to admit to herself, even if it was unattractive—she'd left because the earl was at such leisure, the children were so content and she . . . she hadn't felt as though she belonged. The realization hollowed out her chest.

Of course, she belonged. She was the children's mother, she was the earl's wife—the new countess—but frankly she had not expected to see such camaraderie between them. He'd given the boys very little attention until the last week, and suddenly they were thick as thieves and she was at odds with herself.

What should I do? she asked herself, putting a hand on a tree and taking deep breaths to fully steady herself. She hated feeling this insecure; it was not something she encountered often. For a few minutes she vacillated between returning to the house or reapproaching the group as though she had just come. *Join them*, she told herself. She could not overcome her feelings of not having been invited, however.

She had decided to return to the house when she heard voices coming toward her. Diane quickly amended her plan—again—and began walking toward them so that it would seem as though she had just arrived. Benjamin was walking ahead of the group and when he saw her, his face lit up and he ran ahead of the others. His excitement to see her was a balm for her rising insecurities, and she was able to smile a real smile. All the shoes and stockings had been replaced, and the earl had put on his waistcoat and coat, though his cravat was gone and the neck of his shirt lay open. She looked away from the dark hair she had only ever seen in the moonlight and hoped he would not see the flush of her cheeks.

"I caught two fish!" Benjamin declared when he reached her.

"You did?" she asked, ruffling his hair. She looked past him to where the earl held a basket in one hand—the fish must be in there.

Benjamin nodded vigorously and held up his hand, the

thumb wrapped in a strip of linen that looked like a piece of the earl's missing cravat. "And stuck the hook in my thumb!"

She gasped, thinking back to her fear of that very thing happening.

"Tabby fell in the water!" Alston said, coming up to her from behind his brother and throwing his arms around Diane's legs.

"She did?" Diane's heart was in her throat as she gave Alston a reciprocating embrace. She looked past her sons to the earl, who held Tabby on his hip. They were close enough for Diane to now see that the little girl's dress was wet. She'd predicted that too! She unwound Alston's arms from her legs and hurried to take Tabby from the earl's arms. "Are you all right, little one?"

"I fe-wl." Tabby reached her chubby arms around Diane's neck.

"I can see that," Diane said, fussing over her hair and dress as she repositioned her—she really was too big for Diane to carry. "Are you hurt?"

"I cwy."

Diane frowned, then pulled her close again. "I'm sure you did, you poor thing." She caught the earl's eye. He was grinning until he saw that Diane was not. She turned back toward her sons, still cradling Tabby in her arms. He had reprimanded her for taking the children swimming, without injury, but grinned over this chaotic fishing trip? The hypocrisy burned like hot sand beneath her feet.

"Let me see your thumb," she said to Benjamin. He was happy to take off the linen wrapping and show her not one but two puncture marks.

"Oh my goodness!" she exclaimed. "It went all the way through?"

Benjamin nodded proudly. "And it bleeded all over!"

"Bled," she corrected. "Does it hurt?"

"Nah," he said, sounding beyond his nine years as he lifted his chin. "It was just a fishhook. Every fisherman will get a hook in his thumb at some point—that's what Papa said."

Papa! she thought. They are calling him Papa now? He was "my lord" a few days ago.

"Benjamin cried," Alston said, nodding. "I am the only one who did not cry."

"You did not get a hook in your thumb because you would not touch the fish!" Benjamin accused.

Alston's cheeks turned red.

Diane smiled at her sons, looking between them both. "Now, now, let's not argue. Come back to the house and we'll get everyone all fixed up." She took hold of Alston's hand and turned her back on the earl.

Tabby wanted to be put down, so Diane released her but kept hold of the girl's hand for the rest of the way home, the earl walking behind. Once there, they entered through the kitchen, and soon Mrs. Steadman and Nanny were clucking over the ducklings and plying them with salves and fresh biscuits. By the time Diane had thought of the earl again, he had disappeared. *Good riddance*! She wiped at a spot of mud on her dress, and gave in to the fact that she would need to change into a clean one. She kissed each little summer-and-sunshine-smelling head before excusing herself.

When she pushed through the door that separated the kitchen from the rest of the house, the earl straightened from where he'd been leaning against the wall. Waiting. She felt the muscles in her body tighten.

"The children are all right, Lady Avery," he said, just enough of a chiding tone to spike her anger a degree higher. She clenched her teeth together to keep from saying anything that was not her place to say as she passed him in the narrow hall. She passed by him so close that she could smell the summer and sunshine on him as well. Her awareness amplified her annoyance.

"They are fine," he said defensively, turning to follow behind her.

She kept walking, reminding herself of their arrangement. He was the earl, she was his new countess. She did not have the space to share contrary opinions or question his judgement.

"They had a good time," he said, following behind her. "We all did, and I do not appreciate your accusing looks and pointed annoyance."

She reached the stairs, and he took hold of her arm. She spun around quickly, wrenching her arm from his grasp so quickly that he pulled back in surprise, his eyes wide. "How dare you defend yourself to me!" she hissed through her teeth. "You were not being attentive!"

The words escaped her lips before she could think better of them, her anger increasing with each word. She could feel the heat rising into her chest, neck, and face.

They stared at one another for several seconds, her heart pounding like a fist on a door inside her chest. Had she truly accused him? Had she actually said those words out loud? Plenty of other words began building up behind her teeth, which she had clenched shut again.

"Fishing is not a parlor game, Lady Avery," the earl said, surprising her as she expected he would back away from the fight. "It is in the outdoors. There is mud and hooks. Getting wet is more common than not, and though the hooked thumb was unfortunate, I can promise he will respect hooks a great deal from now on."

They will not be fishing with you ever again! she screamed in her mind, though she said nothing he could hear. He continued to stare at her, his eyebrows furrowed.

She took a deep breath, using all her energy to pull in her composure, and turned to head back up the stairs. She could not risk staying in his proximity and losing her temper again. Already the embarrassment and regret was replacing the anger.

He followed her.

"We all had a grand time together, the hooked thumb and Tabby's tumble into *very* shallow water, notwithstanding."

She thought back to the scene she had seen through the trees. They *had* been having a grand time. Was that part of what bothered her? That they had been having a grand time without her? That the boys had enjoyed the earl's company that much?

Papa.

Having a father was what she'd wanted for her sons. It was a big part of why she'd agreed to the marriage proposal. Why would the realization of that goal bother her?

None of her feelings made sense, and she was embarrassed to have let this madness take control of her.

"If you will excuse me, my lord, I need to change my dress." She was speaking as though they were still face-to-face, rather than having transitioned into the pursued and the pursuer.

He sighed, clearly frustrated, and stayed one step behind her on the stairs. "I would like us to talk about this."

"We have talked, Lord Avery. Please accept my apology for my inappropriate behavior. It shall not happen again." She reached the top of the stairs and within ten steps was at the door of her bedchamber. She pulled open the door and slammed it behind her—which said too much, again. She headed for the bed so she could scream into her pillow.

Chapter Eight

LORD AND LADY AVERY attended a dinner together the next evening. Lord and Lady Mannington's fine estate was located a few miles north of the cottage, and they suffered through a silent carriage ride there and back—it truly was insufferable with the tension swirling about their heads like vaporous snakes. They had avoided each other all day, neither of them willing to be the one to attempt a repair of yesterday's disagreement.

"I am glad you're back," Nanny said, meeting them at the base of the stairs once they had come in, then turning her attention to the earl. "Tabby isn't feeling well, she's been crying for you for nearly an hour. I've tried everything I—"

The earl immediately headed up the stairs, taking them two at a time. Diane hung her light cape on one of the pegs near the door before assuring Nanny they would take care of things, and then followed the earl to the nursery. The poor child was likely traumatized from her dunking in the pond yesterday. As Diane climbed the stairs, she remembered the delighted laughter she'd overheard through the trees. It had not sounded traumatizing at all.

It turned out that Tabby was crying because she had a

tummy ache, which Alston eventually confessed was due to the fact that she'd eaten everyone's pudding. Because Benjamin and Alston did not like sultanas, they had traded plates with her when Nanny wasn't looking. The earl sat on the side of Tabby's bed while the confession was made. Diane stayed in the doorway, not feeling particularly invited.

"You do not like sultanas?" the earl asked, looking across the room to the boys whose beds were along the wall that had the windows. "I have never heard such a thing. They are sweet and burst in your mouth."

"They look like bugs," Alston said.

The earl laughed a true, full laugh that moved through Diane like the sound of a violin. She had heard his company-laugh, much as he had heard hers throughout the months at social events. She had only ever heard this laugh, however—a real laugh—through the trees when she'd come upon them yesterday. It was even more powerful this close. "But they do not *taste* like bugs," he said. "I mean, I suppose roast beef looks like tree bark, but I still find it delicious."

Alston pulled his eyebrows together, seeming to be quite struck by this comparison.

"They stick in my teeth," Benjamin said, defending the shared distaste for sultanas, which Diane suspected was something she had passed to them. She made a mental note to inform the cook to leave them out of future puddings.

"Caramel gets stuck in one's teeth as well," the earl said to the boys while rubbing Tabby's back. "You enjoyed those yesterday, did you not?"

He gave them caramels?

"Mama does not like sultanas either," Alston said.

The earl flicked a glance toward her, proving that he did indeed know she was there. He turned back to Tabby. "There are only two remedies for what ails you, little one. First, you must simply give it time; it will hurt for a bit but will eventually go away. The second is you must always remember what this feels like and not eat more than is wise in the future."

"I shall fetch some soda water," Diane said. "That is the only *other* remedy."

The earl nodded while keeping his eyes on Tabby. Diane left to the kitchen and returned a few minutes later, soda water in hand.

The earl tried to get Tabby to drink, but she refused, pursing her lips tightly together and turning her head away from him. With a glance, the earl and Diane traded places. Diane managed to convince her to drink, though Tabby sputtered and gagged. Still, she took a few more sips before claiming her stomach felt better. Diane began to hum while stroking wide circles around the little girl's back. The earl took the glass from her hand, their fingers barely touching as the cup transferred between them. Did she feel something with that touch? Was it the same thing she would have felt with any other person? Was she more affected because they had been at odds with one another?

With the boys, she drew letters on their backs in situations like this to further distract them, but Tabby did not know her letters. The earl whispered with the boys on the other side of the nursery, making them laugh, but Diane did not look his direction. Finally, after nearly ten minutes, Tabby was asleep. Diane pulled the blanket to her chin, then went to the boys and kissed each of their foreheads.

Once the nursery door was closed, Diane looked past the earl toward the door to her room with longing—she was bone-tired and her hips hurt from the long walk in the woods the previous morning.

"I did not know of the soda water remedy," the earl said.

Diane shrugged. "I am not sure if it is a remedy or simply

propels the affected to say they feel better because it tastes so awful."

The earl smiled.

She could not smile back and stepped to the side to go around him and find refuge in her room.

"Why are you angry with me?" he asked as she passed him in the hall.

She stopped and looked at him. "I am not angry. You explained yourself regarding the fishing trip, and all is well between us."

"You were angry before I took the children fishing. You have been simmering since my arrival and are practically seething now."

She stared at the floor of the hallway. *Do not say anything!* she scolded herself as she tried to construct an adequate explanation. Why was he doing this? Why was he trying to pick a fight?

When she could find no words, she started walking again, aching to hide behind the door of her room.

"Very well," the earl said from behind her. "If this is the way of things between us, I will leave for Reddich tomorrow."

She turned toward him in surprise.

He held her eyes as he continued. "I am quite clear now where we stand, Lady Avery, and shall leave in the morning. I shall take Tabby with me as I have missed her terribly these last months. I shall see you when you return to Bentmore House. Goodnight."

He walked past her and let himself into the room beside hers. The door shut, leaving Diane frozen in the empty hallway, knowing she had managed this very badly indeed.

Chapter Nine

DIANE PACED IN HER bedchamber by the light of her oil lamp, forward and back, forward and back. Each time she turned from the far side of her room, she looked at the light beneath the door that connected her room to the earl's, then shook her head and paced again. She was not wrong in having wanted her holiday, did not even feel that she was wrong in having been upset about the careless fishing expedition, but those rights did not mean that she hadn't handled this wrong. He'd sensed her irritation with his arrival even though she'd said all the right things—well, except yesterday when she'd lost her temper. Regardless, he'd known. He'd felt it. And he cared. That was the most surprising part. He cared that she was irritated—what sort of husband cared about such things?

Beyond that, she had made the earl feel unwelcome in his own home, and that was never something a wife should do to her husband. Her job was to encourage, support, and assist her husband in every way—be his helpmeet—and she had not done her job. She would tell him she was sorry, blame it on the pregnancy, assure him she would like him to stay. She did not want to, but yet she also did want to. Distance was something she'd accepted as a normal part of marriage, but discord was very different and she did not want that. It was her family, her future, her security.

Finally, when she feared she would worry a rut in the floorboards if she kept pacing, she went to the door between their rooms and knocked even though wives did not knock on the connecting doors to their husband's room; it was the husband's prerogative to make a visit, and he had not made one in months. Having broken so many of the unspoken rules today left her feeling very uncertain of herself. It was several seconds before the knob turned and the earl pulled the door open. He was wearing trousers and an untucked shirt that hung nearly to his knees. She was reminded of the scene in the clearing yesterday when she had spied on the fishing party and felt so removed from them. It was shallow and petty to have let things come to this, and she committed to do whatever it took to repair things.

"May I have a moment, my lord?" she asked.

He did not answer but stepped out of the way and waved her into his room. The bedchamber was a mirror image to her own: a fireplace, a bureau, a bed, and a chair. She turned to face him but kept her eyes apologetically downcast.

"I owe you an apology for my behavior yesterday and today," she said, keeping her eyes on the floor. "I perhaps should have warned you that pregnancy sometimes brings my emotions to the surface, but I had no right to speak to you as I did and want to assure you that it will not happen again."

"Look at me."

She lifted her eyes to meet his for a moment, then lowered them again.

"Look at me, Lady Avery."

She looked at him, but it was uncomfortable. This was too raw. Too close.

"You do not want me here."

"That is not true, my lord, I only—"

The New Countess

"I would have the truth," he said evenly. "I want us to be on good terms with one another, but if I have to choose between false accord and honesty, I will choose honesty."

She did not look away from him, and felt a shift inside her, a resolution that both terrified and invigorated her. Mostly terrified. Honesty and truth could be deadly weapons.

"You do not want me here. Why? What have I done?"

Done?

"You have not done anything, my lord," she said, shaking her head slightly. She was grateful, and a bit embarrassed, to have spoken the truth. He hadn't done anything wrong; he'd simply interfered with how she wanted things, and though she thought she had responded as she was expected to, he'd sensed her irritation and cared that she felt it.

"Then why are you so angry with me?"

"I am not angry with you."

"That is a lie."

The accusation took her off guard once again, and she felt her defenses rise as they stared at one another. How dare he call her a liar! And yet he was right. It was a lie.

"Tell me the truth," he said.

"All right," she said carefully, looking back at the floor. "I was angry that you took the children fishing without anyone to accompany you. When I learned of it, I feared someone would be hurt and, in fact, Benjamin was hurt, and Tabby fell into the water. I was upset about that as I care a great deal for the children and their welfare."

"And my explanation that fishing sometimes brings such minor perils did not remedy your anger."

Her response was immediate and sharp. "No more than my explanation that I am well enough to swim with the children remedied yours."

They stared at one another across the distance between

them. Having told the truth did not set her free of her irritation, rather she felt it coiling in her chest.

"That explains some of your anger since the swimming incident," the earl said. "But not why you were angry when I arrived."

Diane said nothing. She did not trust herself to open her mouth again.

"I do not want to be a ruler," the earl said. "I want a partner who will speak her mind, who will be a . . . a participant in our marriage and our family. That means we will have differences of opinion. We will have to talk things through—we might even argue. I accept those terms; they are far more comfortable than eggshells and rage-filled silence."

She stared at him, her mind a summer storm. He could not mean what he'd said. Could he?

"I want to know your thoughts, Lady Avery, your true thoughts."

Something popped, shifted the shifting that had already been taking place. Diane raised her chin. "I am not sure you truly want that, my lord."

Something sparked behind his eyes. "I assure you that I do want the truth from you. It is all I want."

The last of her resistance disappeared. "And dinner parties and riding lessons and fishing trips and pudding and help with political connections and household management. Forgive me, my lord, but the truth is not *all* that you want. You want a wife who does as you ask, when you ask, without complaint. You want *your* way, in everything."

He pulled back, his eyes wide.

The freedom of having spoken so boldly pushed her forward even more. "You asked me to marry you because you knew that I would be a good countess, and I feel confident that I have fulfilled that role. I chose to summer here in Southwood because being a countess is not who I am. At my core, I am a mother and a woman who likes long walks and late mornings. Now you have come, without any warning, and I am back to being your countess and seeing that you are accommodated."

She stopped speaking and the room was silent, save for the sound of her blood pounding in her ears. She'd said too much—she'd crossed a line, but it felt so good to have finally released the pressure that had been building.

For about ten seconds.

Then the relief turned into dread. Had she truly said those things? Had she spoken those words out loud to the earl? The blood began pounding even harder, and her hands and toes tingled.

"I see," he said, with a nod. "I have ruined your holiday."

She opened her mouth to say otherwise, but . . . he *had* ruined her holiday and she had said as much. She could not very well take those words back, and frankly, she did not want to. She did, however, want it to end differently than this.

"I shall continue to rise to my responsibility, my lord, but, in the future, it would be very helpful if we could make a plan in advance. It is far easier to execute expectations when I've had time to prepare."

He was the one avoiding her eyes this time. He folded his arms over his chest. "Very good, Lady Avery. Thank you for your honesty. Good night."

That was it? She shifted her weight, certain he wanted to say more, but he turned away from her, walking toward the dark window. She left the room and closed the connecting door between their bedchambers. With her hand on the knob and her back against the door, she reviewed what she'd said but did not feel the level of regret she would have expected. There was no telling whether or not he'd truly heard her, but having said it was empowering.

Come what may.

Chapter Ten

THE WHISTLING STARTED JUST after the birds the next day, but Diane took a deep breath and settled her nerves—one more week, that was all. Unless he still planned to leave today. She hated that he might take Tabby with him if he did.

Rather than try to sleep, she called for her breakfast tray and then reviewed the day while she ate, detailing out each hour to make sure that every task was accomplished. She dressed in her light blue dress with the square neckline, and Mrs. Steadman helped her do her hair in a braided crown around her head.

She was tying on her shoes—a feat that became more difficult each week—when there was a tap at the connecting door. A rush of nerves shivered through her. He'd had the night to think of what she'd said and had crafted a response.

"Come in," she said as she straightened and caught a quick look in the mirror to make sure she looked alright. A trunk of her better dresses should arrive by tomorrow, and not a moment too soon since she'd already worn every passable gown.

The earl entered the room, dressed to the height of formality as he always was—did that mean he was leaving after all? She inclined her head, and he gave a small bow.

"I have thought a great deal about what you said last night, Lady Avery."

She felt her body bracing.

"I want to apologize for having dominated your plans and interfered with your holiday. I assure you it was not my intention. I do not want you to be angry with me."

"I am not angry with you, my lord," she said, because she wasn't. Not anymore. She'd said her piece and he'd listened.

"I would like to make it up to you by spending the rest of my stay according to your expectations."

She looked at him with raised eyebrows. "My lord?"

"I have asked Mrs. Steadman to make a list of all those we have invited, or accepted invitations from, and I will be visiting them this morning to share our regrets. You did not seek out society when you arrived here, and I have brought it to you, which is unfair. You have earned this holiday, and I am sorry for not realizing that you had crafted it to be the holiday you wanted it to be."

Diane's mouth fell open but no words came out. The earl began to pace, showing his anxiety—had she ever seen him anxious before? "When I return, I would like to participate in the week you had expected to have, if you'll have me."

"If I'll have you?"

He stopped pacing and faced her. "You have been exceptional in your role as countess these last months, Lady Avery. I have appreciated your efforts and admired how diligent you have been as my helpmeet and partner. I had not considered, however, that it was a sacrifice for you to represent me so well. That was shortsighted of me and I apologize."

Apologize? Was he teasing her? Men of his stature did not apologize.

"I would like to enjoy this week with you and our family however you had planned before I came and changed those plans."

She held his eyes, trying to see through them to what he was feeling—was he angry? Was this a trick? She saw nothing but humble sincerity, and she decided to do something mad—*trust him.*

"Perhaps you should know what my expectations for this holiday were before you agree so unilaterally."

He considered this, then nodded. "That is probably wise."

She took a breath, checked her courage to make sure it was high enough to proceed, and spoke. "I want to sleep in late each morning and walk to the beach every day—some days we have a swimming lesson, other days we play on the shore. We go to church and collect rocks or bugs or flowers depending on how we feel. The beauty of the plan is that there is not one."

He nodded to show he'd heard her, though his expression showed his reluctancy.

"I enjoy dinner with the children each night in the dining room and—"

His eyebrows shot up. "The dining room?" he asked, pointing over his shoulder in the general direction of the room that, ordinarily, would not accommodate children.

"I have used the opportunity to teach them table manners, and it has been quite lovely—they all feel so very grown up and responsible to have been invited."

He took a breath and she saw the anxiety in his features again. This breaking of protocol was hard for him, which made it that much more of a gift if he could accept her terms.

"We eat simple meals—porridge, bread, stews, soups, sometimes just bread and milk. We have pudding twice a week."

"Yes, about that, why do you limit pudding?"

"Because pregnancy gives me a sensitive stomach, and I think it is good for the children to eat basic foods from time to time. I like pudding to be an occasional delight, not a daily expectation."

"I do not understand the point of that," he said, shaking his head.

"Are you saying that you shall abide by my schedule and limitations only to the point where you no longer agree with them?"

He took a breath and let it out, taking enough time, apparently, to make his decision. "No, you're right, simple foods will be fine. What else?"

"That's all."

"That's all?"

She shrugged. "That is my idea of a holiday. Having no schedule, enjoying the simple pleasures of the seaside and relishing in the company of my children. Some days we go to town and look at the shops, some days we swim—as you have already seen." Remembering her standing there in her wet shift caused her neck to get hot again. "Mrs. Steadman said there is a farmer with some young lambs the children could play with sometime, so we will take an expedition there one day I expect. Aside from that, I have no set expectations. It is simple and easy."

She could tell by his expression that he did not see the pleasure of it that she did. She felt a stab of disappointment but pushed it aside. His opinion did not matter to her . . . except that it did. They were married. If they could not find common ground in anything except her duties as a hostess and bearer of children, it could be a tedious journey for them both. She could not stand the idea of him suffering through the next week, however. That would take every comfort away from the arrangement.

"We do not need to keep to my schedule," she said, though she was angry at herself for giving in. "You did not know what it would be when you agreed."

"No, it is fine," he said. "There is nothing... wrong with it. It is simply not a way I have ever spent my time. But, perhaps, that is the best reason to do it." He forced a smile that did not hide his discomfort. "I shall embrace it and do my very best to make this an enjoyable week for you."

"For me?"

His smile fell but his discomfort did not. "There *was* a fire at Bentmore, but it did not cause such significant damage that I could not have stayed. I . . . I suppose that I missed you." He paused and she did not breathe. "And the children, of course," he hurried to say.

"Missed me?"

She sounded like a dolt, repeating him like she was, but she had never imagined hearing such words from him and did not know what else to say. He had missed her? What did that mean? Missed what, exactly? She wished she dared to ask.

"I want to know you, Lady Avery. I had hoped that, now that Parliament is closed and Bentmore has not demanded my time, I might have that chance."

She swallowed an unexpected lump in her throat as old hopes tried to break through the carefully constructed boxes she had sealed them in a long time ago—long before she'd married the earl. He wanted to know her? He had missed her? Did this mean that this marriage could be more than it had been? Did she want that?

She did. Instantly she knew that she did. She'd hoped as much with Jacob but learned quickly that he wanted distance, space, and each of them to fill their roles in the marriage, nothing more. She'd adjusted and found her place in that marriage. When she'd accepted the earl's proposal, she had accepted the same terms, or so she thought. She'd adapted and could live that way for the rest of her life if need be. It would be different if they could be friends. Which would only happen if she was a full participant. She would have to share her opinions and preferences; she would have to take the place of his equal instead of his subservient.

She smiled, a true and honest smile instead of her London-made one. "Perhaps the first step might be using our given names for one another."

The earl smiled too. "I supposed that would be a good first step . . . Diane."

Had he ever said her Christian name? She did not think that he had. His did not roll off her tongue any easier. "I agree, Michael. Now, shall we visit with the children before you make your calls and let them help us plan the day?"

"Let the children . . . uh," he paused, and she kept watching him, waiting for him to adapt to this new paradigm. "Um, of course, Lady—*Diane*. That sounds . . . perfect."

"And one more thing," she said, her whole body tingling with nerves. "You must stop whistling in the morning. The space is too small, and it makes me want to slap you."

Chapter Eleven

DIANE SLEPT IN THE next morning—there was no whistling from the other side of the door—and took a breakfast tray in bed, but she felt oddly on edge. They had had a nice day yesterday, at least she thought they had, but he hadn't loved having the children at the table. Never mind the boys were particularly rambunctious and Tabby fell out of her chair . . . twice. She wasn't sure if they were always that ill-behaved, or if she was simply more aware of it because of the tight expression on the earl's face. She went to the nursery after dinner and helped get the children to bed, then read in her room even though she knew the earl was hoping she would join him in the parlor. It had been more difficult than she'd expected to keep to her routine, but she was determined to hold her ground. He said he was willing, and if they were going to change the expectations of their marriage, she could not cater to him as she had. She understood that this might not work—he might suffer through the week and determine that he would not miss her company if it required so much adaptation. She was willing to take that risk, however, for the hope that it might make everything better.

The earl was riding when she came out of her room, so

she checked on the children who were tidying the nursery, then read in the parlor until they were ready to go to the beach. She retied Alston's shoes, fastened a child-sized bonnet on Tabby's head, and opened her parasol before they started on the path to the beach. She looked behind her twice, second-guessing whether they should have waited for the earl, er, Michael, but finally faced resolutely forward. Her schedule. His adaptation.

They were just reaching the cliffs when a sound from behind caught Diane's attention. She turned to see the earl running toward them—*running*.

When he reached them, he doubled over, hands on his knees as he tried to catch his breath.

"Gracious, my lord," Diane said, putting a hand on his heaving back. "What is wrong? Has something happened?"

"N-ooo," he said in between two breaths. "I—just—did not—want—to miss—the beach."

Diane straightened and pulled her eyebrows together. He turned his head and squinted up at her.

"You ran as though the devil were at your heels because you didn't want to miss going to the beach?"

"Precisely." He stood but winced and pressed his hand to his side. "And I believe you are supposed to call me Michael. We are at the seaside, you know. And life is different here."

She wasn't sure how to respond until he smiled at her and winked. Winked! She smiled and shook her head as she faced the path again.

Tabby ran to her father, and he threw her in the air before catching her, squealing, and spinning her around. Soon enough she wanted to be put down and quickly ran up to her brothers.

"I am glad the children get on so well," Michael said after a few steps in silence.

"As am I."

"I worried, you know, before we married, that they would find a little sister tiresome."

"Did you?" she asked, looking up at him from beneath her parasol.

"Did you not?" he asked.

"Not for an instant," Diane said, facing forward again. "My brother had two young daughters, and, when we were living on his estate, the boys adored playing with their cousins."

"It is exactly what I wanted for her, a family."

"It is what I wanted for the boys as well. They have each other, of course, but I wanted a father for them. Fishing and riding—those are things I cannot give them."

"Ah, but you give them something a man could never give—a mother's love. That is the greatest gift a child could have."

She glanced at him again, not sure how to feel about all he was sharing. He had never been so open before. But then, neither of them had ever found the time to speak so casually. Now, here in Southwood, time was precisely what they had. "As you had from your mother."

He smiled, looking ahead as the breeze, which got stronger the closer they got to the sea, began to tousle his hair. "Precisely. I had little time with my father, and no brothers or siblings, but I had an excellent mother who never missed the chance to encourage me. When Margaret . . . well," he looked at the ground and kicked at a rock. "I was heartbroken for Tabby when Margaret died, knowing I could never fill that role."

"And frightened, I can suppose. I understand Tabby came rather early."

Michael nodded, his mood turning somber. "She was so

incredibly small," he said. He held out one arm. "I could hold her head in my hand, and her tiny feet only just reached my elbow."

She looked forward, imagining her healthy and hale sons at such a size. Few children born so small survived. "It must have been a very difficult time."

He nodded and lowered his arm while squinting at the sun that was at full power today. "Indeed."

How he must miss Margaret, Diane thought. The woman he'd loved, the mother who gave her life to leave behind a baby for him to provide for. "I am sorry, my—Michael. For your loss."

He turned to look at her, and she could not read his expression before he turned forward again. She thought he might return the sentiment, but he said nothing and she did not press. Diane was not jealous of Margaret; they were entirely different women who had accepted Michael's proposal for entirely different reasons. But she was curious sometimes.

"Tell me something about you I don't know," he said after they had walked a few minutes in silence.

She startled slightly, having become comfortable with the silence. "That covers a wide range of details. Can you narrow down the scope?"

"Alright, tell me about your family—I know you have two brothers. Any sisters?"

She told him about her sister, Eliza, who had died when she was six—Diane had been ten. Her brothers were a fair amount older than her and Eliza, so she had been raised much like an only child would be. He asked thoughtful questions, and it was not until she had stopped talking that she realized how much she had said.

"That was likely more than you bargained for," she said,

keeping her focus on the children. They had navigated the cliff trail while she'd spoken and were now at the beach where the children were inspecting every piece of driftwood that had washed ashore since the last time they had visited. They had not gone in the direction of the swimming pool because Diane did not want to tempt them. "Now you must tell me something about yourself that I don't know."

"Ah, well, like you said, that covers a broad range of topics. Would you like to narrow it down for me?"

"It is only fair for you to tell me of your childhood, I suppose."

He nodded, then explained that he was an only child, not simply raised as one. His father stayed very busy, though the way he spoke reflected his respect for the man. His father had never been the earl—he had passed away two years before Michael's grandfather had.

"Was it difficult, taking your place with the title?"

"Incredibly difficult," the earl said, watching a bird as it circled upward on the air currents. "I was thirty years old but felt like an absolute child." He smiled a protective sort of smile and looked at her. They were standing side by side, watching the children draw in the wet sand. "But," he said with renewed energy, "I was a quick study and I think I have done rather well."

"Very well," she said, wanting him to know she thought so. "You have an excellent reputation. Everyone knows you are a man of good character and integrity."

"Thank you, that is very nice to hear."

"You are welcome," she said, then faced forward again. She inhaled sea air, holding it deep within her lungs and feeling the magic of it. She put down the parasol so she could feel the sun on her face. "People travel the countryside to take the waters and attempt this healing action or that one," she said in a reverent tone. "I cannot think of anything more restorative than the sea. The sound of the waves, the salt on the wind," she let out a breath. "There is something so sacred and timeless about it. Five hundred years ago people stood just as we do now. Five hundred years in the future others will be doing the same." She inhaled deeply again, closing her eyes and relishing every sensation. A shriek from Tabby led her eyes to pop open, and she quickly located the children who were walking down to the waterline, then running away from the waves as they washed upon the shore. Tabby had not moved quickly enough, and her shoes were soaked.

"All right," she said, putting down the parasol and clapping her hands to get their attention. "You know the rules—no playing in the water until your shoes are off."

She set the example by taking off her own shoes and then, without looking at the earl, pulled the back of her skirts through her knees and tucked the tail into the waistband above her belly. If the earl thought it uncivilized, he did not say so, and she noticed from the corner of her eye that he began removing his boots while she rolled up Alston's and Benjamin's pant legs.

For well over an hour they played on the beach, and after the first several minutes, the earl relaxed into the games. When she ran out of energy for the play, Diane untucked her dress and settled herself on a log; she wore out a little bit faster every day now it seemed. Watching the children play with their father was another sort of magic. The earl's laugher was as soothing as the sound of the waves washing onto the shore.

Diane had completely lost track of time—they could have been at the beach for half an hour or half the day—when she realized the tide was changing. She determined it was time to head back, and since she was opposed to feeling rushed for anything on her schedule, they took their time meandering toward the house. The children started to whine about being tired and thirsty as they neared the house. The earl picked Tabby up and laid her against his shoulder.

The boys' complaints were grating on Diane's nerves, but she wanted to be as positive as possible so she used her most patient tone to encourage them forward.

"And here we are," she said as they rounded the bend to the stables. "Let's get washed up so that we can enjoy dinner."

"I don't want to wash up," Benjamin said, picking up a rock and throwing it at the barn, where it made a great noise that startled the horses into running across the paddock.

"Benjamin!" Diane scolded. "That is enough. We always wash up after the beach. Why would today be different?"

He frowned but did not continue his argument.

"What about Tabby?" Michael asked, looking sideways at the disheveled head of a sleeping Tabby. "Should we wake her?"

"Yes," Diane said, moving toward him to shift the child to her arms. "If we do not, she will not sleep tonight. It is too late for a nap."

Tabby woke up cross, and all three children's moods deteriorated as she turned them over to Nanny who had the unenviable task of bathing three children who did not want to be bathed. Diane used a basin in the kitchen to wash off her face, arms, and feet, deciding to indulge in a long warm bath after the children had been put down for the night. She would make sure not to stay at the beach so long in the future—she was worn out too.

The children were washed up in time for dinner consisting of bread and milk.

Diane felt a pang of conscience as Mrs. Steadman set down the bowl in front of Michael. He blinked at it, and Diane wondered if he'd ever eaten such a simple dinner.

Benjamin pushed his bowl away and laid his head on the table. "I don't want dinner," he whined. "Can I go to the nursery?"

"No," Diane said, reaching over to push him back to sitting. "We shall eat at the table, and you will show the earl what good table manners you have." Last night's unimpressive display could be forgotten if tonight went better. "Pick up your spoon."

Benjamin picked up the spoon but began to tap it against the bowl instead of eating. Alston was eating obediently, thank goodness. Tabby pushed her bowl away too.

"Come on, little one," Michael said. "If I can tolerate this, you can."

Diane glared at him, but he was staring dejectedly into the bowl and therefore didn't see her. "Benjamin, stop hitting the bowl with your spoon. Stand up straight."

Benjamin jumped from his chair and stood straight as a soldier, which made no sense until Diane realized she'd told him to. "I meant sit up straight."

"You told me to stand."

"Benjamin," she said strongly and pointed at the chair. "Sit."

He grumbled and returned to a slumping posture in his chair.

"Now eat."

"I don't like bread and milk. Can we have pudding?"

"Pudding!" Tabby said excitedly.

"No pudding tonight. It is Tuesday," Diane said.

Benjamin started tapping his spoon on his bowl again. Diane reached over and grabbed the spoon out of his hand, glaring at him.

"I wan' pudding!" Tabby wailed. The earl tried to shush her while Diane argued with Benjamin, then gave up and began eating his bread and milk faster.

"Eat," Diane said to Benjamin, handing him back his spoon.

"I am eating, Mama," Alston said proudly, milk dripping down his chin.

"Don't talk with your mouth full," Benjamin said to his brother, then turned to Diane. "It is bad manners to eat with his mouth full, isn't it, Mama?"

"Yes, but at least he is eating." She turned to Tabby. "Now, Tabby, darling, you need to eat your dinner."

"No! I hate it."

"Tabby," she said, more reprimand in her tone. "You do not speak to me that way."

Tabby glared at her and gave her bowl a good shove, strong enough that it slid across the table toward her father who was not paying attention. Tabby's bowl hit Michael's bowl, which made him jump and hit the edge of his bowl, flipping it into his lap. Michael yelped and jumped to his feet, bread and milk dripping from his trousers as the chair flew backward into the wall, and the bowl fell to the floor where it shattered into a dozen pieces.

All five occupants at the table froze, then Tabby began to cry again. Diane looked at the mess, then met the earl's eyes that were absolutely furious. She looked away and stood, hurrying over to Tabby. Alston started crying. Benjamin finally started eating but kicked the leg of his chair in the same rhythm he'd been hitting the bowl before. The earl stood still, fists at his sides, trousers and coat dripping, for several seconds, then turned and left the room without a word.

Diane tried to get dinner on track for a few more minutes, then poked her head into the kitchen where Mrs. Steadman and Nanny were having their dinner and asked for help.

It took nearly an hour to get the children cleaned up and

The New Countess

ready for bed—all three of them were ridiculous, and it was with complete relief that Diane finally closed the door of the nursery behind her. Of all the nights for the children to stage a mutiny...

"May we talk?"

Diane looked up to see the earl dressed in clean clothes standing in the hallway. He was not happy.

Diane nodded and turned toward the stairs. The earl followed her into the parlor.

She took a breath and turned to face him.

"That was horrid," the earl said simply.

She opened her mouth to defend herself, then closed it. It had been horrid. She could not defend it. "I fear we stayed too long at the beach. The sun and the playing, it wore us all out."

"And I'm starving," he said, crossing his arms over his chest. "Bread and milk for dinner—do you truly eat that as a meal, or did you exaggerate the fare in an attempt to make a point?"

"I exaggerated nothing," she said, insulted. She dropped her hands to her sides. "The children love bread and milk for dinner. We have had it a few times a week throughout our entire stay."

He eyed her suspiciously.

"You don't believe me?" She put her hands on her hips. "You think I would lie to you?"

"It wouldn't be the first time," he quipped.

"When have I ever lied to you?"

"You told me you were not angry at my arrival, when, in fact, you were very angry."

She let out a breath and shook her head. "I have not lied to you, ever," she said, though she had been irritated. "The point at hand is that we eat bread and milk for dinner fairly often. Some nights, we have apples and cheese. Or soup. I told you we eat simple meals."

"That is not a meal!" he threw up his hands. "I am all for abiding by your schedule, but honestly, Diane, bread and milk is not a meal. I am a grown man." He put both of his hands on his chest. "I need sustenance!"

He ran his fingers through his hair, keeping his hands on his head as he turned to walk toward the fireplace.

"Then go into the kitchen and find something to eat!" Diane snapped. "Gracious, is it not enough that I have had three overwrought children to manage all evening, but I must coddle you too? If you are hungry, eat."

He turned and looked at her as though he hadn't considered that, but his shoulders relaxed and he lowered his hands. "Very well," he said with a sharp nod, then turned on his heel and left the room. She heard the hinge for the kitchen door squeak, which was when she was reminded that amid the chaos she had not eaten either. She argued with herself for a few minutes, then made her way to the kitchen. Mrs. Steadman was still cleaning up the mess in the dining room.

The earl was sitting at the small table, eating what looked like half a loaf of bread with butter and jam. He glared at her, then looked down at his food as he ripped off an additional chunk of bread and dipped it in the jar of jam like a regular heathen. *Had he ever had to make his own meal?* she wondered.

Diane pointedly ignored him as she went to the pantry and removed some salted pork and a basket of eggs. She spent the next few minutes stoking the fire in the small stove and frying eggs and ham in a skillet. Mrs. Steadman came in at one point, paused, looked between them, and then went about her tasks without a word, leaving as soon as she could, Diane assumed.

When Diane finished making the simple meal, she dished a portion of the eggs and ham onto a small plate and put the rest on a larger plate in front of the earl. He had nearly finished the bread by then but was still chewing as he met her eyes.

"Goodnight, my lord," she said, then turned and took her plate with her. She would eat in her room. It was an undignified end to an undignified day.

Michael said nothing, but she heard the sound of the plate being pulled toward him as she left the room.

Chapter Twelve

THE EGGS AND HAM were delicious and filling, and once Diane was satiated, she could more fairly consider the situation as she changed out of her clothes, washed her face and neck again—they still felt gritty—and put on her nightdress. The earl had never had children at the table—not when he was a child and not while being a parent. He loved good food and had only ever done things one way all of his life. Mealtimes were formal. Schedules were set. Roles were kept. Last night had been a strain with the children, and tonight everyone had been overtired from the beach and, apparently, hit their limit. Yet she'd insisted a grown man be satisfied with bread and milk. It was not fair, but it wasn't necessarily unfair either. It was poor circumstances, and if that was more than the earl could handle, well, then—

A knock at the connecting door interrupted her thoughts, and she straightened from where she sat in bed, leaning against the headboard with a book in her lap she had planned to read. The thrill she'd always felt when he tapped on her door before washed through her, but then she narrowed her eyes. Of all nights, tonight was the night he decided to visit her. When they were at odds with one another?

The New Countess

He knocked again and she realized that she hadn't answered the first knock.

"Come in," she said, straightening her back and trying to look formidable in her ruffled night dress. The baby kicked and she pressed against her belly, willing it to be still. Now was not the time for distractions.

The earl came into the room fully clothed, which was her first clue that he had not come for a visit but instead wanted to talk. She immediately wished it was the former. She was tired of talking. Tired of the tension. "I owe you an apology," he said.

She had not expected that.

"At dinner, tonight, I should have helped you with the children and I did not. I was so caught up in my own feelings, I gave little credit to yours or to theirs. I am sorry and will work hard to do better."

Diane was silent for several seconds as she processed what he had said and felt herself relax. "I thought you would apologize for the tantrum you threw about starving to death."

He shook his head. "That was completely understandable. I was starving." He held her eyes, his expression neutral, then quirked a smile.

Relief flooded through her so strongly that she covered her mouth to suppress the laughter that rose up. He smiled fully and shook his head as he walked farther into the room, sitting himself in the chair by the fireplace. "So, do you make yourself an additional meal every night after the children go to bed?"

"No," she said, still keeping her tone carefree. "But I was so busy managing the little devils tonight that I didn't eat any of my own, which, of course, I did not realize until after telling you off."

He nodded. "Well, then, I feel a bit redeemed. Is there always ham and eggs in the larder?"

"I don't know, this is the first time I have had to make myself an additional supper."

"I cannot survive on the food you are content with—there is no flavor, no appeal, and I am quite sure I could eat bowl after bowl of bread and milk and never be full. We must negotiate this point, or I shall be an absolute bear to deal with."

"Well, that will never do."

"Exactly," he said with a nod. "What if I go to the pub in town for dinner every night?"

"And leave me to eat with the children on my own?"

"You are the one who wants so much to eat with them in the dining room and teach them table manners—which I agree they are in dire need of but do not feel capable of enduring in the meantime. When they are, say, eighteen years old, I shall be willing to join you at the table with them. In the meantime, I would prefer greasy sausages and dry potatoes. Or, they could eat in the nursery, and we could have full meals together in the dining room."

She did not know how to defend against the evidence of the failed dinners. And so she chose not to. "You may do whatever you like for dinner, Michael, but I would like to continue having the children at the table. I truly believe it is good for them. I won't hold it against you if you don't want to join us, but I enjoy eating as a family."

"I like the *idea* of eating as a family. It is the reality of such a plan that is proving difficult for me to understand. It has been madness."

"Because they are overtired, as I said. It has not been like that on past nights . . ." She thought about that and the fact that Michael had accused her of lying before. She did not want to be dishonest. "Well, not very often, I should say. Never twice in a row like this."

"You won't consider having dinners like we had last week?"

"No," she said with resolution. "This is how I want to spend my holiday."

He let out an exaggerated sigh, at least she hoped it was exaggerated. "Very well," he said, spreading his hands in front of him. "You cannot say I did not try."

He pushed himself from the chair. "Goodnight, Diane. I am glad we were able to resolve this."

"So am I," she said, realizing that it was quite an accomplishment. They had never argued because they had never needed to, but they had handled this rather well. She was proud of them, and it gave her hope.

Chapter Thirteen

FOR THE NEXT FEW days, they went to the beach or walked through the woods as a family and enjoyed their time together. When dinner came, the earl disappeared, and though Diane was disappointed, she did not make a fuss about it. She invited Nanny to have dinner with them, feeling the need to improve the lessons on manners but wasn't sure things improved that much. With Michael's perspective to consider, she could see that the meals were chaotic, and though she was making progress with things, like teaching the boys how to hold a fork and sit up straight, it took constant attention. She wondered, especially in regard to three-year-old Tabby, if her expectations were not realistic.

After dinner she would put the children to bed and go into her room. The earl would come in sometime later, and she would listen to him move about his room and wonder if he might knock on her door. He did not.

On the third night, after closing the nursery door, Diane made a different choice and went down the stairs to the parlor instead of into her room. She settled in a chair and began to read, though she kept an ear trained on the front door. When she heard it open, she adjusted her sitting position and lifted her chin slightly. Would he see the candlelight and come in, or would he go directly to his rooms?

"Good evening, Diane."

She looked up as though having not expected him. "Good evening, Michael. How was your dinner?"

"The sausages were extra greasy and the potatoes were extra dry, but the ale was excellent and my belly is full." He patted his stomach and smiled as he came into the room. "You are reading in the parlor tonight?"

"Um, yes, I . . . I suppose I wanted a change of scenery."

"I find I get too tired when I read in bed," Michael said as he wandered to the bookshelf and began perusing titles. "My body seems to realize where I am and demand that I sleep."

"That is what I like about it," Diane said, watching him without his knowing it as he moved to review another section of titles. "My body relaxes, and when I'm ready to sleep, I simply turn down the lamp and drift away."

"Hmm," he said, "that does sound rather nice." He pulled a volume from a shelf and turned toward her, opening the front cover and assessing whatever was there, which she assumed was the vetting process of him determining whether he wanted to commit to read the book or not. He apparently approved because he moved toward one of the chairs in the room and began to read. Diane moved her attention back to her book as well and noticed that she felt much more relaxed now that he was home and all was well between them. Yet, there was a continued awareness of him that kept her from being able to fully lose herself in the pages of her book. She wanted conversation, and after several minutes of resisting the desire, she gave in.

"What are you reading, Michael?"

He glanced up from his book and held her eye a moment, then held up the book so that she could see the cover.

"Are you enjoying it?"

He opened the book again. "I am," he said. "I had a great deal of instruction regarding history in school, of course, but it did not draw my curiosity back then. Since taking my place in Parliament, I have become much more interested in how governments are formed and what, ultimately, leads to their demise. The Greeks kept one of the longest formal governments than any other society, and they had great minds that influenced their decisions. I enjoy seeing how they did it."

"Oh," she said, completely at a loss of what else she could say. She had little interest in the Greeks. Or governmental history.

"And you?" he asked, closing his book again. "What are you reading?"

"*The Black Dwarf*," she said, then held up her book. "I am trying to be captured but am struggling."

He pulled in his eyebrows. "*The Black Dwarf*? I am not familiar."

"Well, it is a novel. Part of the Waverly series by Sir Walter Scott. He only publicly acknowledged himself as the author last year."

His expression showed that he had no knowledge of this. "Ah, I see. I am afraid I have not read many novels."

"And I do not read much history."

They held one another's eyes for a few seconds, then Diane dropped her eyes to her book, disappointed that her attempt to find common ground had instead led to yet another lack of commonality between them.

The baby kicked and she startled at the strength of it, unable to hide a smile as she rubbed the place on her belly that he—or she—had targeted.

"What?"

She looked up to see Michael watching her.

"Are you alright?" he asked.

"Oh yes," she said, smiling as the baby kicked at her hand still pressed on her belly. "I fear our child will be resistant to bedtime once it is here—it's always quite energetic this time of night." She set her book to the side and moved her hands to feel the contour of a knee or elbow. The baby kicked on the opposite side and she laughed.

"What does it . . . what does it feel like?"

"It is like . . ." She struggled to describe something that he had no capability to experience. "Well, at first it is just a fluttering, almost like when you feel nervous anticipation, though lower in the body, of course." She felt her cheeks flush to be talking about her body this way, but his expression did not show any discomfort, only curiosity. She let that spur her forward. "And then, as the baby grows, the movement becomes more pronounced, and something I have no comparison to. Their movements have only just become strong enough for me to identify specifics—such as an elbow or a kick."

"You can tell such details?"

She nodded. The baby kicked again, and she had an idea. It made her feel that fluttering of nerves she'd just described to him, in addition to the kicks and squirms of their child. "Would you like to feel it?"

He pulled his eyebrows together again in confusion.

"Did you ever feel Tabby when . . ." Her voice trailed off, still unsure how to talk about Margaret.

"I don't know what you mean."

"Here," she said, waving him over to her. He hesitated, then put down his book, stood, and crossed to her chair. When he was close enough, she reached for his hand and guided it to her rounded belly. Before he touched her, he pulled back slightly, and she looked into his eyes and smiled reassuringly before tugging at his hand again. He did not resist, and a moment later, the warmth of his hand seemed to cover far more of her belly than seemed possible. There was an intimacy here that she had not expected, and even more fluttering began within her chest. Of course, now that it had an audience, the child was still.

"I don't feel anything," he said and tried to pull his hand back. She was still holding his hand at the wrist and did not let him pull away. She moved his hand to one side, then to the other.

She heard his sharp intake of breath, which he held until the baby turned beneath his hand. He moved from standing at the side of the chair to kneeling in front of her and placed both hands on her belly, covering the whole of it. He stared at his hands, and when the baby kicked again, he laughed and looked into her face. With her sitting and him kneeling, they were eye level with one another and close enough that she could see the complete rapture of his expression.

"That is . . . it is . . . I . . . I don't know how to explain it."

"I know," she said, putting her hands over his. When the baby kicked next, she could only just feel the vibration through his hands. He stared at their hands layered on her belly, staying there for nearly a full minute as his child moved and kicked within her.

"Thank you," he said softly after a long while that was not nearly long enough.

"It is not fair for me to be the only one to experience the miracle of this." She wanted to ask if he truly had never felt Tabby within Margaret's belly, but the ecstatic joy on his face told her this was his first experience.

He met her eyes, and she did not look away. Their child moved again, and she thought of those nights when he had come into her bedroom, kissed her neck, stroked her hair, and held her in the darkness as their breathing came back to normal.

"May I kiss you, Diane?"

His request shivered through her from head to toe as the words connected to the memories she'd been entertaining. The kisses they had shared before now had only taken place in the dark, and she wondered how a kiss in the light of a dozen candles, in the parlor of the simple cottage, could feel so much more personal and intimate than what happened there. She nodded and he leaned in, withdrawing one hand from her belly so that he could put it behind her neck. His touch was warm and soft, making her shiver again. When his lips met hers, the warmth of his touch filled every part of her.

She lifted her hands to his shoulders and kissed him back in a way she hoped explained everything she felt and thought. The kiss deepened, expanded, until he finally pulled away. He rested his forehead against hers as they both attempted to catch their breath.

"I am sorry," he said, still breathless.

Diane pulled back. "Sorry?"

"I know it is not wise, forgive me." He pulled away, though his expression showed reluctance. He stood and took a deep breath as he turned to face the window. If she did not know better, she would think he was angry, but she did know better.

"What do you mean, it is not wise?"

He looked at her long enough for her to see his cheeks flush, then he turned toward the doorway. "I think I shall take a walk, work through my . . . um. Goodnight, Diane, thank you."

He left before she had thought of anything to say, and though she tried to read after the front door closed behind him, it was quite impossible. Her blood was running hot through her veins as she reviewed the exchange over and over again. Each time she thought over his apology, she felt she understood a little bit more why he'd stopped himself.

After waiting nearly an hour for him to return, she went to her room and readied herself for bed, her stomach aflutter as she planned how to address things when he returned. She brushed her hair and braided it over one shoulder. She put a touch of perfume behind each ear.

When she finally heard him come into his room, she walked to their connecting door and listened to the sound of his boots falling to the floor before she knocked.

Everything on the other side of the door went silent, and she remembered how uncomfortable she'd felt when she had knocked on his door the first time. Was it only a week ago? The level of comfort between them had changed dramatically since then.

The door opened and Michael stood before her, fully clothed except for his stocking feet. They held one another's eyes for a few seconds, then his eyes traveled down the rest of her—clad in a modest, though perhaps somewhat sheer, nightdress. She was aware that perhaps her misshapen body would not draw his attention, but she was equally aware that she could not know for sure unless she asked.

"May I come in?"

"Of course." He moved to the side so that she could enter and closed the door behind her as she turned to face him. The energy that had built between them had not dissipated, which she found invigorating.

"If this is about what happened in the parlor, I am sorry. I would never do anything that would endanger our child."

Without knowing it, he had confirmed her suspicion. "You believe that . . . passion would endanger the baby?"

"Of course," he said as though it were as true as the moon in the sky.

"That is why you have not knocked on the door since I told you?"

"I am not a barbarian, Diane," he said, sounding insulted. "I can control myself."

She smiled at his determination. He pulled his eyebrows together. "And what if you did not have to?" she asked.

His face relaxed in the way of having heard something he had never considered before. His lips parted but he said nothing.

Diane took a step toward him, then another, until she stood right in front of him. Then she lifted her hand and traced his lips with her finger. "There is no danger in our being together, Michael, and I have . . . missed that part of us very much."

His hands came around her back, but his eyes did not leave hers. "You are certain?"

"Absolutely certain," she said in a whisper. "As long as you have no other objections."

His eyebrows furrowed again. "What other objections could I possibly have?"

"I have no figure to speak of and—" He silenced her with a kiss, his broad hands circling her back as he pulled her close to him. What happened in the dark had never been a struggle for them, but this was different. New. Connected in ways they had not experienced before. Diane kissed him back, letting her fears, anxieties, and formality melt away.

This.

This is what she'd never dreamed of having in a marriage. This was what she wanted for the rest of her life.

Epilogue

"Diane?"

She blinked open her eyes, so exhausted she could barely focus until she realized it was Michael's face before her. She smiled and relaxed back into the pillows, every muscle in her body aching the way a new mother's body always did. She reached out a hand and he took it, bringing it to his lips and kissing it, letting his lips linger.

"You are alright," he said, not phrasing it as a question and not releasing her hand, though he lowered it to the bed. His relief was evident in his expression.

"I am fine, did you see him?"

"I did," he said, his tone reverent. "He is perfect. You're sure you're alright?"

She laughed, as much as she could, and patted the bed beside her. He followed the invitation and went around to the other side, removed his boots, and climbed in behind her. He carefully wrapped his arms around her, the way they had slept every night for the last few months. She melted into him, closing her eyes and enjoying his warmth. "Have the children seen him?"

"Mother took them on a walk to the vicarage. They'll be back soon."

"And is she terribly disappointed that the next earl was not born at Bentmore?"

Every other earl had been born at Bentmore House: Michael, his father, his father's father, and so on. Diane had fully expected that this child would also be born there, at the holdings that would one day be his. It had been Michael who had asked her, only a week before the intended trip north to Bentmore, if she would prefer to stay at the cottage. They had discussed the benefits and drawbacks—Diane loved the idea, and Michael loved her. Enough to explain to his mother that he was breaking tradition, enough to interview the local midwife at length to be sure she was capable of whatever might come.

And so, it was decided; she finished growing the next Earl of Avery at the cottage by the sea. She had gone into labor early this morning, and, just after two o'clock, had delivered a healthy baby boy who was, as his father had pronounced, absolutely perfect. She'd already fed him—he'd taken to the breast very well—and now the nurse was washing and swaddling him while Diane rested.

The warmth of Michael's body against hers lulled her into a hazy sleep where she relived the last year of her life and all that had changed and blossomed and grown. What if she had never come to this holiday cottage by the sea? What if Michael had not followed her?

There was no point in wasting energy on such questions because, in fact, she *had* come here, and he *had* followed her, and they had created the family she had always dreamed of.

"Thank you," she whispered.

"Hmm," he said, startling and betraying that he had been on his way to sleep as well.

"Thank you, Michael, for asking me to be your countess, for wanting to know me, for making us a family."

"Mmm," he said, nuzzling her neck as he buried his face in her hair. "It is a very good life we have built, Diane, and I look forward to everything that comes next."

A very good life indeed.

Josi S. Kilpack has written more than thirty novels, a cookbook, and several novellas. She is a four-time Whitney award winner, including Best Novel 2015 for "Lord Fenton's Folly, and has been a Utah Best of State winner for Fiction. Josi loves to bake, sleep, eat, read, travel, and watch TV--none of which she gets to do as much as she would like. She writes contemporary fiction under the pen name Jessica Pack.

Josi has four children and lives in Northern Utah. For more information about Josi, you can visit her at:
Website: www.josiskilpack.com
Blog: www.josikilpack.blogspot.com

Mishaps and Memories

~~~~~~

Martha Keyes

Chapter One

THE VALUE OF A large, well-placed plant in a drawing room could not be overstated, for it was in just such a place that a man seeking to escape an unpleasant encounter might hide himself for a short time. Though *hide* was not the word James Carlisle would have preferred to use. He was merely sipping his champagne in solitude at his leisure, leaning against the wall, which just so happened to be concealed by an obliging plant.

"There you are." The frowning face of James's father, Henry Carlisle, appeared. "What in heaven's name are you doing in the corner of the room, hiding behind a tree?" He brushed at a few protruding leaves with an impatient hand.

James finished off what was left in his glass and stood straight. "I am not *hiding*, Father."

His father scoffed lightly. "Then what *are* you doing?"

James's mouth turned down in a frown as he contemplated his response. "I am"—he stroked a leaf with a finger—"enjoying nature."

"What you *should* be doing is asking Miss Garrett to dance."

James had made sure to remain in his corner until Miss Garrett was engaged for this set. Through the leaves of the tree, he could see her performing the beginning figures of a cotillion on the ballroom floor. "She appears to be well-entertained without my interference."

"My point precisely," his father said testily. "At this rate, she will have three offers of marriage before you have even emerged from this ridiculous corner." He swatted the leaves that sat against his shoulder. "Sir William leaves in the morning for his estate, and he shall be gone a fortnight, after which he will be paying Miss Garrett's father a visit. All you need do is exert yourself a little in the meantime—snatch her up before he does."

"I have never been terribly fond of *snatching*, as you so elegantly phrase it, Father."

His father's lips drew into a thin line. "I am running out of patience for your aversion to marriage, James. What reason can you possibly have to be so set against it?"

James stepped away momentarily to set his glass on the tray of the passing footman, biting his tongue as he did so. He didn't have an aversion to marriage, and he was not set against it. But he didn't particularly care to explain to his father why he was reluctant to offer for someone like Miss Garrett. His father would have no patience for the sentimentality that made James wish for something more than a practical match.

"It is merely the joy you take in defying me, no doubt," his father said with obvious resentment.

James smiled sardonically. "How well you know me, Father."

His father's frown deepened, and he glanced around at the chattering crowds lining the ballroom floor. "You could have the pick of the young women here—no doubt half a dozen of them came here with the express hope of being asked to dance by you—but instead, I find you paying your addresses to a . . . a *fern!*"

James frowned. "That is not fair, Father. I would never pay my addresses to a common fern. I am tolerably certain this is a fig tree."

His father was not amused. "Your mother and I wish to see you settled. Prosperous!"

James offered no response to this.

"Bah!" his father grumbled. "You never did care for anyone's wishes but your own. But mark my words, James. You *will* marry. And since you refuse to choose a bride, I have taken the liberty of choosing one for you." And with that, he turned on his heel.

James's smile faded as he watched his father disappear amongst the crowds. James *did* care what his parents thought. He merely wished that their desire for his prosperity was centered more on his happiness than on his marrying well.

Perhaps James was foolish to hope for more than a strategic marriage. Perhaps only the most fortunate managed to marry for more than necessity. Surely, that opportunity would have presented itself already after so many years of being introduced to the Season's most promising and highly regarded young ladies.

Thinking perhaps it had been a mistake after all to attend tonight's dinner, James emerged from his corner, only to be confronted by his friend, Philip Langham.

"Your father said I would find you here." Langham peered around James, as though he expected to see someone behind the tree. "Thought he might snap my head off just for asking."

"I am in his black books," James said.

"Have you ever been out of them?"

James cocked his head to the side, frowning. "Not that I know of. Tonight, he finds me too lazy on the subject of marriage—and Miss Garrett. He insists I come up to scratch and—how did he phrase it?—*snatch her up* before Sir William manages to." James's gaze traveled to Miss Garrett again, only to find that, despite being engaged in conversation with Mr. Coombs, her eyes were on him.

"Miss Garrett?" Langham said with a hint of distaste. "The one who stares?"

James held Miss Garrett's gaze, but as she showed no sign of embarrassment at being caught in the act of looking at him, and because he found her gaze particularly unnerving, he admitted defeat and looked away first. "Yes, the one who stares. But what is the inconsequential habit of gawking in comparison with her father's barony?"

"I don't know, Carlisle," Langham said incredulously. "I imagine you would find it consequential enough if you found her forever staring at you when you were trying to read *The Times* in peace at the breakfast table."

James suppressed a shudder.

"Just so," Langham said. "Her entire family has a strange kick to their gallop. Her sister married that devilish poor fellow from Yorkshire. They won't hear a word against him, though. Nothing more certain to set up their hackles than maligning the working class. I tell you what, Carlisle. Your problem is that you are too charming by half. You must take a leaf from Miss Garrett's book and acquire some undignified habit—an obscenely loud laugh or perhaps pretending to be hard of hearing. If you would but set your mind to it, it would be easy enough to give her a reason to prefer Sir William."

James cursed under his breath. His parents were approaching, with Miss Garrett and her father at their side.

"Gads," Langham said as his eyes followed James's gaze. "One would think she would have to blink every now and then. What a lovely evening you have ahead of you, Carlisle. I understand all of the courses are to be fish, too."

James's head whipped around, looking in vain for any sign that his friend was joking. But Langham only gave a sympathetic grimace.

"Our dear host wished to pay tribute to the sea before he leaves back to Shropshire for the summer."

James stifled a groan. Coming this evening had decidedly been a mistake. He couldn't abide fish—not since he'd become violently ill after eating some as a child.

"For someone who so enjoys being in a boat on the water, your hatred of the fish that dwell in that water is quite ironic."

"I am aware of that," James said, unamused.

Insensitive to his friend's predicament, Langham slapped James on the back and strode off.

Miss Garrett's eyes were still on James—though, to be completely fair, so were those of his parents and Lord Linscott—and he pasted on a smile to receive them.

"Ah, son," his father said, the pleasant expression on his face giving no indication of the bad terms they had parted on just minutes ago. "I was just telling Lord Linscott how anxious you are to pay him a visit. He and Miss Garrett said they would be happy to receive you once they are settled back in at Linscott House. What date was it you said, my lord?"

Lord Linscott inclined his head. "I believe it was the twentieth. If it is convenient to you, of course."

James could feel Miss Garrett's unblinking eyes boring into him with even more power than usual. Did they never become dry? He opened his mouth to express his regrets at not being able to agree to the date in question, but his father spoke over him.

"Yes, yes. The twentieth will do perfectly, won't it, James? And now, I believe they are about to ring the bell. You will, of course, take Miss Garrett in to dinner, son."

James smiled through gritted teeth and offered Miss Garrett his arm. "Of course, Father."

Mishaps and Memories

Perhaps it was time to see just how willing the young woman was to look past his faults—or stare past them, rather.

Chapter Two

JUDITH JARDINE PUSHED ON the fabric at the fingertips of her borrowed gloves, hoping to force them farther down. Anne's fingers were much longer than hers—and much more elegant, certainly. Only when she had seen Anne's hands deftly working a needle earlier that day had Judith realized how coarse her own hands were in comparison. She was glad they would be covered—until dinner, of course. She must simply hope that people would be too focused on eating to notice.

The glow of the ballroom ahead spilled out of the doors and into the candlelit corridor, the music along with it. The smell of violets swept by as a young couple brushed past, arm-in-arm, with laughter on their lips.

Judith's cousin, Anne Dawes, patted Judith's arm with a smile full of eagerness. "You must leave the gloves be, Judy. No one shall take notice if they are a little long. Not when you are looking so ravishing." She nudged Judith with a teasing elbow.

Heat seeped into Judith's cheeks, and she shot Anne an annoyed look. She had never been to such a fine gathering, and she was sorely conscious of how little she belonged, from her drooping gloves and unpolished hands to her ill-fitting gown.

Mishaps and Memories

"This is your chance," Anne whispered excitedly. "I am so thrilled your father agreed to let you come. A week is not terribly long, I admit, but I am very hopeful we shall find someone for you."

"Oh, hush, Anne," Judith said. "Our efforts are better spent finding someone for *you*. Just being here is reward enough for me. Besides, no one here would seriously consider marrying someone like me."

She said the words as much for her own benefit as for Anne's. She couldn't deny that her hopes were high for this short visit in Brighton. Never again was the opportunity to rub shoulders with so many eligible gentlemen likely to come her way—not as the daughter of a country vicar. It had been a difficult enough task to receive permission from him to come—he worried about her head being turned by such frivolity and that she would return home with a dissatisfaction for her life.

And perhaps he was right. As Anne and her mother introduced Judith to person after person, she could see their evaluative gazes taking her in and the subsequent approbation in their eyes as she made her curtsies and greeted everyone the way her mother had taught her.

Anne was delighted with Judith's success, and Judith felt both relief and pleasure, tempered only with the suspicion that everyone's interest and esteem would flounder when they came to know of her family's reduced circumstances.

"Given how things are going tonight," Anne said with a squeeze to Judith's arm, "a week will be more than enough time to secure the interest of *several* gentlemen." She was more than happy to spend the time between introductions making Judith acquainted with the eligibility of the gentlemen in the ballroom, starting on one end and moving toward the other.

Judith secretly made note when Anne mentioned men of respectable stock who were neither titled nor particularly wealthy. If Judith had any chance of success, it would certainly be with them and not the barons and sons of nabobs in attendance.

"And *that*"—with a nod of the head, Anne indicated the corner of the room where a group of a few people stood—"is the one and only Mr. James Carlisle."

Judith's gaze took in three older people and a beautiful young woman, finally settling on a younger gentleman. He stood one dark-haired head above the others, and though he was inarguably handsome and his smile charming, the latter had a pasted-on look about it.

"The most sought-after gentleman in attendance, I think," Anne said, obvious admiration in her eyes.

"More so than the viscount you mentioned?"

"Well, I suppose it depends on whether you wish for a man with a title empty of money, a disagreeable appearance, and the awful habit of winking *or*," Anne said, her head tilting to the side as she admired Mr. Carlisle, "a man with an obscenely large fortune—made in the East Indies, mind you, but that unfortunate fact we can easily overlook—a baron for an uncle, and the most pleasing face you ever did look upon. Not that it matters. I understand he and Miss Garrett are intended for one another. She is the one he is speaking with."

Judith didn't disagree with her cousin's assessment of either man, but neither of them were worth a second thought. Not for her, at least. Anne might have some hope with a viscount or a man like Mr. Carlisle, but for her part, Judith would happily settle for a young man who could give her a few new dresses each year and put a smile on her face.

Two such men had already stood out this evening, and both had shown clear interest in Judith upon their introduction. She had great hopes that she would enjoy a set with both after dinner—perhaps she would even be seated next to them if she was fortunate—where she would have the opportunity to gauge just how genuine their interest in her was.

But fortune chose not to smile on her in such a way. In fact, it seemed to frown heavily upon her, since she found herself seated at the very far end of the table, with Anne across from her, Mr. Carlisle to her right, and no companion to her left. What a waste of a perfectly good opportunity to continue her acquaintance with Mr. Brown or Mr. Doyle.

Judith sighed and resigned herself to the situation. Had she not told Anne that simply being here was reward enough?

Her eyes fell upon the host of dishes covering every inch of the dining room table, and they widened in dismay. She had anticipated they would be served by footmen, but apparently the hostess preferred to have the guests serve one another. She swallowed down her silly fear. She would not be the one doing the serving, at least. Mr. Carlisle would be expected to perform that task.

Whether he forgot about her or was simply too occupied with responding to Miss Garett's continuous flow of conversation on his other side, Judith couldn't be certain. Whatever the reason, she was obliged to either starve or serve herself more often than not, and even when Mr. Carlisle *did* turn to ask whether she desired a particular dish, it was with a look of such distaste on his lips that Judith couldn't help but color up and wonder whether perhaps he'd had word of her ineligibility and was disgusted to be seated beside her. At least he would not notice the coarse state of her hands when he could barely spare a glance in her direction.

Anne sent Judith frequent, significant looks, prodding her to engage Mr. Carlisle in conversation. But Judith could see no purpose in such an endeavor, nor had the two of them been introduced properly. It was highly awkward.

"I admit I was glad to hear of the match between them,"

Miss Garrett said loud enough that those around could hear. Her eyes were locked on Mr. Carlisle, wide and blue, as though she couldn't bear to look elsewhere.

"Oh," Mr. Carlisle responded in a voice just as loud, "but for him to marry so far below his station cannot but offend finer sensibilities. Good breeding cannot be bought, of course, but it does go hand-in-hand with money."

Judith clenched her jaw. What an insufferable man! Be he ever so good-looking, he did *not* deserve that so many young women should be wishing for his attention.

At one point during the second course, there seemed to be a lull in the conversation between him and Miss Garrett, and to Judith's surprise, he turned toward her. However attractive she had found him in the ballroom, the look of exasperation he wore as he faced her—as if she was an intolerable obligation—drained him of any appeal to her.

He held a plate of fish in his hands. "Would you care for any, Miss—" He frowned.

"Jardine," Judith said. "And yes, please. Just a bit of the sardines, if you would be so kind." That he had already forgotten her name from the first time she had relayed it to him said more than enough about him. How he presumed to speak about good breeding when he showed so little himself was beyond her. If this was what people of the *ton* were like, she was glad not to be counted one of them.

Mr. Carlisle served her from the platter with the same look of distaste he had worn whenever he turned to her, and with hot cheeks, she noted his eyes flick to her hands as she held her plate at the ready to receive the food. But when he looked to set the platter down, there was no room for it—the gentleman across from him had set a plate of salmon in its place.

"Oh, here." Judith reached for the platter he held. There

was a large enough spot for it at her end of the table. But Mr. Carlisle had not heard her. Her attempt to take the dish surprised him, and he pulled it back toward himself. The platter tipped, spilling three sardines and their juices onto his lap.

Mr. Carlisle jumped up from his chair in a failed effort to avoid the spill, and Judith's eyes widened in horror at the sight of his soiled breeches and waistcoat.

His face screwed up as all gazes turned to him, and he let out a frustrated gush of air from his nose.

"Thank you, Miss Jardine," he said with an ironic smile. "Or was it Miss *Sardine*?"

There was a veritable fire blazing on Judith's cheeks as chuckles rippled around the table at the pun.

Mr. Carlisle brushed at the spill with his napkin, but the smell of sardines filled the air around him, and he tossed down the cloth onto the table with a resigned sigh.

"If you will excuse me." He bowed and left the room, which teemed with light laughter, punctuated by the words, "Miss Sardine."

Chapter Three

BUCKET IN HAND, JUDITH walked the path that led from her sister Mary's house to the beach. She could see the coastline, stretching west toward Eastbourne and Brighton. The water shimmered, reminding her momentarily of the dress she had worn to her first real ball. What a disaster.

She looked away, refusing to acknowledge the warmth the memory brought about. She had been foolish to think a week amongst the set who frequented such a ball would amount to anything.

If the week there had been a foray into a new, glittering world, her arrival at her sister's seaside cottage had been the equivalent of a slap in the face. Mary and George Bradford's home and circumstances were even more humble than those of Judith's family, and when Judith had arrived yesterday, it was just as the sole maid, Jane, had been leaving—dismissed for theft.

The sound of giggling brought Judith's head around. Three young girls stood in front of the small house next to the path, their heads together.

"Miss Sardine!" one called. More giggles ensued.

Judith's eyes widened momentarily. She gave a pretend

smile and turned her head away with a clenched jaw. They were only children, but that didn't make the words any less unwelcome. She had sincerely hoped that, in leaving Brighton, she would also leave behind the nickname that had dogged her entire week there.

Apparently that had been too much to hope for. Mary must have told one of the neighbors of Judith's unfortunate experience, and in a small place like Portsbury, word always spread like a fire in a field of dry crops.

Father had been worried at the effect of Judith's Brighton visit on her pride. Well, his worry had never been so unwarranted. She doubted she had any left to her.

She let out an irritable sigh as she kneeled down next to the small stream that emptied into the ocean, dipping the dirty bucket to clean it of the grimy water inside from scrubbing the hearth. She looked out to the beach wistfully. She had known her time in Portsbury would be full of tasks—she was here to help Mary before her confinement, after all—but she had not been prepared to take on the work of a maid as well. She had envisioned at least a few walks on the beach.

The waves lapped up against rocks and boulders of varying sizes, their bases covered in thick moss. The water was rougher than usual today. A small boat knocked against the rocks with each incoming surge. She squinted at a heap of clothing on the sand as the foamy fringe of a wave gathered around it. Her eyes widened, and she hurried up from her knees, dropping the bucket and running toward the heap. It was no pile of clothing—it was a person.

She lifted her skirts as her feet kicked up damp sand. Whether the man was dead or simply unconscious, she didn't know, but her heart hammered against her chest as she came up beside him. A wave approached, and, overcoming her fright at the sight that might await her, she pulled on the man's shoulder to bring him from his side to his back—and his face away from the approaching water.

He slumped onto his back, head lolling at an uncomfortable angle. Judith stilled.

It couldn't be. She blinked, then searched the face of the man before her—the man who had dubbed her "Miss Sardine," who had looked at her with disgust, who had ruined her chances of a match. It was Mr. Carlisle. The prig.

A wet chill seeped into Judith's boots, and she sucked in a breath of surprise, tearing her eyes away from Mr. Carlisle to note the gathering water. She took both of his arms and pulled with all her might, so that his body slid away from the water and onto the sand the waves hadn't yet reached.

Panting, she kneeled down beside him. Was he alive? His face had plenty of color, and his eyes were closed—thank the heavens for that.

"Mr. Carlisle," she said softly. There was no response.

"Mr. Carlisle," she said more loudly. Still nothing.

What could she do? She looked at the state of him—dirt, seaweed, and moss covered his clothing. Her gaze moved to his unbuttoned waistcoat and the sopping shirt beneath, plastered to his skin. Her lips drew into a thin line, but she lowered her ear to listen.

It was there—a soft heartbeat—and she breathed more freely. He was alive, at least.

But now what? How was she to wake him from this state? She had once seen a senseless, drunken man slapped to consciousness. It was certainly tempting.

But, no.

Instead, she put a hand to his cheek and said his name as loud as she could without shouting. It was no use, though. He would have to be carried, and she certainly wasn't strong enough to do it.

Mishaps and Memories

Mr. Carlisle showed signs of stirring as Mary's neighbor, Mr. Barry, brought him into the house, heaving from the effort of carrying such a load. He had been obliged to stop more than once to rest. After a moment of consideration inside Mary's house, Judith instructed that Mr. Carlisle be set down in her own bed. He would need to be seen to, and it would be easiest there.

On more than one occasion during the last week, she had considered what she would say to Mr. Carlisle if she were ever to see him again. None of the things she had come up with were civil enough to be uttered aloud, but that was just as well, for she'd had no anticipation of the opportunity presenting itself. It most certainly hadn't occurred to her that she would be offering up her own bed to him.

She thanked Mr. Barry, asking him to see that the surgeon was called for, and Mary entered soon after, a hand on her round belly and questions pouring forth. But there was no time to explain anything. Mr. Carlisle was coming to.

He groaned softly and reached a hand to the crown of his head, wincing. The fingers came away red.

"You've injured your head," Judith said. She hadn't noticed the blood until now, hidden as it was amongst his drying hair.

He blinked rapidly, eyes fixed on her as though trying to bring her into focus.

She waited for any glimmer of recognition, but recognition never appeared. Of course, he didn't remember her—the pompous pig had hardly glanced in her direction at the dinner.

His gaze flickered around the room—small, cramped, and bare of furnishing as it was. "What is this place?"

Judith had been wrong. She *did* have a bit of pride left in her, and the dismay in both his expression and voice as he took in his surroundings fanned the flame bright. He was horrified by where he found himself.

"You are in Portsbury," Judith said in a clipped voice.

"Portsbury," Mr. Carlisle repeated softly, forehead drawn into a deep frown. "Do I live here?"

Judith glanced at Mary, but Mary had no idea who this man was. Did Mr. Carlisle truly not remember?

"Do you know your name, sir?" Judith asked.

Mr. Carlisle's gaze was fixed on her, though he seemed not to be truly looking at her. "I . . . I . . ." He put a hand to his head again. "What happened? Who are you?"

Part of Judith felt bad for Mr. Carlisle. But another part of her wanted the first thing he remembered to be how terrible he had been to her. His memory would undoubtedly return to him once he'd had some time, but for just a moment, she wanted him to know what it felt like not to be the most desired and eligible bachelor. How fitting it would be for the tables to turn—for someone as insufferable as the dashing Mr. James Carlisle to wake, finding himself in just the sort of life and lowly station he had deplored at dinner.

She spoke before she could think better of it. "You were out fishing for sardines."

She watched him, ignoring the way Mary tilted her head to the side with her questioning gaze on Judith.

"I was fishing?"

Judith nodded, nostrils flared, enjoying the confusion in Mr. Carlisle's expression. "You must have been knocked over by a wave—they are frightfully large today. I hope this doesn't mean you shan't be able to carry out your duties."

"Duties?"

Judith donned her most innocent, wide-eyed expression.

"Yes, duties." She gave a little laugh. "Oh dear. Has your injury truly made you forget everything? I *have* heard that a blow to the head can do strange things."

Mr. Carlisle rubbed at his forehead with a hand. "Forgive me—I find my brain is very muddled—but am I a *servant*?"

Judith did her best to suppress a smile, blinking. "Why, but of course! You have served here for two years now. Ow!" A forceful hand squeezed Judith on the shoulder, and she whipped around to look at Mary, who stood behind her, a significant and unamused expression on her face. Judith felt a pang of guilt at her sister's expression.

"Might I have a word with you, Judith dearest?" Mary asked through clenched teeth.

Judith rose reluctantly and allowed her sister to pull her into the short, dark corridor.

"What in heaven's name are you doing?" Mary hissed, gripping Judith's arm tightly.

Judith pulled it from her grasp. "Making the world a more just place! If only for a few glorious minutes."

"How in the world is telling such a lie justice for that poor, injured man?"

Judith scoffed. "Oh, don't tell me you have become a victim to his beautiful face as well."

"What on earth are you talking about, Judy? What has his face got to do with anything?"

Judith leaned in closer to ensure her voice could not be heard in the bedroom. "Do you know who that is, Mary?"

"I have never seen him in my life."

Judith smiled with faux-sweetness. "Well, *Miss Sardine* has."

Mary stared at her, then glanced at the gap in the door, where Mr. Carlisle could be seen staring blankly at the wall. "*That* is him?"

"It is. The very *gentleman* himself."

Mary said nothing for a moment, still staring at Mr. Carlisle. Finally, she looked to Judith. "But you cannot seriously mean to persuade him that he is our servant, Judith. That is utter madness."

"It is a bit of harmless fun, Mary. He has hit his head. He will regain his memories before Mr. Sharp arrives, and perhaps he will learn a valuable lesson in the meantime."

Mary shot her a severe look. "Or perhaps you will ruin your reputation for the sake of some silly attempt at retribution."

"Reputation?" Judith gave a caustic laugh. "What reputation? I am known now as *Miss Sardine*, even here in Portsbury, thanks to that man. Any hope I had of securing a match was ruined when he made me into the joke of Brighton Society." She took in a deep breath, trying to calm herself. "I will tell him the truth, Mary. You needn't worry. Only let me have a moment to enjoy the world as it should be. Heaven knows men like him could use a little dose of humility."

Mary held Judith's gaze silently. A baby's cry sounded in the next room, and Mary sighed. "You will do as you please, Judy. You always do. But I will play no part in it. I must go get Charlie now." She gave Judith a final, sober look, then made her way to her bedroom.

Judith stood in the corridor for a moment, eyes on the gap in the door and Mr. Carlisle within. She hated knowing Mary disapproved of her behavior, but Mary had not been there for the continuous teasing—harmless as it may have seemed to those engaging in it—that Judith had experienced while in Brighton. No one had been able to take her seriously after Mr. Carlisle's mockery.

Judith's jaw tightened, and she stepped back into her bedroom, where Mr. Carlisle had begun to shiver.

Chapter Four

JAMES CLENCHED HIS EYES shut, straining at his name, a memory, at anything to help ground him and tell him this was not a dream.

The door creaked, and he opened his eyes. The same young woman appeared who had been sitting next to him. The hem of her dress was wet, and her soft brown hair, though tied back in a bun high on her head, had come loose in places, falling onto her forehead and temples in a becoming way. James's pounding head hurt even more when he reminded himself that he was this young woman's servant.

"I am very sorry," he said apologetically, "but along with my own name, I seem to have forgotten yours. Well, everyone's, really. But I should know the name of my mistress." The words sounded strange on his lips. But *all of this* felt strange. He had no recognition whatsoever of this room nor the two women he had seen since waking from the accident—while fishing for sardines, evidently.

She reached for a blanket in the corner and brought it over to the bed. "Oh, I am not your mistress. That would be my sister, Mary. Mary Bradford. Her husband, George, is away right now, I'm afraid, which makes the timing of your accident all the more lamentable."

"Indeed," he said. "How should I address you, ma'am?"

She glanced at him with a frown, and there was a pause before her response. She almost looked displeased. Had he said something unacceptable? How could a man wake, able to speak, but with no more memory or knowledge than a newborn babe of how to go on with people he had been serving for years?

"It is miss. Miss Jardine," she finally said. She didn't move, gaze fixed on him watchfully.

He reached for the blanket as another shiver racked his body. "Thank you, Miss Jardine."

She put out a hand for the blanket. "We should change your clothing first, otherwise the blanket will not warm you for long."

He stared at her.

"*You*," she said, and her cheeks looked more pink than they had before. "You should change your clothing first. That is, if you are able. I can see whether Mr. Barry might come help you if you are in need of assistance."

"No," James said. "I can manage. Though, would you mind helping me up?"

Miss Jardine nodded curtly. Apparently, servants were not supposed to ask their superiors for help standing. He made mental note of the fact. How many blunders would he make as he tried to fulfill what was expected of him?

Miss Jardine came over to him and hesitated a moment before sitting beside him. She slipped her hands behind his back to push him up from his lying position. He felt weak, but she pushed him forward with more strength than he had anticipated. He shifted his legs so that they swung over the edge of the bed, and Miss Jardine set his arm around her neck to help him to a stand. He kept a hand on the bed to stabilize himself, and she extracted herself from under his arm.

Mishaps and Memories

"Thank you, Miss Jardine," he said.

"I shall just go retrieve your clothing," she said, and she left the room.

He looked around and sighed. For some reason, the view depressed him.

Miss Jardine returned shortly with a pile of folded clothing in hand.

"Here," she said, setting the clothing on the bed. "Freshly laundered—by you, earlier today." She wore a smile on her face now—one that James could only describe as satisfied—and it enhanced her beauty. "I shall leave you to change. If you are in need of assistance, you need only call out. When you have finished, knock three times on the door to apprise me of it."

James nodded and picked up the trousers that sat on top of the clothing pile, sincerely hoping he wouldn't be obliged to call for Miss Jardine in the middle of changing them. He might have been overly confident in his assertion that he would need no assistance.

"Miss Jardine," he said as she reached the door.

She turned to look at him, and suddenly, he felt sheepish.

"What is my name?"

She didn't respond immediately. It was almost as if she was considering whether to respond at all. "James," she finally said.

There was a familiar ring to that, and he welcomed it gladly—a glimmer of hope that perhaps his memories were still intact somewhere inside his head.

He managed to peel the wet clothing from his skin and don the new ones without being obliged to call for help, but by the time he had finished, his head was pounding, and he had become aware of other injuries on his body. He stumbled over to the door, shutting his eyes against the pain, and rapped on it three times, making his way back to the bed, where he sat and waited.

Miss Jardine arrived shortly, but she stopped in the doorway at the sight of him, putting a hand to her mouth. It didn't quite cover the edges of her smile or the laughter in her eyes.

James followed her gaze down to his clothing and grimaced.

"It seems as though I lost half of my body along with all of my mind," he said with a rueful smile. His shirt hung loosely around him, and if not for the straps that held them up, his trousers would have fallen to the floor.

Miss Jardine stepped into the room, shutting the door behind her. "Yes, well, we have all slenderized a bit of late, what with our straitened circumstances. You more than anyone, though. Thankfully, it has made you quicker about your duties."

His duties. What *were* his duties? "I am sure this is all quite troublesome to you," he said, "but can you help me remember what exactly my duties are? You said I was fishing when I hit my head? And that I did the laundry earlier?"

"Yes," she said as she sat and smoothed the covers on the bed. "Before that, you had come from cleaning the privy, I believe."

James's eyes widened. "Cleaning the . . ."

Miss Jardine looked at him with a wide, clear gaze. "Yes, normally, you wake before sunrise to light the kitchen fire, sweep, prepare breakfast, of course, then on to the carpets and dusting. While we eat breakfast, you see to the beds, and—" She stopped. "Is there something wrong?"

James swallowed. "No, that is, well, it is just . . . one would think I would have some sort of memory of these things, but everything you are saying sounds so . . . foreign."

She patted his hand. "I am certain it will all come back to you as you carry out the tasks." Muffled voices sounded somewhere nearby, and she straightened. "I believe the surgeon has arrived. I will show him in."

James gave a reluctant nod as Miss Jardine went to the door. He didn't know whether to hope his memory returned or not.

Chapter Five

JUDITH SHUT THE DOOR to her bedroom and immediately covered her mouth with a hand to stop the irrepressible laughter that rose to her lips. The chagrin on Mr. Carlisle's face—the look of utter horror when she had mentioned the privy. It felt almost like justice had been served for the humiliation he had caused her. *Almost.*

She let out a sigh as she heard Mary greet the surgeon. The fun was over now. She had assured Mary she would tell Mr. Carlisle the truth, and she would be as good as her word once the surgeon saw to him. No doubt it was for the best. Judith couldn't deny the guilt that lurked behind her amusement. Mr. Carlisle *was* injured, after all, and to take advantage of that was not something she anticipated being proud of in retrospect.

Mr. Sharp stayed with Mr. Carlisle for a matter of ten minutes and, as Mary was occupied with Charlie, it fell to Judith to confer with him afterward. The surgeon was a man of somber demeanor, with thick, gray eyebrows that curled up at the top like the wings of a bird about to take flight. She tried to suppress her nerves at the somber look on his face. Did he know what she had done? Would he scold her?

He shook his head, a troubled expression on his face as Judith stood with him just outside the door to her room. "He seems to have lost all recollection of the past. Nary a memory left!"

Trying to conceal her relief and surprise, Judith shook her head soberly. "Very sad."

"I have seen cases like this before. A blow to the head is an unpredictable thing, and I urge you to take the utmost caution with him, Miss Jardine."

Judith swallowed and nodded quickly. "Of course."

"We must hope that his memories return, but they must do so at their own pace." He turned a severe eye on her. "You mustn't, on any account, force them upon him. It might overset him." He shook his head regretfully. "I once knew a woman in just such a situation. Her family attempted to remind her of her past."

Judith waited. To no avail. "And what was the result?"

"She died in Bethlem Hospital, raving mad."

Judith's eyes widened and her stomach dropped.

Mr. Sharp seemed content with her reaction, and the severity in his gaze lessened slightly. "I have great hope that his memories will return with time, but they must be coaxed out gently. Let him rest today, but do not leave him alone for long periods of time while he is so disoriented. See to his wounds. Then, slowly but surely, encourage him to engage in the activities he was accustomed to before the unfortunate accident. *That* is the best method for assisting him in regaining normalcy."

Judith managed a nod, but she was beginning to feel sick inside. Mr. Sharp moved to walk toward the door, and she followed.

"I shall come check on him soon to see how he is getting along. We can reassess the situation then. Good day, Miss Jardine."

"Thank you," she said, hoping the panic building within her was not evident.

"Oh, Mr. Sharp!"

He turned toward her, bushy eyebrows sloping down in a frown.

"You said *wounds*," she said. "I was only aware of one—on his head."

"He received some cuts and bruises as well. I recommend replacing the strips and the salve with fresh ones in two hours or so. Good day."

Judith shut the door behind him and stared blankly at the wood grains on the door. What in heaven's name was she to do?

"Judy?"

She whipped around to find Mary looking at her, face full of concern. "What did Mr. Sharp say?"

Judith took in a large breath and grimaced.

Chapter Six

MARY LISTENED WITHOUT SAYING a word as Judith recounted what the surgeon had said. When she had finished, Judith waited for the chastisement she knew she deserved. But she was treated instead to her sister's ill-suppressed amusement.

Judith frowned, waiting impatiently for her sister to gain control of herself.

"I am sorry," Mary said, still covering her mouth, "but you cannot deny it is diverting."

"Diverting?" Judith said incredulously.

Mary nodded, wiping at one of her eyes, which had begun to leak with her laughter.

"Do you not understand, Mary? I cannot tell him the truth now without the risk of condemning him to lunacy—or death."

Mary waved an impatient hand. "Mr. Sharp does so enjoy his dramatics."

Judith's brows knit. "So, you think I should tell Mr. Carlisle the truth?"

"No."

Judith let out a snort and folded her arms, waiting for her sister to expound on her contradictory remarks.

"You should follow Mr. Sharp's counsel, of course, but I expect Mr. Carlisle's memory shall return shortly on its own. After a night of good sleep, in all likelihood."

Judith chewed on her lip. She was trapped in a cage of her own making. "*This* is what comes of trying to help people."

Mary raised a brow.

"What?" Judith said defensively. "I could have left him on the beach. Someone else would no doubt have come upon him, and then *they* would be saddled with his care."

"And were you trying to *help* Mr. Carlisle when you informed him he was a servant here?"

"Yes," Judith said, lifting her chin. "For what could help an insufferably proud person more than to give them a dose of humility? It was for his own good."

Mary gave a decisive nod. "No doubt. And now, as a result, *you* have learned a lesson about the dangers of telling falsehoods, however justified or well-meaning they may be. I simply find a bit of amusement in the predicament you have created for yourself. May it be of great benefit to both of you in the end."

Judith gave a snort. "What, then, do you propose, *sister dearest*? Mr. Sharp instructed that Mr. Carlisle slowly engage in the activities he was accustomed to before his accident. Perhaps you failed to notice, but I am not the most fit person to chaperone a man to balls and dinner parties—or whatever it is he spends his time doing."

"No, of course not." Mary shrugged her shoulders. "You said yourself that some humility would benefit the man. If he believes himself to be my servant, then, by all means, let him see what it means to be a servant."

"Mary!" Judith cried. "You cannot be serious."

"It shan't harm him. We certainly could use the help until we find someone to replace Jane, and I cannot do that until

George returns. Besides, the presence of a strong man in the household will let *me* sleep more soundly. The Barrys had a window broken and their silverware stolen the other night."

Judith said nothing, staring down the corridor at the bedroom door and chewing on the tip of her thumb. They *did* need help, even if it was something as simple as watching Charlie or helping with washing up after dinner. Mary needed rest if she was to keep the baby in until George returned in ten days.

Mary nudged her. "A bit of lowly work may coax the memories out of him more quickly than lazing around at some club would do. Every bone in his body will revolt at being made to do such work if he is the sort of man you've described."

Judith smiled slightly. *That* was also true. What was the wording Mr. Carlisle had used? *For him to marry so far below his station cannot but offend finer sensibilities.* Yes, well, perhaps the offense of living below his station would help him remember his own fine sensibilities.

With Charlie in Judith's arms, she and Mary went to Mr. Carlisle. He was lying back on the bed, head bandaged and eyes closed, but they opened with the creaking of the door.

Together, Judith and Mary conveyed Mr. Sharp's orders.

"And, as you seem to be struggling to remember much of anything," Mary said, "Judith has agreed to help with your duties until you have regained your confidence."

Judith whipped her head around to Mary.

"I would be very grateful for that, Miss Jardine," Mr. Carlisle said. He looked at Judith, who hadn't yet managed to regain her composure, and frowned. "If it isn't too much to ask, I mean."

"Not at all!" Mary said brightly. "She *did* come visit for the sole purpose of being helpful to me, after all. And helping you is helping me." She turned her sweet, speaking smile on Judith, who returned her own false smile. She might have expected Mary would do something like this.

Mary turned back to Mr. Carlisle. "But for now, you must rest."

"Indeed," Judith cut in. "For the more you rest now, the sooner shall you be able to return to your duties."

"Yes," Mary said. "And in view of that goal, Judith kindly offered to make some of her delightful chicken soup. She can bring that to you when it is ready, then change out Mr. Sharp's bandages once you have eaten."

Judith rubbed her tongue roughly along her teeth, sending Mary a look full of promised revenge, then left the room to make the soup.

Judith carried the tray down the corridor, stopping just before the door to her bedroom, where she balanced it carefully on one hand and knocked on the door. It grated her pride to be forced into serving Mr. Carlisle in such a way. Even if the reward for all this was humility for Mr. Carlisle, the cost to Judith was proving to be very high as well.

"Come in," Mr. Carlisle said, and Judith pushed the door open and entered.

His overlarge shirt was buttoned at the throat, but because of its size—Mary's husband was shaped more like a pumpkin than a green bean, after all—it gaped open, providing a view of the bandages Mr. Sharp had placed on Mr. Carlisle's wounds. Despite drowning in someone else's shabby clothing, Mr. Carlisle managed to look as handsome as ever, and the fact did nothing to endear him to Judith.

As she set the tray on his lap, he eyed the bowl of soup with a hint of wariness that set up Judith's hackles, reminding her of the expression of distaste he had worn at the dinner party. He would have been well-served if she chose to spill the soup all over him again, but she refrained.

"*Bon appétit*, James," she said ironically, and made her way from the room.

But Mary was waiting just outside the door, and she raised a brow and shook her head as Judith emerged. "Mr. Sharp said he is not to be left alone for long periods of time. He was already alone the entire time you were making the soup."

"If you were so concerned, you could have sat with him then, and you are welcome to do so now."

Mary heaved a great, if somewhat dramatic, sigh and put a hand on her belly. "I am feeling quite done up, I'm afraid."

Judith pinched her lips together, staring her sister down, then gave a little huff and turned back into the room.

Mr. Carlisle paused with the spoon in midair, looking surprised.

"My sister was so kind as to remind me that you are in need of a nursemaid at your side at all times." Judith sat in the rickety chair in the corner of the room, folding her arms across her chest.

"Am I?" Mr. Carlisle asked, eating a heaping spoonful of the soup.

Judith didn't respond.

"This soup is . . . delicious. Do I know how to make it?"

The corner of Judith's mouth quivered, but she controlled it immediately. "No. I am afraid your cooking skills leave much to be desired." She could safely assume as much.

"Oh. How disappointing. Perhaps you could teach me?"

She glanced at him. The thought of instructing Mr. Carlisle on how to pluck a chicken and cook it was as laughable as it was enticing. And if he had resisted the idea rather than suggesting it, Judith would have been inclined to press the issue. But he had not. How was it possible for someone who had looked at her with so much disgust last week to look at her now with such imploring—and for such a purpose?

"Perhaps," she said evasively. The opportunity would never present itself.

Mr. Carlisle set down his spoon, watching her. "Miss Jardine, I understand that it must put you out a great deal to be obliged to attend to duties that normally fall to me. I sincerely apologize for the trouble I have caused you."

Judith met his gaze. Oh, the trouble he had caused her. She could almost imagine he was apologizing for thrusting a nickname upon her. Either way, she couldn't help but relent toward him at such a frank apology. Had his head injury jolted some kindness into him?

She knew a moment of misgiving as she looked in his eyes. What was she to do with a kind Mr. Carlisle? It had been easy to despise him when he had been rude and neglectful. But what now?

Perhaps he would become more pompous as his memories returned. Judith had an inkling that that might be for the best. After all, how would the *ton* resist a man who was possessed of kindness, handsome looks, *and* a large fortune?

Thankfully, Judith was not of the *ton*.

"I am not upset with you for being injured," she said. "Forgive me if I have seemed so to you. Are you finished with your soup?"

He hesitated then nodded, and she stood to take the bowl, which was empty.

She picked up the tray, then stopped, looking at Mr. Carlisle. "Would you care for more?"

He gave something between a smile and grimace, then nodded.

Mishaps and Memories

She couldn't stop a smile at his sheepish demeanor—nor could she deny the little bit of pleasure she felt knowing he had enjoyed the soup she had made. "There is plenty. I shall bring another bowl."

She fetched another helping as well as two of the rolls that sat nearby, consoling herself with the knowledge that it was in her own best interests and not due to a desire for Mr. Carlisle's approval that she did so. The sooner he regained his strength, the sooner he would regain his memories. That was all.

Judith left Mr. Carlisle to the second bowl of soup and rolls while she prepared a salve and ripped up an old shift of Mary's to use for bandages. When she returned, the bowl was empty, and the rolls were gone.

She moved the tray from his lap to make way for the one she had brought in. "My, but you have an appetite."

"Not a novel occurrence, it would seem." He pulled at the loosely hanging front of the shirt he wore.

Judith laughed and sat down beside him. "Come. Mr. Sharp ordered that your dressings be changed."

"Miss Jardine," Mr. Carlisle said in an apologetic voice, "surely it does not fall to you to do such a thing."

"Oh?" she asked politely. "To whom, then?"

He grimaced but offered no response.

"Now, show me these infamous battle wounds." She tried to keep her voice light and a smile on her face.

He frowned, then gave a little resigned sigh and pulled down the straps of his suspenders.

Judith's heart stopped, and she instinctively looked away.

Mr. Carlisle didn't miss her reaction, and he stopped with his hands on the hem of his shirt, ready to pull it over his head. He let it go and shook his head. "We can leave the dressings till morning. Perhaps then Mr."—he fumbled a bit—"Burns can come assist me."

Judith raised a brow. "Mr. Barry, you mean?"

"That is what I said."

She laughed. "You decidedly did not. You said Mr. Burns. And, no. We will not leave the dressings on until tomorrow. Mr. Sharp would have my head. I am not squeamish." She gave a nod. "Hurry, then."

He wavered a moment, then pulled the shirt over his head, wincing. Two bandages were wrapped around his midsection. Judith focused her attention on the fibers of linen that hung from the strips, though even without allowing her eyes to explore anything else, she had no difficulty recognizing that Mr. Carlisle added athleticism to his accomplishments. A pugilist, no doubt.

The wounds were, thankfully, located on his side and back, which meant Judith needn't look him in the eye at all while she dressed the wounds. It did not, however, save her from a more intimate knowledge than she ever wished for of Mr. Carlisle's powerful build and warm skin. He prevented too much of her focus from resting on such thoughts by asking her questions about his duties and situation, all of which she answered as vaguely as possible, with guilt in her heart and heat in her cheeks.

"Miss Jardine," he said after putting his shirt back on.

"Hmm?" She gathered the old dressings to be washed.

There was a pause. "Am I married?"

She stilled, then slowly set the last dressing on the tray, wondering what had brought about such a question. "You are not."

"Oh."

She looked at him, wondering if he was disappointed or relieved.

He sent her a smile. "Thank you. For everything. I assure you I mean to be back to my duties in the morning."

Mishaps and Memories

She shook her head, but he talked over her. "I will not let you take on all my tasks, Miss Jardine. I can see to them."

"Some of them, perhaps. We can speak of that in the morning, though. For now, what you need is rest, both body and mind." She would much rather he laze about and find excuses not to perform his duties. She would feel less guilty then.

He looked as though he might resist but only nodded.

When Judith had closed the door behind her, she realized that, with Mr. Carlisle in her own bed, she was left without a place to sleep.

She stood in the corridor, brows knit together, eyes on the narrow door in the dark corner at the end. If Mr. Carlisle was to fill the role of servant for a time, he should sleep in the closet—a cramped room with barely enough space for a straw mattress, a wash basin, and a small set of drawers with a tallow candle sitting upon it. It had been Jane's room.

But Judith hadn't the heart to ask him to move there. He was undoubtedly used to sleeping in fairly luxurious circumstances. Judith's bed would be change enough while still allowing him to sleep comfortably enough to aid in his recovery. If he slept well, his memories would hopefully return with the morning, and she could take her room back up again when he left.

The sooner he left, the better. For everyone.

Chapter Seven

BETWEEN THE STRAW POKING her every time she moved and the number of times she had hit her head on the low ceiling, Judith did not sleep well. The lack of a fire in the grate when she woke to a chillier morning than usual did nothing to improve her humor. Mary, on the other hand, was in an irritatingly joyful mood, seeming to take no heed of Judith's predicament. All responsibility for Mr. Carlisle she insisted—very unapologetically—upon placing on Judith's shoulders.

"We need more fish," Mary said as she sipped the tea Judith had prepared. "And potatoes, too."

Judith stared at her, soot from her encounter with preparing breakfast and cleaning the hearth smeared across her dress. "And I am to acquire them?"

Mary rubbed her belly and gave a shrug. "Send Mr. Carlisle to the market. *That* is sure to refresh his memory."

"Perhaps I will," Judith set her teacup down with a *clank*, then rose from the wicker chair and strode purposefully toward her bedroom.

She pushed the door open and halted.

Mr. Carlisle lay asleep upon the bed. The bedcovers were in a tangle around him. Had he slept badly as well? The bandage around his head had shifted so that it was slung at a diagonal, covering one eye completely and pushing up his dark hair above the other eye. It was amusing—and aggravatingly endearing.

She couldn't possibly send him to the market. She sighed and went back out again.

Whatever kindness had motivated Judith's decision to make the trip to the market herself, it had been long since expended by the time she reached the cottage with a basket on one arm and a bursting sack of potatoes and vegetables hanging from the other.

Mr. Carlisle sat at the table in the sitting room, drinking a cup of tea at his leisure and laughing at something Mary had just said as she bounced Charlie on her knee. The bandage had been repositioned on Mr. Carlisle's head, so that gone was the endearing appearance that had inspired Judith's act of selflessness.

"You look to be feeling well, James," Judith said in a brittle, sunny voice. "Have your memories returned?"

His smile faltered slightly. "No. I am afraid not." He rose from his seat and put out a hand to take the sack hanging from her arm. If she had not just spent the last two hours squeezing through a crowded market, trying to make her voice heard over those of other aggressive market-goers, and having her feet trod on, his chivalry might have had greater effect.

"Well," Judith said, "Mr. Sharp encouraged us to give you some light work that might help refresh your memories, and I have just the thing." She plopped the basket down on the table, full to bursting with fish. Having Mr. Carlisle clean twenty sardines would even the scales and, she trusted, be sufficiently revolting to spur some memories.

Mr. Carlisle looked at the fish then up at her, bafflement in his eyes.

She smiled at him, ignoring Mary's pointed look. "I shouldn't think that you are yet well enough to see to beating rugs and some of the more physical tasks you are accustomed to, but preparing the fish—*sardines* today—will not require too much of you."

Little Charlie pulled a face as he peered at the basket.

"Nonsense, my love," Judith said as she pinched the toddler's cheek. "A veritable bundle of deliciousness."

"They needn't be prepared beyond cutting off the heads," Mary said. "We can roast them whole."

Judith waved aside her sister's comment, unwilling to settle for so painless a task. "I cannot abide finding bones in my fish. They must certainly be prepared properly."

"Indeed," Mary said with faux interest. She turned to Mr. Carlisle. "And tell me, James. Do you remember how to prepare fish?"

Mr. Carlisle was still staring at the heap in the basket, where round, glassy eyes stared up at all of them blankly. He blinked and looked up, shaking his head. "I cannot say that I do."

"I suspected as much," Mary said. She looked at Judith with such innocence in her eyes that Judith's smile flickered as she realized what was to come. "Judith will gladly help to refresh your memory. And you, sir"—she faced Charlie toward her, though her belly kept him at a greater distance than usual—"are in need of a washing."

"I can see to that," Judith said eagerly, reaching for Charlie. "After all, you have much more practice cleaning fish than I, Mary. Come, Charlie."

But Mary shifted away from Judith, keeping Charlie from her reach. "All the more reason for you to see to the task. For how will you improve your skill but by practice?" She stood and, taking Charlie by the hand, shot Judith a look that made her want to wring Mary's neck.

Judith took in a deep breath. She had cleaned fish the last time she had come to Portsbury, and she had never wished to repeat the experience. Perhaps it would be worth the pain, though, to see Mr. Carlisle engaged in such an activity.

She retrieved two knives from the kitchen and sat in the chair Mary had occupied, preparing herself for the unsavory task before her.

"Perhaps it will come back to me once I"—Mr. Carlisle swallowed and picked up one of the fish—"have one in hand."

Only with difficulty did Judith control the impulse to laugh at the utter disgust on Mr. Carlisle's face. He shuddered slightly, and juice from the fish dripped onto his trousers. She watched him for any indication that the scenario might feel in the least bit familiar, but there was none. Was his memory truly gone? Or had his encounter with her at the Brighton ball been so inconsequential that he would never think on it again?

Mr. Carlisle took in a fortifying breath and picked up the knife Judith had set on the table beside him. He set it to the fish with hesitation, then looked at her.

She raised a brow.

"It is not coming back," he said, with enough guilt to soften her slightly.

"No." She rose from the chair and pulled it next to his. "I can see that from the way you are holding it. It is dead, James. You needn't treat it as though you intended to give it a name—"

"Mr. Higgins," he said without any hesitation.

She pinched her lips together to stop their unruliness. "—and a place to sleep."

He flashed her a sidelong glance with eyes full of teasing, and it brought her heart up into her throat.

Well, *that* wouldn't do. She reached for a fish, forcing herself to focus on the distasteful feel of it on her fingers rather than Mr. Carlisle's smile. It worked to great effect, and she suppressed her own shudder as she set it on the small wood platter and straightened her shoulders. "You must hold your knife like this—a light hold is paramount, for otherwise, you risk slipping and cutting yourself, and forgive me, James, but I have no desire for you to add such an injury to the ones you have already acquired. Nor do I not intend to go to the market in your place next week because you are recovering from another accident."

"A light hold," he repeated, letting the knife rest on his hand as he bounced his wrist lightly up and down.

Judith recoiled, and he stopped.

"A light hold, James. Not *no* hold at all."

He smiled, but adjusted his grip accordingly.

"Now," she said, "first, we must get rid of the head."

Mr. Carlisle looked down at the sardine before him. "It is staring at me. Mr. Higgins is staring at me."

"He is not." She pinched her lips together. "*It* is not."

He gave her a challenging glance, indicating the fish before her, and she looked down at it. Its large eye gaped at her, daring her to follow through with her threat.

"Are you scared of a dead fish, James?"

His brow and mouth frowned deeply, and he shook his head decidedly, but as he looked back down at the sardine, the head-shaking slowed and turned into nodding.

Judith couldn't stifle a laugh. "Oh, for heaven's sake! All you need to do is *this*." She steeled herself and made the necessary cut with her knife, then she turned the fish over and repeated the exercise.

By the time she had shown Mr. Carlisle how to finish the task, her stomach was churning. "I will go retrieve the salt to

Mishaps and Memories

preserve what we will not be using," she said in an unstable voice.

She hurried up from her seat and toward the small larder at the far side of the kitchen, opening the window that looked toward the sea and breathing the fresh air deeply. When she returned with the salt, Mr. Carlisle looked up at her with culpability in his gaze.

She looked at the table and brought a hand up to cover her mouth, which trembled traitorously. "Good heavens! What have you done to poor Mr. Higgins?" His sardine was, indeed, headless, but the rest was . . . well, mutilated.

Mr. Carlisle grimaced apologetically, his face looking a bit green, and Judith's mirth escaped in the form of a small snort.

His brows shot up at the unladylike sound.

Clearing her throat, she sat down beside him again and set down the salt, taking a new sardine from the basket.

"I shall do better next time," he promised, taking up another fish. "I am determined to learn." He set the knife to it.

"Stop," Judith cried with a hand up, moving her chair even closer to him. "No wonder you are struggling. You are still not holding the knife correctly. It should be held like *this*." She fixed his grasp on the knife and guided him in the cutting process, forcing herself again to focus on the gruesome details of the task rather than her hand on his. There was *nothing* romantic about cutting a fish with a man, whatever her heart might say.

The next hour was one of the strangest Judith had ever passed, full of fish bits, laughter, and frustration as Mr. Carlisle showed no aptitude at all for the task at hand. The salt rested on the table, unused as yet, and only three sardines remained in the basket.

"I think we shall have to content ourselves with picking out the bones for dinner this evening," Judith said resignedly.

Mr. Carlisle was looking sickly after a particularly unfortunate attempt at cutting a sardine, but he nodded. Judith looked at the results of her unsuccessful foray into teaching, and her own stomach swam at the sight. It—and the smell that permeated the air—were overwhelming.

"A fish massacre," Mr. Carlisle said with obvious frustration.

"A one-man fish massacre, no less," Judith replied, looking away from the macabre sight.

"Perhaps you could cut the last ones, and I can simply watch."

She sighed and placed the three sardines on the table, cutting them in turn, her thoughts and feelings conflicting. She had managed to make Mr. Carlisle look green, but the task had not elicited any of his memories as she had anticipated it might, and, worse by far, the more time she spent with him, the more she was coming to like him.

"There," she said. "See how easy that was?" She looked up at him and stilled. His gaze was on her, and a little hint of a smile pulled up at the corner of his mouth. But it was not that which kept her attention. It was the fish bits that had somehow made their way to the bandage on his head—including an eye.

She fought valiantly to control herself, but it was a lost cause, and it was through eyes leaking with tears of laughter that she attempted to explain to Mr. Carlisle the object of her mirth. Through her pointing and unintelligible speech, he managed to gather that his bandage was the culprit, and he lifted it from his head, turning it in his hands with a look of disgust on his face until he found the spark to Judith's amusement.

He gave a start and threw the bandage, which landed on Judith's lap. Her mouth dropped open, and she immediately picked it up with two fingers and tossed it back.

Mishaps and Memories

Mr. Carlisle was smiling now, and he held it up threateningly. Judith reached her hands for the mess of fish on the table and gave him a look of warning. He swiftly dropped the bandage on his lap and put both hands up in surrender.

"Good choice," Judith said, smiling at the genuine dismay in his eyes. "And now, I think it is time both of us cleaned up."

There was a hint of reluctance in the way he agreed. Judith felt it, too, and it struck a chord of fear within her.

A man who could make her feel loath to leave the cleaning of fish was a dangerous man indeed.

Chapter Eight

JAMES HELPED MISS JARDINE clean up his embarrassing efforts at preparing fish. Not only had he no memory of ever executing such a task, he had also obviously lost the skill for it. Beyond that, more than once, he had come perilously near to losing the tea he had drunk just beforehand.

How had he managed to do such a task when the sight and smell of the dead fish made his stomach turn? Had he simply suffered through it for years? Or was the aversion something he had acquired with the accident?

The truth was, nothing about life here felt familiar—nothing felt right. Nothing except Miss Jardine. And that in itself was wrong, wasn't it? In his capacity as a servant, there was no place for the attraction and admiration James had been feeling.

"That will do for now," Miss Jardine said as she removed her apron and motioned for him to follow her down the corridor.

They reached the bedchamber he had been occupying, and Miss Jardine entered, taking a few garments from the armoire in the corner. James frowned as she gave him a polite smile and exited.

"I shall fetch you some fresh clothing," she said. "And once I have changed, I shall bring more strips and the salve I made yesterday."

James nodded, but he was confused. Was this Miss Jardine's room? He had never thought on the subject long enough to wonder. He hadn't recognized the room as his own, but he hadn't recognized *anything*.

When Miss Jardine returned a few minutes later with folded clothing in hand, he took it from her. "Miss Jardine?"

She paused at the door.

"Is this your bedchamber?" he asked.

She took a moment before responding. "Yes."

"Then where are you sleeping?"

A pause. "In one of the other rooms."

"But why put me here, if there are other rooms I might be in? There is no need to inconvenience you."

Miss Jardine looked uncomfortable with the line of questioning. "I thought you could do with a bit of space."

He frowned more deeply still, and the gesture tugged lightly at the wound on the back of his head. "My normal bedchamber lacks space, then?"

Her lips pursed together. "Yes. Yes, it does."

"Miss Jardine," he said. "I have put you out quite enough. And I assure you, I have no need of extra space. I would prefer it if you returned here and I to my own bedchamber."

A flicker of humor danced in her eyes. "Would you really?"

Her strange answer gave him pause, but he nodded.

"Follow me, then," she said.

He did as instructed, and they emerged into the dim corridor, where the smell of dampness was strong. Miss Jardine walked to a small, uneven door at the end of the corridor and put out a hand in a showy gesture. There was an amused smile on her face, and James's eyes lingered on her for a moment before returning to the door.

The door stuck as he tried to open it, but with a more forceful tug, it gave way. It was dark within, and it took a moment for his eyes to make anything out. As they did, his eyebrows went up, and he could feel Miss Jardine's gaze on him.

It was no bedchamber—or not a proper one, at least. There was a small, lumpy bed and a washstand with two drawers, both of which looked to be broken. It lacked a window, so the only light which reached the space was the trifling bit that existed in the corridor.

"This is where you slept last night?" James asked.

"Yes." She tilted her head to the side. "Well, *sleep* is a generous term. Let us say rather that this is where I spent the night."

James glanced at the woman beside him, who looked at him with wrinkles of amusement beside her eyes. It was hard for him to comprehend how she could fit in such a space, to say nothing of his own, taller form. And he was not now anywhere near as large as he had once been, based on the clothing that belonged to him. Just the thought of attempting to fit within made his legs cry out in protest.

"Return to the other bedchamber, James," Miss Jardine said with an understanding smile.

He shook his head, staring again at the mattress. The fabric was threadbare in many places, with straw poking through.

"That is an order," Miss Jardine said. "And might I also suggest that you take advantage of your time there? For I doubt I shall be feeling so generous tomorrow."

James hesitated, wanting to resist her order but laboring under the force of the knowledge that he had no right to nay say her. He was a servant.

Before he could decide what to do, Miss Jardine was slipping into the small space, hunched over in a way that, in spite of himself, brought a smile to James's face.

"Excuse me," she said as she closed the door. It refused to shut all the way, and there were sounds of struggle.

James gave the door a push, and it slammed into place.

"Thank you," came her muffled voice.

James stared at the door another moment, then sighed and went back to his temporary bedchamber to change his clothing.

His injuries felt less painful and tight than they had the day before, but it was largely owing to the generous size of both the old and new garments that he was able to change them with so little trouble.

Ten minutes later, he sat on the edge of the bed with no sign of Miss Jardine. It must be difficult, indeed, to do anything in the small space she had been in, to say nothing of changing clothing. He had little doubt she would air her grievances on the subject to him. She was a strange woman—hot and cold by turns.

She was likely occupied with helping care for her nephew. He could hear the ear-splitting sounds of Charlie's displeasure being made known.

Presently, there was a knock on his door, and he shot to his feet. His head throbbed at the overzealous action, and he shut his eyes, taking in a deep breath. He shouldn't be so eager for her company.

He opened the door and blinked. Mr. Sharp stood before him, spectacles perched halfway down his nose. His leather bag was slung over his shoulder, a copy of a newspaper sticking out.

"Mr. Sharp," James said, trying to infuse his voice with pleasantness instead of disappointment. "Come in."

Mr. Sharp was not one for exchanging civilities, and he set right to the task of asking questions and examining James's wounds.

"These should be bandaged," he said, displeasure evident in his voice. "I gave precise orders on the subject."

"I was just waiting for Miss Jardine to come with fresh ones when you arrived."

He gave a grunt and opened his bag.

"Mr. Sharp?"

Another grunt.

"None of my memories have yet returned. Do you anticipate they will?"

"I believe so."

The curt answer was hardly invitation to continue, but James couldn't help himself. "I just find it so strange how unfamiliar everything continues to be."

Mr. Sharp offered no response, only continuing his inspection of James's head.

"May I give you an example?"

Receiving no refusal, he proceeded. "Just today, I attempted one of my regular duties—cleaning out and preparing fish. One would think that doing something which should be so familiar to me would have roused some sliver of a memory at least, no?"

A small grunt.

"But it did not. And not only that, sir, but I was hard-pressed not to retch with the sight and smell of the fish. And furthermore, even with Miss Jardine's aid, I could not manage to carry out the task properly even *once*." He shook his head, troubled again at the memory.

Mr. Sharp moved to the injuries on James's side and back, moving his bag of instruments to the floor so he could sit down. "Blows to the head can be life-altering. I have seen them change people in very strange ways. Your speech, for instance."

"What do you mean?"

The surgeon chuckled. "I have never met a servant with such proper speech." He shrugged. "It wouldn't be the strangest result of a head injury I have ever heard of."

James didn't respond. He might have asked Mr. Sharp a hundred more questions, but the man's answers only led to even more questions. Would James never remember life before the accident?

Mr. Sharp stood and reached for his bag, eyes on James's head. "Whatever Miss Jardine put on the wounds, it seems to have worked well. The injury on your head should remain bandaged tonight, but you may remove it tomorrow if you are feeling well enough." He began to move toward the door, then turned. "As for your memories, don't despair just yet. Sometimes, it only takes something insignificant. It is merely a matter of finding that spark. Good day."

James sat on the edge of the bed for a moment, pondering on the surgeon's visit. The sound of Charlie's cries had dissipated, yet there was still no sign of Miss Jardine.

He stepped into the corridor, intending to go to the kitchen, where he could hear the clamor of preparation occurring. But he stopped short, listening.

No, he wasn't imagining it. He hurried to the door at the end of the corridor and yanked it open.

Miss Jardine fell forward, and he caught her under the arms. She smelled of straw and violets—a strange combination—and she hurried to push herself to a stand, using James as a bolster.

Her eyes sparkled, and she brushed roughly at her skirts with a huff. "Is *everyone* in this house deaf?"

James's eyebrows shot up, and his mouth trembled with

laughter. He covered it with a hand, well-aware of how unwelcome his reaction would be. "Were you in there that entire time?"

"Do you find that amusing?" she asked.

He pulled his lips between his teeth, shaking his head and hoping his own eyes didn't betray him by laughing the way Miss Jardine's sometimes did.

"I suppose you expect my thanks for releasing me"—she kicked at the door, which hit the frame at its odd angle and rebounded, forcing her to hasten to the side—"but as you were the one who entrapped me in the first place, you will, I am afraid, have to do without."

"Entrapped you?" he asked. "I thought *I* was the one with the faulty memory! Perhaps you will recall that I expressed my desire that you should return to your own bedchamber."

"And then promptly cemented me into the closet." She gave another huff. "You may sleep in my bedchamber tonight, James, but tomorrow, you will have the doubtful pleasure of occupying this space again." She strode toward the kitchen, leaving him in the corridor.

He smiled as he watched her disappear, but she returned quickly with the salve and strips of fabric. He followed her into the bedchamber and sat down upon the bed, watching Miss Jardine's fiery movements with wariness. "Perhaps we should wait until . . ."

She raised her brows challengingly. "Until?"

"Until your desire to harm me has subsided a bit?"

"I can quite easily separate my feelings for you from my actions, James." She tore a piece of fabric to make it smaller, and his eyes widened.

But she proved to be correct. So correct, in fact, that James almost wished otherwise. Her light touch on his wounds, the soft hand she used to stabilize herself on his skin—it did nothing to help James toward his goal of smothering his attraction to her. Was the draw he felt to her new, or had he felt it before his injury, too?

Thankfully—*and* regrettably, somehow—she made quick and silent work of it. There was no trace of anger left in her eyes afterward. In fact, James could have sworn they were troubled. But it was not his place to pursue such a subject.

"Tomorrow morning, I will resume my duties," he said.

Her lips pinched together in dissatisfaction, though why, he couldn't tell.

"You object?" he asked.

"I do if you perform them like you performed your duty today."

He let out a rueful laugh. "Your patience for teaching me is understandably spent."

She looked at him, silent for a moment. "I will *try* to teach you. And I trust you will be rested enough after another night in this luxurious bed to enable your most exemplary work."

"I would gladly take my rightful place in the closet," he pointed out.

Those intent eyes fixed on him again, searching his face. "No. I gave you an order, James. I trust I will not be obliged to repeat myself again." She gave him a haughty look—the type that was entirely undermined by her insistence upon taking the cramped closet for herself.

However little James remembered of life before he had woken in Miss Jardine's bed, he was grateful that he *had* woken to find himself employed in the home of women as likable as Mrs. Bradford and Miss Jardine. What if he had woken to find himself the servant of a man like Mr. Sharp? He hoped Mr. Bradford would be as amiable as his wife and sister-in-law, whenever he returned.

With the help of both women, James learned how to

prepare potatoes and sardines—or what was left of them, anyway—for dinner. And though he did resist when Mrs. Bradford insisted that he join them for dinner, his protestations were easily overcome. "You have oft sat down to dine with us in the past," she had said. And when he entered Miss Jardine's bedchamber to settle in for the night, it was with a strange sense of contentment.

He reached to pull off one of his boots, and his hand brushed something at the base of the bed. It was a newspaper, and he picked it up with curiosity. It must have fallen out of Mr. Sharp's bag earlier.

The first page was covered in fine print, lists of advertisements for servants. James read through a few of them, wondering if he himself had answered just such a notice. There were so many questions about his past. How had he learned to read, for instance? Did he have family still living? How old was he? Why was he not married?

As for the last question, a part of him wondered if the attraction he felt for Miss Jardine was one of the few things connecting him to his past. There was something that felt so familiar about her. Had he felt before as he did now, always wishing to spend more time near her?

He sighed and opened the newspaper, letting his eyes run over the next page—two notices of impending marriages, a number of paragraphs devoted to bills coming up for debate when Parliament resumed and—he frowned at a paragraph in the center of the page.

"Information sought regarding the whereabouts of Mr. James Carlisle, son and heir of Mr. Henry Carlisle and Mrs. Margaret Carlisle of Lower Birchmouth, who was last seen in Brighton on the twelfth of June. A reward of five pounds is offered to anyone in possession of reliable intelligence on the subject, to be presented at . . ."

Mishaps and Memories

James's mind whirled, and he stared at the name: James Carlisle.

And with such a spark, the flicker of memory fanned into a small flame.

Chapter Nine

JUDITH TURNED OVER SLEEPILY in bed, only for her head and arm to hit against the wall. She groaned softly and rubbed the spot on her forehead with a hand.

Thunk thunk. The sound forced a greater awareness onto her.

Who in the world could be knocking on her door in the middle of the night? Her eyes flew open. Perhaps it was Mary, and the baby was on its way.

She stood, careful not to let her head hit the steeply sloped ceiling, and slipped on her wrapper before opening the door hurriedly.

Mr. Carlisle stood before her with the sort of smile on his face that, to be quite frank, was unsuitable for such a time of night.

"What is it?" she asked, brushing aside both her irritation and the vain worry she felt over her appearance.

He hesitated a bit. "You said to wake you when the cock crowed, did you not?"

Was it truly morning already? She had spent a great deal of time the night before berating herself for ever having offered up her own bedchamber to Mr. Carlisle. So far, very little about her desire to teach him a lesson had gone according to plan, and she owed at least a portion of that to her own pesky—and oft-regretted—moments of charity toward him. She was finding it difficult not to like Mr. Carlisle—and to like him more than she cared to admit.

When she emerged a few minutes later, dressed for the day, he was leaning against the wall, humming softly, and she knew a bit of anticipation at the prospect of spending the day with him.

"Is it not cold in that closet during the winter months?" he asked quietly as they passed the door to Mary and Charlie's room.

"Yes," she said. "That is when you sleep by the fire in the sitting room." Or, at least, that was what Jane had done.

He looked over at her, his dark eyebrows raised.

She felt an annoying need to defend her sister's circumstances. "If Mary's husband manages to be offered the position he is seeking, their lodgings would be much improved."

"Would you go with them? With us?"

She shook her head. "I am only here to help during my sister's confinement."

"But you have visited on other occasions? While I have been employed here?"

She glanced at him warily. It was natural for him to have questions, of course, but she disliked having to answer them—to perjure herself.

"I only ask," he said, "because very few things have struck a chord in my memory as of yet. But you . . ." He looked at her thoughtfully, searchingly, and her blood flowed warmer. "There is something familiar about you."

Her heart pattered more quickly, and she knew a certain dismay at the thought that he might recognize her and discover the truth. That would mean the end of things, and while she had been wishing for that precise thing since Mr. Sharp had forbidden her from oversetting Mr. Carlisle, she found that just now, she wasn't quite ready for it. It must be due to the simple fact that she enjoyed being in a position of superiority. Her entire life, her family had lingered on the fringes of polite society, looked down upon by people like Mr. Carlisle. Of course, she would find some enjoyment in the tables being turned.

There was nothing else to her feelings. She wouldn't let there be.

She changed the subject. "You have removed the bandage on your head." It was unfortunate, really. It had been easier to forget how handsome he was with it covering part of his face and pushing his hair up at awkward angles.

"It still smells of fish."

She laughed as they came to the hearth. "Then I am glad you have removed it. I have no desire to be smelling you all day." She turned to the hearth. "Now, the first task is to light the fire." She took the flint box from the mantel and handed it to him.

He stared down at it, then up at her, a blank look in his eyes.

Judith let out a dramatic, resigned sigh and took the box back. "What would you do without me? You cannot remember even the most basic of tasks." She crouched down, and he followed suit.

"*Or* perhaps I am simply finding excuses for your company."

Judith whipped her head around to look at him. He was teasing her—it was written in his laughing eyes as clear as the stars in the sky, and it nettled her.

"In misplacing your memory," she said severely, "you seem to have misplaced your sense of propriety as well."

"Did I have one before the accident?" he asked.

Judith's mind flashed back to the way he had ignored her almost entirely at dinner. "Not much, no."

"Then what has induced your sister to keep me on as a servant?"

Judith drove the striker along the flint so that Mr. Carlisle could see. She handed it to him. "She hasn't the heart to send you back to the life you had before."

"The life I had before..." Mr. Carlisle said, watching her. "What was it like?"

She chose not to respond directly to the question. "Despite your episodes of impudence, you are much improved since working here."

"Am I?" The words themselves were harmless enough, but they were said with a dose of teasing—one might have even said *flirtation*—that affected her far more than was fair.

"You mustn't sound so puffed up about it," she said. "Transforming a pig into an ass may be an improvement, but both beasts leave much to be desired."

Mr. Carlisle let out a laugh and attempted to emit a spark with the striker and flint. He failed, and Judith was obliged to guide him. He showed no indication of ever having performed the duty required of him, and little wonder. It was very possible he had never had to light a fire in his life.

And while Judith was quick to express her frustration with his ineptitude, Mr. Carlisle was just as quick to make her laugh, and she found that the normally tedious tasks of cleaning the stove and the carpets were much less so with him for company.

The latter activity was the first he showed any natural aptitude for. They set the rugs, which were full of dirt from the dry summer roads, to hang over the branch of the tree behind Mary's house and, with the fresh sea breeze assisting them, took turns beating them.

Mr. Carlisle clapped at Judith's more forceful attempts, and she accepted the praise with the sort of graceful curtsies she had given the night of the Brighton ball. She pretended to give him instruction, as well, but in truth, he needed none.

Breathless after a dozen turns each, they rested their backs against the crooked trunk of the tree, which offered a view of the sea beyond. The sun-kissed water stretched on for miles, until the horizon became so shrouded in mist, it was impossible to see where the sea ended and the sky began.

"I have a question," Mr. Carlisle announced. "Does it still count as impudence if I warn you of it?" The trunk of the tree was wide, but not so wide that they could both lean against it without standing up against each other.

"Yes, James." She shot him an unamused look. "It does."

He gave a *humph* and crossed his arms.

Judith tried to fight off her curiosity at what he had been about to say. She could feel her feet on dangerous ground, and it wasn't a question of whether the ground would give out, but when.

"Although," Mr. Carlisle said, sending her a sidelong glance, "one cannot expect an ass to act like anything other than an ass . . ."

She tried to control a smile.

He paused a moment, and his expression became more pensive. "You are not married."

She stiffened involuntarily, and her smile disappeared. "A comment fit for an ass, indeed." She stepped away from the tree.

"No, no," Mr. Carlisle said, and he pulled her back by the hand.

Judith's heart leapt into her throat.

"You mistake my meaning," he said, and the teasing in his eyes was gone. "I was only wondering if there was a particular reason for the fact."

"Must there be a reason?" She cocked an eyebrow at the hand he still held, and he dropped it. The regret she felt when he did bothered her deeply.

He shrugged. "I lost my memories, Miss Jardine, not my senses, and it stands to reason that a woman with as much to recommend her as you has had opportunity to marry."

She gave a little snort, and he frowned.

"What? Why do you scoff?"

Judith didn't respond immediately. How could she explain that she might have received an offer of marriage if it weren't for him? He had no memory of their encounter. Perhaps, though, when his memories returned, he would remember what she said now, and her words would encourage him to act with less arrogance toward other women in positions like Judith's.

"Impudence is still impudence when it is couched in flattery, James." She stared at the waves rolling in toward the shore. "In any case, you betray your lack of understanding when you say such things. I live in a world in between—too humble to deserve the notice of those above me in station, but just lofty enough not to be noticed by those below me in station."

"Well, there, you're wrong, Miss Jardine."

She looked at him.

"You were the first thing *I* noticed when I woke," he said.

She gave another scoff. "You could hardly have noticed anything else. I placed myself directly in your line of vision."

"But I haven't stopped noticing you since."

She swallowed, all too aware of her heart thundering. If a week ago, she had been told she would hear such words on the lips of Mr. Carlisle—the man who had taken no notice of her at all—it would have been with the anticipation of feeling undeniable pride and a sense of victory. But that was not what she felt now. She felt hope. And she felt as though, of all things, she might cry. Both things terrified her.

In any case, a servant should be slapped and dismissed for such presumption.

But Mr. Carlisle was not her servant, nor was he her sister's servant. He was *no one's* servant at all.

"I think these rugs have been sufficiently beaten," she said. "And we have much left to accomplish."

The best thing would be to ignore his flirtation and make it clear to Mr. Carlisle—and herself—that her role was that of mistress instructing a new servant, because less and less about their interactions felt like those of servant and mistress.

Chapter Ten

JAMES PAUSED AT THE door, watching Miss Jardine inside her sister's room as she aired out the sheets. The afternoon light poured through the open window, illuminating her from behind. She was humming lightly as she saw to her work, and James felt a little ache in his chest at the idyllic image. Even with the return of his memories, what it was that was so familiar about her still eluded him.

He had begun the day with several objectives in mind. Firstly, he wished to postpone his return to normal life, as that would entail facing the expected visit to Miss Garrett, and he was not at all certain how he intended to approach that meeting. He shuddered every time he pictured her stare fixed upon him, but he also shuddered at the thought of his father's disappointment if he should fail to "come up to scratch." He would use the day to ponder on that dilemma.

Secondly, he had hoped to seek enlightenment—very carefully, albeit—regarding Miss Jardine and Mrs. Bradford's objectives in making him believe he was their servant. A servant, of all things! In his initial anger and bafflement, he had nearly gone to demand an explanation from Miss Jardine last night. But could he count on her telling him the truth? A person who would deceive someone as she had been deceiving James was clearly not to be relied upon.

The entire situation was so incredible as to be lunatic—and yet, simultaneously comical and intriguing. In the end, his curiosity determined his final aim for the day: to turn the tables on Miss Jardine. He had considered other options, of course: berating her, leaving the house without a word—he would have been justified in either. But those options would both be so fleeting and dissatisfying.

No, he would amuse himself much better this way, making Miss Jardine regret the promise she had made to guide him through his so-called *duties*. It seemed only fair, given what she was doing to *him*. And certainly more enjoyable than facing the realities of his life.

But teasing Miss Jardine was proving to be even more entertaining and agreeable than he had foreseen. And as he watched her for another moment, broom in his hand, he made a decision.

Based on the date he had seen on the newspaper Mr. Sharp had left, he had a week until the meeting his father had arranged with Miss Garrett and Lord Linscott. What would happen if he never appeared for it? No one could blame him for being too indisposed to attend such an engagement—he *had* lost his memory, after all. And if he waited long enough, Sir William would offer for Miss Garrett. She would be well taken care of, and James would be liberated from the undesired connection.

He would stay. And he would find out what Miss Jardine was about while he was at it.

Mr. Sharp called the next day and, despite the niggling

guilt in James's stomach, he gave the surgeon no indication that his memory had returned.

"As for injury to body," the man said to James and the two sisters, "he is well on his way to recovery. As regards injury to mind, I cannot deny that I am disappointed. We must begin to consider the possibility that the memories shall not return."

James looked at Miss Jardine, whose eyes were round with . . . was it dismay? The news certainly did not seem welcome, and her reaction perplexed him. If she had been trusting that his memories would return, what in the world was she about? Why not simply tell him the truth?

She knew at the very least he was not her sister's servant—there was no doubt at all about that. But did she know his real identity? He suspected she did, and the fact that he couldn't think *how* they might have become acquainted grated him unbearably. They were not the sort of people he would have had occasion to meet in Society, and he was certain he had never before been to Portsbury. If he had not taken it in his head to go out rowing that fateful morning and subsequently found himself in increasingly rough waters, he never *would* have been to Portsbury.

He was determined to untangle the whole mess.

That determination was certainly tested, though, for life as a servant was anything but easy. His time from dawn till dusk was occupied with chores, and the closet—fiend seize that blasted closet!—was a trial, indeed, to sleep in, if he was fortunate enough to sleep at all. His experience there made him all the more appreciative of Miss Jardine having slept there the first two nights of his stay.

Evenings were the most difficult for James. It was then that he seriously considered ending the baffling charade they were all living, for it was then that he was alone. His time during the day was often spent in the company of Miss Jardine as she oversaw his tasks and instructed him in improving them. He made sure that there was enough progress in the performance of his duties not to raise questions or lead to his termination as a servant—ha!—but little enough progress that Miss Jardine was obliged to assist him from time to time. He took great joy in teasing her and in flirting with her just enough to discomfit her. He enjoyed her company.

Once or twice, he wondered whether the sisters shared a hope of forging a connection between himself and Miss Jardine. This was largely due to Mrs. Bradford's apparent eagerness to throw them into tasks together. Perhaps they hoped to arrange for a match between the two of them before he could become aware of his true situation in life?

But such a belief was unsustainable. James had heard Miss Jardine plead with her sister on more than one occasion to allow her to take on the care of Charlie in lieu of engaging in a task alongside James. He was baffled—and a little hurt, if he was being honest—by those instances. But Mrs. Bradford was always quick to insist that she wished to keep Charlie to herself so that she might spend as much time with him as possible before the new baby arrived.

Miss Jardine was difficult to puzzle out, in truth. She could be impatient with James—and often was—but this he found easy to forgive. After all, he had made it his goal to make her life more difficult. In addition, her shows of wit pleased him, and it became an ambition of his to make her laugh. He always felt exhilaration and satisfaction when he succeeded.

At other times, though, he knew a desire to do much more than make her laugh. He had caught himself with the impulse to take her in his arms. His wish to tease and torture her had become confusingly mixed up with other developing feelings.

Mishaps and Memories

The ease of being with her and the knowledge that she and Mrs. Bradford would struggle to get along without him made the uncomfortable nights more bearable. Every now and then—usually when he had just hit his head on the unforgivably slanted ceiling in the closet—James would fall into a fit of laughter at the absurdity of his current situation.

Just shy of a week after his arrival, James sat on a stump outside the cottage, just under the kitchen window, letting the sea breeze ruffle his hair and cool the sweat on his brow. It was a particularly hot day, and he had nearly finished beating the rugs when he had noticed a stain upon the one from the sitting room—compliments of Charlie having managed to steal a few blackberries undetected.

More and more, Miss Jardine had begun leaving him to perform tasks on his own, only coming to check on the final result of his work. He disliked the development, but he could only pretend incompetence for so long.

Her voice sailed through the open window above him. "And what if his memory never *does* return, Mary?"

James stilled, cocking an ear, though he could easily hear their voices without doing so.

"Then I will happily keep him on as a servant," Mrs. Bradford said.

Miss Jardine let out an impatient noise.

"To be sure," Mrs. Bradford continued, "I had my doubts he could learn how to be a satisfactory one—particularly with the fish-cleaning debacle—but he has improved significantly, you must admit."

"Yes," Miss Jardine said incredulously, "but only after great pains have been taken on my end."

"And I applaud your efforts, Judy. I think members of the *ton* in general would benefit from knowing what a day in the life of a servant is like."

"Undoubtedly," Miss Jardine replied, "but you cannot seriously mean to keep him on, Mary! To deprive him of his family and his family of him, to say nothing of keeping him from the life he was born into. You must be joking."

"*You* certainly seem not to mind spending time with him." James could hear the smile in Mrs. Bradford's voice, and his heart beat more quickly.

"What in heaven's name are you talking about?"

"Oh, Judy, don't pretend! Not with me. I can see how things lie with you, plain as day."

James leaned closer, cursing the beating of his heart, which had grown so loud in his ears, he feared he might not hear what was said next.

"You are being ridiculous," Miss Jardine said in a clipped voice. "Though that should come as no surprise to me, I suppose. You are hardly subtle in your efforts to throw us together, as though anything could come of that."

"And why not?"

Miss Jardine scoffed. "Enough, Mary. I know you are only amusing yourself, but no more, please. It is time to tell him the truth."

"No, no," Mrs. Bradford said hurriedly. "I am sorry for teasing, Judy. I can see you do not find it funny, which can only mean your feelings run deeper than I had thought. But please do not tell him. Not just yet. When George returns, you have my blessing, but . . ."

"But what?" Miss Jardine sounded exasperated.

"I feel much safer with him here while George is away," Mrs. Bradford said in an apologetic voice. "Only think! What if the baby were to come? My time is drawing near, and I have been feeling pains for a few days now. *You* would be obliged to go fetch someone, and *I* would be in no fit state to care for Charlie."

There was a pause.

"Just a few more days, Judy. That is all I ask. And then you are free to tell him whatever you wish."

There was silence, finally punctuated by a sigh from Miss Jardine.

Footsteps sounded, approaching the door that led to the back of the cottage and out to where James was seated.

He picked up the stick he had been using to beat the rugs and hurried to his feet, rushing over to the branch where a rug was still draped and beginning to hit it. He hoped Miss Jardine didn't realize that the sound had been absent for the past few minutes.

As for what Mrs. Bradford had implied about her sister's feelings for him, he hardly knew what to hope for.

Chapter Eleven

AS SHE APPROACHED, JUDITH chose to look at the rippling rug in order to keep her eyes from admiring the man beating it. It was something she had been catching herself doing far too often—admiring Mr. Carlisle—and it frustrated her to no end. When had her disdain for him turned to admiration? And how had she hidden it so ill that Mary had noticed?

Mr. Carlisle turned toward her, wiping a dirty, hanging sleeve across his brow as he met her gaze. A discarded cravat hung from one of the smaller branches, and sweat glistened on the part of his chest visible through the gap in his overlarge shirt. In all her plans to humiliate him, she had never anticipated he would look so utterly charming and unruffled as she did so.

"You might have left this task for this evening when it is cooler," she said.

He shrugged. "There is something rewarding about perspiring after a job well done."

She raised a brow. How would the Mr. Carlisle of two weeks ago feel about hearing such words on his own lips? "A job well done, you say? I think *I* shall be the judge of that." She stepped over to the rug to inspect it. Her lips pinched together. It *did* look well-beaten.

Mishaps and Memories

Mary was right. Mr. Carlisle had improved greatly in the past few days. She looked at him, only to find his gaze fixed upon her, watching her carefully. Was he so anxious for her approval?

"An acceptable job," she said begrudgingly.

He inclined his head in a formal gesture. "You overwhelm me, Miss Jardine. Tell me, now. Does this mean I have reached new heights? Am I no longer an ass?"

She was finding it harder and harder to stop her smiles around him. Or perhaps he was getting better and better at eliciting them. "Let us not be premature."

"This is all?" Judith asked in dismay.

Mary's shoulders lifted in a helpless gesture. "The fish you bought were meant to last much longer than two meals, Judy."

They stood in the kitchen together, Charlie tugging on his mother's skirts while the two of them looked at the last of the potatoes and the empty larder.

"But market day isn't for two days," Judith replied.

"I know."

Judith stared at the three potatoes—the smallest ones, which had fallen to the bottom of the sack—and bit her lip.

Mr. Carlisle appeared, holding an empty water basin in the crook of his arm. He smiled at them as he approached but, seeing their expressions, his gait slowed and he frowned.

"Is something the matter?"

Judith looked at Mary, avoiding Mr. Carlisle's eye. It was silly, and she knew it, but she was hesitant to explain the situation to him. Not because it was his fault the sardines hadn't lasted as long as they had been meant to. Her hesitation was because of her pride. What had he said at the dinner?

Good breeding cannot be bought, of course, but it does go hand-in-hand with money.

Whatever the state of Mr. Carlisle's memory, his prejudices must be lurking beneath the surface. And when he knew that there was no food—and no money for food in the house—what would he be left to infer about Judith and Mary?

But Judith didn't want to care for Mr. Carlisle's opinion. A man who would assume such things didn't deserve that she should allow his opinions to hold any weight.

"We have no food left," she said. It came out sounding more like a challenge than the simple statement of a fact.

His eyebrows went up, and he blinked. "Oh."

Judith felt her pride flare up again at the expression on his face. "I'm afraid that the massacre upended Mary's plans for dinner."

She immediately regretted the words at the look of guilt on Mr. Carlisle's face.

"Of course," he said. "I should have thought of that. I sincerely apologize, and I assure you, I will . . . I will make amends."

Mary shook her head. "You needn't concern yourself with it, James. There is nothing you can do."

"I can fish," he said suddenly. "I will catch them myself."

Judith tilted her head to the side, her worry and pride giving way to amusement. "You think you can fish? Surely, you haven't forgotten what happened last time you attempted that?"

He smiled responsively, though there was still a hint of guilt in his eyes. "I can try." He raised his brows. "Or I could be taught."

Judith scoffed. "I'm afraid our need for food is rather more urgent than the time it would take for you to relearn such a skill."

He shrugged. "I should like to try."

Mishaps and Memories

He was serious, and Judith couldn't help but like him the better for it, even if the mere thought of trying to teach him such a skill exhausted her. Had they been so successful in convincing him of his past as a servant that he truly thought he had once possessed such an ability? What would his reaction be to discover that his only accomplishments were dancing cotillions and making bows?

"We *do* have the equipment for it," Mary said.

Judith shot her an annoyed look.

"What?" she said defensively. "We do. It is on the side of the cottage."

"I cannot blame you for having little desire to teach me," Mr. Carlisle said to Judith. "I can make the attempt on my own. Or perhaps there will be a kindly fisherman who will take pity on me."

As he left the room, Mary shot Judith a look that could only be described as that of a chastising mother. "It is not wise for him to go alone, Judy."

"Why must he go at all?" Judith retorted. "No one asked him to."

"We must eat," Mary said significantly. "And it is very kind of him to offer, even if he is unsuccessful. You *did* want him to learn humility, did you not?"

"Yes," Judith said, resignedly reaching for her pelisse. "I did. But if eating is our goal, I should likely have better success fishing on my own."

She hurried to catch up with Mr. Carlisle, who had reached the side of the house and was gathering the fishing equipment together. He glanced up as she approached.

"Have you come to help me or dissuade me?" he asked.

"To protect you," she said, reaching for the bucket. "And ensure that we have something to eat for dinner. You left without even inquiring about a vessel for your expedition."

He smiled mischievously. "I hoped you would follow."

She scoffed and set the bucket down again. "You deserve that I should leave right now."

"Very likely," he said, giving no indication at all that he expected her implied threat to be carried out.

She hesitated another moment, then grabbed the bucket and led the way to the path that would take them to the beach.

Mary and George owned a small boat of somewhat questionable integrity which, when not in use, was kept hidden in the reeds just above the beach. Judith and Mr. Carlisle set their equipment inside it and together pulled it down the grassy slope to the sand below.

"So, you leave the invalid to push you out to sea?" Mr. Carlisle teased as she climbed in.

"Whatever your skill with a fishing pole, you can at least manage this part of the process, can you not? It *will* take a great deal of strength. You will simply wait for—"

Mr. Carlisle gave a great push, and the boat slid forward, unsettling Judith from her seat and into the bottom of the boat.

Mr. Carlisle ran after the boat, making a great splash in the waves, then climbed in, causing it to rock from side to side. Wet from the thighs down, he steadied himself, then extended a hand toward Judith, who was staring at him with all the animus she could muster.

"You were saying?" He waited for her to place her hand in his, a wide smile on his face.

She didn't deign to reply to his provocation and accepted his hand begrudgingly.

He pulled her up with the same strength he had used to push the boat, and the force brought her right up against him. She stopped herself with her hands on his chest, but she needn't have, for he held her in place with a firm hand around the waist.

Too flustered for speaking and afraid he could feel her heartbeat with their sudden proximity, Judith pulled back in a hurry, sitting down on the board behind her in a less-than-elegant shuffle.

Mr. Carlisle sat down opposite her so that they faced one another, and he took the oars in hand. "Now, then. Where do we go, Miss Jardine?"

Hoping her cheeks weren't as hot as they felt, she cleared her throat. "Just past that cliff. The fish tend to gather in the pools nearby."

Mr. Carlisle seemed to need no instruction on the subject of rowing, and Judith secretly marveled at the speed with which he took them to their destination. She tried to keep her eyes trained on the water, even though they strayed time and again to the rhythmic movement of his shoulders. There was a contentment in his eyes, too, that struck her.

The sun was making its gradual progress toward the horizon, lengthening the shadow of the boat on the water, though the light hadn't yet taken on the golden glow Judith so loved.

"This will do," she said, feeling a heightened awareness of their solitude as they rounded the cliff, taking the beach they had departed from out of sight.

Mr. Carlisle laid down the oars and picked up a fishing pole. "Teach me, oh mistress."

She shot him an unamused look but complied, showing him how to thread the line through the loops on the pole, tie the hook to the line, and attach a lure. More than once, she found him looking at her rather than the pole or line. She tried to ignore it, though it made her fingers feel too large for their task and her cheeks warm.

"How very hot it is," she said after fumbling with the knot in the line.

Mr. Carlisle used his hands to fan her face, and she laughed, swatting them away.

"I *am* your servant, am I not?"

She shot a quick glance at him and took one of the poles in hand to occupy herself. "Your duties do not—however regrettably—include such a task."

He picked up the second pole, running a hand along it. "What makes you think everything I do for you is out of duty?"

He had made such flirtatious comments before, and they always left Judith feeling somewhat unhinged and flustered. She forced herself to wave them off, but she had seen in his eyes a growing glimmer of admiration—or perhaps something more.

Whatever it was, it wouldn't—it couldn't—survive the inevitable reckoning that the truth would bring.

"As for casting your line—"

In a deft movement, Mr. Carlisle whipped his rod in the air, sending the line sailing several fathoms away.

She stared at him, and he glanced at her.

"Was that wrong?" he asked.

"No, but . . . well, it was very disobliging of you. You might have at least waited for me to explain it so I could attribute your success to my instruction."

He laughed. "How *do* you know how to fish? Is that something most young ladies are practiced at?"

"Playing the pianoforte, stitching a sampler, catching and cleaning a fish," she said. The sound of his laugh gave her just as much pleasure as did her line reaching nearly as far as his. "I am not what one might call an *accomplished young lady*. George taught me to fish when I was here for Charlie's birth."

He pulled his line back in and recast it. "Surely, fishing is a more valuable accomplishment than stitching a sampler?

Unless, of course, someone has found a way to subsist entirely on samplers, in which case London might be fed for years."

She laughed and looked at him thoughtfully. "And what do *you* know of London and Society?"

He glanced at her and shrugged as he pulled in his line. "Nothing, really."

"As much as you know of anything, then," she teased. "Have none of your memories returned?" Why did she feel such anxiety to hear the answer?

He looked her in the eye for a moment, then shook his head, and they fished in silence for a time, the only sounds the water lapping gently against the wood and the *plop* of their lines dropping into the water as Judith sat with troubling thoughts of what the future held.

Mr. Carlisle was the first to catch anything—a mackerel—and Judith tried to rein in her surprise.

"Beginner's luck." He grimaced as he pulled the fish from the line and set it in the bucket.

"Remembering Mr. Higgins?"

"Always," he said.

Judith managed to catch another mackerel shortly after, and Mr. Carlisle a second, after which a lull occurred. They sat in silence some of the time, but it was a peaceful silence rather than an awkward one, and Judith sighed contentedly as she took in the view around them.

"This is my favorite time of day," she said.

"Is it?" He looked at her with eyes slightly narrowed—sincere interest reflected in them.

"The water almost glows orange, and on a day like today, it is calm enough that it sparkles as it moves. There is nothing like it."

He gazed out at the vista around them. "I think you are right." Silence reigned for a moment. "Thank you."

She frowned and glanced at him as she readjusted the hook on her line. "For what?"

His gaze rested on her, soft and warm like the glow of the water. "For everything, Miss Jardine. For tending to me in my injuries, for giving me a place to recover, for sleeping in that miserable closet"—he smiled ruefully—"for being patient with me in my ineptitude. Not every mistress would do as much."

She looked away. "I am not your mistress, James."

"Not in a strict sense of the word, no."

Not in *any* sense of the word, she wanted to say.

He glanced at her with an amused smile. "Do you always turn off compliments and thanks when they are offered?"

"No," she said with a hint of defensiveness and even less persuasiveness.

He raised a brow at her, drawing his line back in. "I don't believe you."

"Well, you are wrong not to."

"Am I? Let us see about that." He set down his fishing pole and turned toward her purposefully.

"What are you doing?" she asked warily.

"Putting your assertion to the test. Let us see if you *can* accept a compliment—if you can look me in the eye and simply accept it rather than make some witty retort."

Judith scoffed and looked away. She should put Mr. Carlisle in his place. But that was the tricky thing about the situation she had created—what *was* his place? Her heart needed the protection afforded by insisting on a servant-mistress relationship, but her conscience balked at the lie.

Her hand was taken up, and she whipped her head around.

"There," he said as her eyes met his. He held her gaze as he took the rod from her hands and set it down next to his own.

She wanted to look away, but his eyes kept her there, rooting her like an anchor. She expected to see teasing there, but instead, she saw sincerity and the admiration that so terrified her—terrified her for how much she wanted it to be real, for it not to crumble the moment Mr. Carlisle realized where he truly stood in relation to her and what she had done to him.

"You are the most extraordinary woman I have ever met," he said.

Her first impulse was to turn away, but Mr. Carlisle had anticipated it, and his hold on her hand tightened, reminding her of what she was tasked with doing. She gritted her teeth and fixed her eyes on him.

"You hold others at a distance with your wit and sarcasm," he said, "but you cannot hide the heart behind. It is softer and kinder than any I have ever encountered."

To her dismay, tears began to well in her eyes, and she turned her head away. "Says the man with no memories."

He laughed and put a hand to her cheek, guiding it to face him again. "You truly *cannot* do it, can you? Why is that?"

She blinked quickly. "Perhaps I doubt the sincerity of the compliments being offered." It was true, in part. She didn't doubt that he meant them now, in this moment. She merely doubted they would survive the return of his memory.

His brows knit together, and he searched her face, his own lit from behind with a sunny halo. "Then allow me to reassure you." He moved closer, taking her other cheek in hand, the intent in his eyes clear.

Judith should have pulled back immediately, but her heart revolted. It wanted the reassurance he was offering, and she shut her eyes. The boat listed gently, and she grasped his wrists to steady her.

The touch of his lips was felt first on her own—soft,

warm, unlike anything she had ever experienced. But its effects rippled out over her skin, down her back, and deep inside her—everywhere. She let go of his wrists, reaching her own hands around his neck, pulling him closer. The truth she had been holding in, all of the feelings she had been suppressing, demanded escape through the only medium offered to her, and Mr. Carlisle responded in kind, as if he had only been waiting for her invitation to give more.

One of his hands left her cheek, and she felt it next on her waist, pulling her nearer. The boat rocked with the shift, unsettling them, and Judith's eyes flew open. She broke away, reaching for stability on the sides of the boat.

Chapter Twelve

JAMES GRIPPED THE RIM of the boat with one hand and steadied Miss Jardine with the other. She was staring at him, dismay building in her wide eyes.

Had he been wrong to kiss her? If so, he had never wanted so badly to be wrong again—and again. He didn't know what had motivated her to take him in and convince him he was a servant, but he knew her well enough to know she was regretting it. And whatever doubt there might have been in his mind about the nature of his feelings for Miss Jardine, it had slowly crumbled over the last few days.

But her eyes were full of such doubt now, and he felt guilt ripple and build inside him as he wondered what she was thinking, what she wanted.

"We should go," she said.

"But . . . we have only caught three fish."

"It will be enough. I am not hungry."

He watched her for another moment. "Miss Jardine," he said. "Forgive me—"

"No." She looked at him and smiled, but it was a counterfeit smile. "There is nothing to forgive. Here, allow me to row us to shore. You should not be exerting yourself so much. You are still injured, after all."

He grimaced and reached for the oars. She clearly did not wish to speak of the kiss. "I am fully capable of rowing, Miss Jardine."

James wondered if they might pass the time it took to reach the shore in utter silence, but what happened was worse. Miss Jardine kept up a monologue full of polite but vacuous remarks, while James only responded when a response was required of him. His mind was too full for anything more.

His heart urged him to tell her the truth—to tell her what he knew. But what would happen? The entire world they had constructed over the past week—absurd and ludicrous as it was—would shatter instantly.

I feel much safer with him here . . . Just a few more days, Judy. Those had been Mrs. Bradford's words. They needed him, servant or not. And he was not fool enough to think Miss Jardine would let him stay once the whole truth was laid before her. She had far too much pride for that.

When they reached the shore, he jumped out of the boat and into the chill water as he pulled the vessel onto the sand. The afternoon's glowing, orange hues had given way to ambers and deep reds as the sun settled on the horizon. Miss Jardine's talkativeness seemed to have dissipated with their arrival on shore, and after putting the boat in its place, their walk to the cottage was undertaken in silence.

But James couldn't pretend nothing had happened, and as they set the equipment back in place, he finally spoke.

"Miss Jardine, I cannot let things lie so easily as you."

"James, please," she said, shaking her head. "*Please* do so for my sake. I shall not tell my sister what happened, but if you insist on speaking of it, I shall have no choice."

He stared at her. She was threatening him with dismissal—dismissal from a fictitious position.

"You kissed me back." He couldn't stop himself.

Mishaps and Memories

She swallowed. "You are mistaken. Now, please. Say nothing more on the subject." She turned and walked to the cottage, disappearing through the door with only the briefest of glances at James.

~~~

James didn't eat dinner. He spent the evening cleaning and made do with a cup of ale at the table after the others had retired to bed and the house was dark and silent. The table was still laid, the dirty dishes before him, and a single candle lighting the room. There had been no time to clean the fish upon their arrival at the cottage, so they had been cooked whole.

One of the three plates contained the better part of a fish—picked at but largely uneaten. James had no doubt that it belonged to Miss Jardine. The head was intact, and the eye stared forward grotesquely, reminding James forcibly of Miss Garrett. He shuddered.

Tomorrow was the date of his expected meeting with Miss Garrett's father, and James found himself at a crossroads. He had been running from his life since his memories had returned, but he could only run for so long—particularly when he wasn't certain of his destination.

That he had fallen in love with Judith Jardine was no longer deniable—and in a shockingly short amount of time. That she returned at least some of his regard, he didn't doubt. But she was resisting it, and James could only assume it was her conscience that held her back. So, why the ruse?

His stomach rumbled, and he stared at the fish on Miss Jardine's plate, considering whether he should finish it off. Its juices glistened in the candlelight. It looked even less appetizing than had the fish at the dinner he had attended in—

He stilled.

The dinner. Fish juice.

His eyes widened, still fixed on the half-eaten fish as flutters of memories flapped around elusively in his head.

The woman beside him at dinner—the one he had hardly spoken with due to Miss Garrett's incessant talking. She had spilled on him, and he had nearly vomited, goaded beyond endurance by the sequence of undesirable events that night—until he had seen his opportunity to escape the dinner he had regretted almost since arriving at it.

He shut his eyes, trying to recapture the face of the woman beside him. It couldn't possibly be. Could it? She had told him her name at one point, hadn't she? She had, for he had elicited laughs from the table when, in his aggravation, he had turned her name into a joke.

Miss Sardine.

James performed his duties in the morning with almost more impatience than he could manage to contain. But despite the fact that he could hear the sounds of her movement within, Miss Jardine was slow to leave her bedchamber. She was still inside when the front door opened, and a man stepped into the house.

Kneeling at the hearth, James stared up at him, taking in the man's large girth and the way he looked on James with an expression of confusion.

"Who are you?" the man asked, eyes taking in James's task.

James stood just as Mrs. Bradford stepped into the room, followed by a toddling Charlie. She rushed toward the man. "George!"

Mr. Bradford wrapped his arms around his wife, and they kissed. James looked away out of politeness, feeling a little surge of envy. Charlie was anxious for the embrace to end, though, and Mr. Bradford picked him up with a laugh, planting a kiss on the boy's round cheek before turning to James again.

"Who is this?"

Mrs. Bradford looked at James with a great deal of anxiety in her eyes. "Oh," she said with a nervous laugh, "that is James. Come set your things down, George, and I shall explain it all." She ushered him out of the room with a firm hand, and James was left to himself again, smiling wryly. Mr. Bradford was clearly not complicit in the ruse.

As for James, he was suddenly deprived of his final excuse for staying; he was no longer needed in the Bradford household. His head whipped around at the sound of a door opening, and Miss Jardine appeared in the corridor, eyes sweeping the area. But the door to Mr. and Mrs. Bradford's bedchamber was closed.

Miss Jardine walked toward James. "Did I hear George?"

He nodded, feeling a great deal of nerves now that the opportunity he had been waiting for was finally before him. "He just returned. Went to set his things down and speak with your sister." He dusted off his hands and swallowed. "Could I speak with you outside, Miss Jardine?"

She looked at him with wariness.

"It is important," he said.

She gave a quick nod.

He opened the door for her, and she thanked him curtly, stepping into the refreshing morning air and walking the short path that led to the main road. She extended a brief greeting to a man driving a donkey cart there. Her arms were at her sides, somewhat rigid, and her fingers fiddled with her skirts.

"Miss Jardine," James said, his mouth feeling dry.

She turned toward him abruptly. "Let me speak first."

James frowned, looking at her intently. Was she going to tell him the truth? She *had* told her sister that she would only wait until Mr. Bradford returned. "I—"

"Hallo there!" The shout was nearly drowned out by the sound of horse hooves and carriage wheels, which soon decreased in volume, then stopped.

James turned toward the newly arrived chaise as the door opened, and a man stepped out—Philip Langham.

Chapter Thirteen

JUDITH COULDN'T MOVE. THE stranger who had just appeared could not have come at a more inopportune time. It had taken her all night to garner the courage to tell Mr. Carlisle everything—the courage to accept that, whatever visions of possibility she had created, they would only ever be dreams. George's arrival had decided things.

"I am devilishly relieved to find you here," the stranger said to Mr. Carlisle. "The first report I followed turned out to be a hum! I admit, I had my doubts when the fellow spoke of a man without a memory, but—" He clapped a hand on Mr. Carlisle's shoulder and surveyed his clothing with obvious distaste. "Good heavens, Carlisle. What in heaven's name happened to you?" He looked at him through narrowed eyes. "You *do* remember me, don't you?"

Judith's gaze shifted rapidly between the two men. Mr. Carlisle was watching her, though, a somber expression on his face. His gaze lingered on her for a moment as he turned to the man by his side.

"What are you doing here, Langham?" Mr. Carlisle asked.

Judith's heart plummeted. He knew the man. His

memories were returning, and she hadn't been able to explain everything.

"What do you *think* I'm doing here?" the man called Langham said as he laughed. "People had begun to think you dead. But I knew better. Knew you didn't want to offer for the Garrett girl—figured you had found something more entertaining." He glanced at Judith finally, chuckling again. "And all this time, you have been having a little dalliance with Miss Sardine, of all people!"

Judith stiffened, and her face flooded with color on hearing the nickname. She looked to Mr. Carlisle, and the guilt in his expression answered the questions she had only just begun to ask herself. He *knew*. He knew everything.

"Your father will be mad as fire when he knows the truth of it, I can tell you that much. Come." Mr. Langham took Mr. Carlisle's arm. "You can stay with me at the Red Lion"—he glanced at Mr. Carlisle's clothing again and shuddered with disgust—"and we can find you a tailor until you return to London."

"Stop, Langham," Mr. Carlisle said, not budging from his place.

Mr. Langham paused, and his brows shot up.

Mr. Carlisle gently took his arm from the man's grasp. "I am not coming with you."

"Eh?" Mr. Langham gave an uncomfortable laugh.

"I am in the middle of a conversation just now. You will have to wait."

"No," Judith said in a clipped voice. "We have finished our conversation. You should go."

Mr. Carlisle turned to her, searching her face, a frown on his brow. "Miss Jardine."

Mr. Langham covered a chuckle, and Judith's nostrils flared, well aware that her name was a source of amusement to him.

"You knew!" she shot at Mr. Carlisle, unable to contain herself any longer. "You knew this entire time!" What did it matter if Mr. Langham heard what she said? She was done caring for the opinion of such people.

"No," Mr. Carlisle said, coming closer to her and reaching out a hand. "I didn't. I—"

She stepped backward. "Stay away from me. I am nothing but sport to you—a joke from the very first time we met. And you . . ." She swallowed. "I can only hope everyone in England comes to learn the sort of person you are."

She turned on her heel, but he grabbed her hand, keeping her from going. Mr. Langham was watching with wide eyes, but he seemed to come out of his staring trance, clearing his throat and hurriedly stepping up into the carriage. "I'll just be in here, dear boy!"

Mr. Carlisle gave no indication of hearing his friend. "You are not sport to me, Miss Jardine."

"Am I not?" She pulled her hand away. "Miss Sardine has not been your *entertainment?*" She nodded at the carriage Mr. Langham was inside.

"No! I should have told you when my memories returned, but . . ." His shoulders came up. "I didn't want it to end—I wanted more time with you."

She pulled her hand away, shaking her head. "I do not believe a word you say. You have been lying this entire time."

Mr. Carlisle blinked. "*I* have been lying? And what of you? You convinced me I was a *servant.* You had me cleaning fish and the privy, sleeping in quarters one might expect to find in gaol. And for what? Revenge? Because I made a silly comment at a dinner?"

"You think that is all it was?" she cried, incredulous. "A silly comment? You were the most ill-mannered *gentleman* I have ever come across."

His eyes widened, and she could see that her insult had landed. "Forgive me if I have not lived up to the standards of all the gentlemen you have undoubtedly encountered in a place like *this*." He gestured to the house.

Rage ran hot through Judith's veins. "Oh, yes. You made your prejudices against those less fortunate than you quite clear at dinner. But what claim have *you* to the title of gentleman when you ignored me for the entirety of dinner, left me to fend for myself instead of serving me any food, and, as if that was not enough, made a laughingstock of me, ruining any chance I had at a match?" Her jaw hardened, but she couldn't fend off the tears much longer. "You deserved every moment here, and I hope it serves you—and Miss Garrett—well. Please offer her the compliments of Miss *Sardine*."

She wheeled around and stalked toward the path they had taken to the beach just the day before, refusing to wipe the tears that slipped onto her cheeks until she was no longer in Mr. Carlisle's line of sight, her body trembling with anger and feeling.

The path finally sloped downward, and with a quick, bleary glance over her shoulder, she sank onto the sand and surrendered to emotion.

Chapter Fourteen

JAMES WATCHED MISS JARDINE disappear behind the hill that led down to the beach, his chest rising and falling rapidly. He was angry. He was confused. He was guilty. And he was heartbroken. He had anticipated the encounter would be unpleasant, but this? He had not anticipated this.

"Carlisle?" Langham's voice was tentative coming through the chaise window, which had been open the entire time. Langham had heard everything. He and the postilion waiting by the horses for his orders, who fiddled awkwardly with the bridle of a horse.

"It seems my timing has been rather unfortunate," Langham said, clenching his teeth. "I can return later, if you would like. Or not."

"No," James said, not allowing himself a look at the house or the spot where Miss Jardine had disappeared. She had been quite clear what she thought of him. There was nothing for him here. "I am coming with you."

He climbed into the chaise and sank down into the seat across from Langham, who watched him for a moment, then hit a fist against the roof.

The chaise pulled forward, and they rode in silence for some time, James occupied with unhappy thoughts, and

Langham no doubt feeling awkward at the strange situation he had happened upon.

After ten minutes, though, Langham cleared his throat. "Forgive me, Carlisle, but . . . what the devil just happened?"

James let out a sigh and let his head fall back against the tufted seat back. He shook it from side to side, wishing he could forget all of it, unable to put it into words.

"You must be ready to give *some* sort of explanation to people, Carlisle. And better you sort through what to say with me than bumbling through it with your father or Miss Garrett."

Miss Garrett's name made James cringe. But Langham was right. He had decisions to make, and with the bundle of emotions he was still feeling, he was bound to make a muddle of it if he didn't think things through first.

"Start at the beginning, man," Langham said. "Start when I last saw you—before you decided to dress like a dashed hot air balloon."

The chaise slowed as it passed by another equipage, and James shrugged his shoulders, having come to the point of the story where Langham had arrived. He had glazed over a few details—his feelings for Miss Jardine, in particular—but Langham had the long and short of it, at least.

Langham stared at him. "You fell in love with her? With Miss Sardine?"

James's brows snapped together. "Don't, Langham. Don't call her that." He looked through the window at the shrubs that lined the road. "I never knew what effect those words would have."

"Effect?" Langham laughed. "They gave everyone a great laugh. Very clever, it was."

"And thoughtless and cruel."

Langham looked at him under furrowed brows. "You really do love her, then?"

"What does it matter?"

"Don't be a fool, Carlisle. If you love the girl, what in heaven's name are you doing in here with me?"

"It doesn't matter, because she doesn't believe me, Langham. She thinks it's all been for sport—a great lie—and I cannot blame her."

"No one is asking you to blame her, you oaf," Langham said impatiently. "I'm telling you to *make her believe you.*"

James grimaced. "And who's to say that would change anything? She called me"—he let out a frustrated breath as he tried to remember what exactly she had said.

"The most ill-mannered gentleman she had ever come across," Langham supplied.

James shot him a glare. "Yes, *thank you.*"

"Don't look daggers at me. *I* didn't say it." Langham tapped his finger on the hat in his lap. "Listen, Carlisle. If you want a guarantee that she'll have you, I can't give it to you. Can't say I'm an expert on the topic, but love is always a risk, isn't it?"

James leaned forward, resting his elbows on his knees and clasping his hands in front of his mouth. "Even if she would have me, what of my father?"

Langham waved a dismissive hand. "I imagine he will be so happy to know you are alive *and* choosing to marry, he will overlook your slight to Miss Garrett."

"It is not a slight," James said testily. "She is to receive an offer from Sir William."

"True. And that *is* a good match, I say, if only for the fact that she will be able to stare to her heart's content while Sir William is none the wiser. Everyone knows the man is blind—everyone except him, of course."

James could feel his hands sweating and his heart hammering harder and harder as he stared at the chaise floor. Every second he hesitated put more distance between him and Judith, and he felt every inch in his soul.

"Stop the chaise," he said softly.

Nothing happened, and he looked up at his friend.

"Hmm?" Langham said, feigning deafness. "Did you say something?"

"Stop the chaise," James said louder.

Langham smiled. "Confidence, Carlisle. Confidence is key." He hit his fist against the roof. "Now, let us catch you a sardine."

Chapter Fifteen

JUDITH'S ARMS WERE WRAPPED around her knees, and the shoulders of her dress were wet from using them to dry her tears. The tears had stopped, though, and the trails on her cheeks had dried with the sea breeze.

Watching the waves roll in and out, in and out, calmed her, helping her collect the pieces which had come apart in front of Mary's house. Her heart still ached with a sense of loss—not all of her attempts to distance herself from Mr. Carlisle had managed to prevent that.

Nor did knowing that he hadn't been honest with her act as a salve on her conscience, for she knew that he was not the only one in the wrong. Focusing on his mistakes did not erase her own. And it had been the knowledge of her own culpability which had made her temper flare more easily than it otherwise would have, leading her to speak the unkind words she had spewed.

Mr. Carlisle's incivility had begotten the whole situation, certainly, but upon reflection, Judith had to admit that her own behavior was the more reprehensible.

A breeze blew up some of the sand around her feet and made the reeds behind her rustle musically. She glanced at them, and her gaze settled on the boat hiding amongst them.

A few residual tears obscured her vision as thoughts of the kiss she had shared with Mr. Carlisle crept into her tired mind. She shut her eyes for a moment, remembering how it had felt to be held by him and, even more importantly, the look in his eyes before he had kissed her.

All of it had been wrapped up in lies.

"Miss Jardine?"

She jumped at the unexpected voice and hurriedly wiped the tears from her eyes before turning.

Mr. Carlisle stood at the top of the sandy slope, his oversized shirt billowing with the wind in a way Judith might have found amusing yesterday. But just now, it made her heart ache.

He stepped down the slope toward her, boots sinking into the deep sand.

"What do you want, Mr. Carlisle?" she asked in a weary voice as she turned back toward the water.

He said nothing, merely sitting down beside her and putting his arms around his knees just as hers were. They sat in silence, listening to the waves and the grass rustling, watching the white sail of a boat in the distance.

"I am sorry, Miss Jardine," Mr. Carlisle finally said. "For so many things."

She stared straight ahead, even though she wanted to see his face again—to look into his eyes and see whether the sincerity she had seen there in the boat yesterday had been imagined, or if it was still there. If she didn't see him, perhaps she could forget how much she cared for him.

"I am sorry for being so ill-mannered at that dinner. I was so focused on deterring the woman I didn't want that I neglected the only woman I ever *could* want."

Unable to bear it any longer, Judith looked at him, her heart throbbing at the sight. If ever a man had meant what he said, James Carlisle did so now. His eyes said it all.

"I am sorry for the terrible, thoughtless joke I made about your name. And I am sorry for not being honest with you when I began to remember things."

She had seen him degrade himself countless times over the past ten days, but none of that had been as satisfying as she had imagined it would be. His apology, though, filled her in ways she had never anticipated.

She took in a deep breath. "And *I* am sorry. For not being honest with you from the beginning as I should have been." She forced herself to look him in the eye, to face up to her decisions.

"Why *did* you do it?" he asked. "What I mean to say is, well"—the corner of his mouth turned up—"what in heaven's name were you thinking?"

She thought back on that day—on the moment when she had made that small decision that had grown into such a complicated lie. "It was a silly, impulsive decision," she said. "I never meant for it to go on so long. I merely wanted to teach you a lesson for an hour or two. But then Mr. Sharp forbade me from saying anything that might overset you, or from forcing your memories onto you, and"—she lifted her shoulders helplessly—"I didn't know what to do."

He gave a half-smile that flipped her heart. "Your obedience to Mr. Sharp is inspiring, if somewhat unexpected."

She turned herself toward him more, needing to explain. "He told me the most horrid stories, threatening me with the prospect of driving you to insanity—of sending you to Bedlam, where you would die a madman."

"Good heavens," Mr. Carlisle said with a laugh.

She reached for a handful of sand, letting it slip through her fingers. "I thought surely your memories would return when you began to take on the role of servant. But they did not." She looked at him with a frown. "Or so I thought."

He smiled apologetically.

"Why did you not tell me?" she asked.

"I very nearly did—almost boxed your ears. But I decided against it, for a number of reasons. The reason I tried most to believe was simply my wish to escape the duties that awaited me as James Carlisle."

She narrowed her eyes at him. "Surely, those duties were not more unpleasant than cleaning the privy."

He laughed, and Judith watched the reflection of the bright water in his eyes with longing. She had never denied his charm or attraction, but to her, he had never possessed more of either than in this moment, with the sea in his eyes, George's shirt drowning him, and a laugh on his lips.

"That is up for debate," he said. "But it was not the only reason I stayed—and it was certainly not what kept me here. As I look back now, I can admit that the real reason for playing along with the ruse was"—he let out a breath through his nose and looked at her—"you."

Her heart skipped a few beats.

"I wanted to understand you," he said, "to puzzle you out. I wanted to be with you."

She searched his eyes for a moment, then looked away, but he guided her face back with a hand. "Don't turn away, Judith. I need you to believe me. I know I have no right to your trust after everything, but I am asking for it anyway."

She shut her eyes. "I am sorry, James. But I find it inconceivable that you—a man so accustomed to being served that you must hardly notice the people who serve you—chose to continue being a servant just to spend time with *me*." She shook her head and swallowed, but he kept his hand on her cheek, and all she wanted was to nestle into it.

He came to kneel before her, taking her other cheek in hand. "Please look at me, Judith."

She slowly opened her eyes, and he held her gaze intently. "I will be your servant for the rest of my life, Judith, if only it means I get to love you." He rested his forehead against hers. "Please let me."

She shut her eyes, savoring the impossible moment, feeling the warmth of his head resting against hers and his breath grazing her nose and tickling her lips.

"If you still do not believe me, only feel how my heart beats for you," he said softly, taking her hand and placing it on his chest. A quick pattering tapped against her hand, a language all its own, and she lifted her chin, catching his lips with hers.

He responded willingly, pulling her closer until she lost her balance, and they tumbled backward onto the sand. He held her against him, laughing, and they rolled down the slope until the ground leveled out. She found herself on her back, looking into the face hovering above her, lit from behind like it had been in the boat yesterday, gazing at her with tenderness and the smile she had come to crave.

He dipped down for a kiss, and, pulling him closer, she forced him to roll to the side, their lips still locked together. Sand sprinkled from her hair down into her dress and stays, stopping where James's hand pressed against the small of her back. She pulled away, looking down on him now from above, admiring the way his dark eyes and hair contrasted with the sandy backdrop.

"When *did* your memories return?" she asked.

His mouth twisted to the side guiltily, and he waited before responding. "The night we cleaned the fish."

Her jaw dropped open, and he recoiled slightly, as though afraid of what she might do.

"That long ago?" she said in dismay.

He nodded, apology written on his face. "Mr. Sharp's

newspaper must have slipped out of his bag when he came to visit the second time. There happened to be an advertisement within requesting information regarding my whereabouts. It all began to come back when I saw my name." He grimaced. "Can you ever forgive me?"

She considered him through narrowed eyes. "A few more nights in the closet ought to balance the books."

He reached a hand up, threading his fingers through her hair and looking at her in a way that made her heart thump.

"A small sacrifice," he said. "I have become somewhat fond of it, you know."

"What? Of the closet?"

He nodded. "It is full of thoughts of you."

"And bruised heads and pokey straw," she said with a laugh. "Besides, it wouldn't take very many thoughts of me to fill *that* space. I begin to think you have overestimated your affection for me."

He guided her head down until their lips just brushed. "Then allow me to reassure you, my love."

Epilogue

JUDITH AND JAMES WALKED arm-in-arm along the damp sands of the beach at Brighton, waves threatening their feet again and again, only to withdraw. Judith looked to the north, letting her gaze travel along the row of townhouses that lined the coast.

She had been hesitant to come to Brighton after their wedding, but experiencing the seaside town as a new bride was entirely different than experiencing it as Miss Jardine less than three months ago. With the arrival of autumn temperatures, many of Society had begun to trickle out of the seaside town. Judith preferred it a little quieter and calmer. She enjoyed her promenades with James when there were fewer people to greet.

She was also happy to be in such close proximity to Mary and their new baby girl, Sarah. George had received a new position on an estate just north of Brighton, and things were looking up for the Bradford family.

More than anything, though, Judith no longer felt like an imposter here. She didn't wonder anymore whether she fit into Society. She and James belonged together, and that was all that mattered to her. She belonged where he belonged.

Two people approached from the opposite direction, and

Judith and James slowed once they were recognized.

"Carlisle," Mr. Langham said as he came upon them. He walked with a woman of middling age whom, given their similarity in appearance, Judith took to be his mother.

James tipped his hat. "Good day, Langham. Mrs. Langham."

"Mother," Mr. Langham said, "allow me to introduce you to Mrs. Carlisle—formerly known as Miss Sardine."

James cleared his throat significantly, looking anything but amused.

"Miss *Jardine*," Langham corrected himself.

Judith laughed softly and curtsied to Mrs. Langham.

"The notorious Miss Sardine," Mrs. Langham said, but her smile was so warm and her voice so kind that they robbed the words of any offense. "How lovely to finally meet you. I have heard so much about you."

"Oh dear," Judith said with a nervous laugh.

"I just saw your father yesterday, Mr. Carlisle," Mrs. Langham continued, "and he wasted no time informing us of his son's recent marriage."

Judith glanced at James, raising her brows. James's mother had welcomed Judith with open arms, but his father had taken more time to come around to the match.

James smiled down at her, as if to say, *I told you so*. He had been adamant about two things when they had become engaged: first, that his father would be powerless against Judith's charms, and second, that he didn't give a fig for what his father thought anyway.

"You heard about Sir William and Miss Garrett, I imagine?" Mr. Langham asked.

"Married last week, were they not?" James replied.

Mrs. Langham smiled and nodded. "I met them near the Pavilion just yesterday, arm in arm. Very much in love—Miss Garrett could not keep her eyes from her new husband."

Mr. Langham coughed, though it sounded suspiciously like a laugh.

"I can only imagine," James said, holding Judith all the closer.

~~~~~

They parted from the Langhams shortly after, and James sighed as they continued their walk.

"I apologize for Langham," he said. "He can be the greatest of dolts."

"It is quite all right," Judith said, smiling. "I have embraced the name, you know. I find it amusing now."

He looked at her through narrowed eyes. "Do you?"

She nodded.

"And what of Brighton?" he asked. "Do you dislike it here?"

She stopped and took in a breath of fresh sea air, shaking her head. "I quite like it now."

He came to stand before her, playing with her bonnet ribbon, which rippled in the wind. "I am glad to hear that. I thought perhaps your memories of the place had ruined it for you forever."

"I thought so, too. But even those memories are happy now, thanks to you." She took his hand, holding it within hers. "It is funny how that happens, isn't it? Our memories are not really fixed. They take on new shape as the future takes form, and even the worst ones can evolve into something happy, if only they have guided us to a joyful present."

He brought one of her hands to his lips and kissed it fervently. "A joyful present, indeed. I love you, Judith." He wrapped his arms around her waist. "*Miss Sardine.*"

"And I you, Mr. Carlisle."

He smiled softly. "Your servant."

Martha Keyes was born, raised, and educated in Utah—a home she loves dearly but also dearly loves to escape to travel the world. She received a BA in French Studies and a Master of Public Health, both from Brigham Young University. It wasn't until exploring a host of other career opportunities that Martha considered writing a story of her own. She has never looked back. When she isn't writing, she is falling down research rabbit holes, looking for travel deals, and spending time with her husband and rascally twin boys at their home in Utah.

Visit Martha's website here: http://www.marthakeyes.com/

Moonlight Summer

Heather B. Moore

Chapter One

EIGHT TRUNKS AND SEVEN valises packed into two carriages, and still Dottie had the feeling she was forgetting something as she stood in the doorway of a London townhome. Oh, no—all the baggage wasn't for *her* alone. She could only claim one trunk and one valise. A feat for a twenty-year-old lady, to be sure. But Dottie's mother had given her strict instructions to pack modestly. She'd bring along her small sketchbook in her reticule in the morning.

"That way, my dear, you'll have to shop for what you need," her mother had said earlier that day as her pale blue eyes sparkled. "You have a new father now. And he will provide for us."

Her mother's color was heightened these past few months, and her voice had taken on a higher octave. Perhaps it was because of her new marriage? Still a blushing bride?

Dottie didn't want to think about her own mother, at thirty-eight, having a romantic time with Viscount Fisher of Turnberry, Dottie's new stepfather.

But there was no denying it.

Last night after supper, her mother had announced that she was with child.

Well.

Dottie was already feeling misplaced enough with a new home, three new stepsisters, and a new stepfather who said hardly a word to her.

Now, Dottie knew why they were quitting the London season early. A season that was meant for her, at least originally. She'd missed her first season because she and her mother were in mourning for Father. And her second one? Her mother had secured the husband, not Dottie.

One day, Dottie might find it amusing, but at this very moment, she could hear someone crying. Wailing, really.

"Dorothea!" Her mother's voice echoed from the upper level.

Dottie turned from the doorway and all the preparations. She hurried up the stairs, wishing for one quiet moment. She'd never appreciated those moments before, when she was the only child to her parents, Lady Atkinson and Lord Atkinson, who had been the Baron of Rutland.

"I don't want to leave my dollhouse!" This was followed by another wail.

Dottie stepped into the nursery, where her mother, the nursemaid, and the housekeeper were all surrounding six-year-old Alice. The young girl was as fair-haired as Dottie was dark.

"Dorothea, do something," her mother said, touching her perfectly coifed hair as if a piece of it had strayed. "My nerves can't take this. I'm expecting, you know."

I know, Dottie wanted to say, but instead, she crossed to Alice and knelt in front of her.

The child's clear green eyes were filled with tears, and the flush on her cheeks told Dottie she was about a half a minute from a full breakdown. Wailing was only the beginning. Dottie's heart went out to this young girl, though. A child who'd lost her mother last year. Just as Dottie had lost her father.

"What do you want to take on our trip to the seaside?" Dottie said in a quiet, calm voice.

Alice sniffled. "My dollhouse."

Dottie didn't miss the fact that her mother and the housekeeper had quit the room. Only the nursemaid, Mary, remained, hovering by the door.

"This one?" Dottie said, resting her hand atop the roof of the nearby dollhouse. "I love it too."

"You do?" Alice's eyes widened. "But you don't play with dolls. You're too old."

Dottie smiled. "Perhaps. Do you know if you take the dollhouse to the seaside, then we can't take all your favorite dresses? There won't be room for both." She could see the understanding growing in the girl's eyes. "What will you wear? A blanket?"

Alice's small, rosy lips curved upwards.

"Oh, I know. You can wear my shawl."

Alice giggled. "It's too big for me."

Dottie touched a finger to her chin. "Let's see, then. How about you wear one of my dresses?"

"That's too big!" Another giggle.

Dottie held back a laugh. "Oh well, I guess we'll have to bring your dresses. But I have an idea for your dollhouse."

Alice's green eyes rounded. "You do?"

"We'll put a special drape over it so that it will stay here, safe and sound, for you," Dottie said. "Nothing will be touched, and it won't even get dusty."

A line appeared between Alice's eyebrows, but she turned and gazed at the dollhouse for a long moment. "All right."

Dottie's heart did a victory leap. "Wonderful. Now, let's find the drape that you want. It has to be very pretty, just like the house."

Nursemaid Mary leapt into action at this. "I have something that might work. I'll be back in a moment."

"Thank you, Mary." Dottie then smiled at Alice. "See? Now you won't have to wear a pillowcase."

Alice grinned. "I'm too big for that anyway."

"You certainly are," Dottie said, tapping the child on the nose. "You're almost a young lady now."

Alice seemed to grow an inch at the compliment. Her astute gaze rested on Dottie. "Why can't *you* be my new mother?"

Cold prickled Dottie's skin. This wasn't the first time Alice had said such a thing. The good news was that her mother wasn't in the room. "Oh, Alice, I'm your *sister* now. That's even better. We can have more fun together, and I don't have to get after you when you try to wear a reticule as a hat."

Alice's belly laugh burst out.

This time, Dottie laughed with her. Being an older sister wasn't so bad after all.

"Dorothea, I must speak to you." Her mother stood in the doorway again, wearing lavender from head to toe. "Come to my chambers. Blanche and Nora will be joining us as well."

Dottie's two other stepsisters. She hid a sigh. Spending time with little Alice was one thing—something enjoyable—but Blanche and Nora were ages eighteen and sixteen, respectively, and one would think they were grand duchesses for the airs they put on.

"Very well," Dottie said, just as Mary returned.

A lively discussion ensued between Alice and her nursemaid of how to drape the dollhouse, and Dottie decided it was a safe time to leave the nursery.

She followed her mother to the next level of the house, their footsteps silent on the luxurious carpet. Although her father had been a baron, he hadn't had as much wealth as her new stepfather, a viscount. Dottie knew the whispers about the *ton* over how the age difference between her mother and new husband was vast—twenty years—and he only married her to sire another child.

Well, that had happened. Her mother seemed happy, though. So Dottie would make do. Maybe next season, she'd come into her own and secure a husband herself.

Blanche and Nora were both waiting in her mother's chambers already. Blanche was the eldest, and at eighteen, she always dressed as if she were on display for royalty. Nora tried—oh, she tried. But there was always something amiss—a falling ribbon, a torn hem, a soiled glove.

Both girls were as blonde as Alice, and looked to be the picture of angels, until one got to know them.

"Girls," her mother said with a clap of her hands. "Listen up." She settled onto the edge of a wingback chair. "In light of my announcement last night, you know that I will not be up to the task of chaperoning you to every social event. Therefore, it will fall to Dottie."

All eyes turned to Dottie. She opened her mouth to reply, but in truth, she was too shocked to comment. *Her?* A chaperone? She wasn't a married woman or a matronly aunt. She should have her *own* social calendar to attend to. One that didn't involve chaperoning two others.

"I will, of course, accompany you when I can," her mother continued, "But it will not be seemly for me to do so as I progress." She placed a hand on her stomach, as if she were actively progressing. "And now, Dorothea, I have another matter to discuss with you." Her pointed look shifted to Blanche and Nora. "Privately."

Even though the two sisters left the room and shut the door, Dottie had no doubt one of them, if not both, would be listening at the door.

"Have a seat, my dear."

Dottie took the chair opposite, suddenly feeling overwarm. Her mother plucked a letter off the nearby end table and unfolded it. "Father received this correspondence just this morning."

Dottie hid a wince at the way her mother said "Father." *Her* father was not Lord Fisher. But now, she had to listen to the man as if he were.

"His close associate, Lord Edgar Marshall, Baron of Wildenhall, will be on holiday in the same area as we are staying." Her mother smiled. "He's an older gentleman, but fifteen years is not such a leap. He's very well thought of in the *ton* circles, and he's in need of a wife."

Dottie swallowed against the dryness of her throat. She was privy to this information . . . why?

Her mother's smile grew. "Father says he is quite pleasant and well-spoken, and has a tidy fortune. Upon our arrival, we will draw up the marriage contracts."

Dottie shot to her feet. "Mother!"

Her mother lifted a hand. "Do not speak in haste, Dorothea. Not now. Not when we've been given so much. We need to be grateful for—"

"Mother," Dottie repeated, keeping her voice lower. "I will not agree to w-wed a man I've never met."

Her mother's pink flush returned. "Of course not. You will certainly *meet* him before anything is signed, but I trust Father's judgment completely, and so should you." She rose to her feet as well. "A year ago, we were nearly destitute. Your father—bless his soul—had debts that you very well know almost sent us to Scotland, begging a living off my cousins. If it wasn't for my husband, we wouldn't have any of this."

Dottie's breathing had gone shallow. Perhaps she'd prefer living in a cottage in Scotland if she could make her own choice of whom to marry. Her mother's gaze seemed to pierce straight into her heart. The woman across from her seemed a different person, a different mother than she remembered.

Joining two families hadn't been easy, and they'd all made concessions, but that didn't mean Dottie's future had to be decided by her stepfather.

"I thought I would h-have another season," Dottie said quietly. "Be able to choose a man closer to my age—a man whom I can love and have children with and look forward to spending a lifetime t-together with."

Her mother pursed her lips.

Dottie knew she'd started stuttering, an awful thing that happened when she was upset or nervous.

"Father would like you settled sooner than later," her mother said in an overly calm voice, as if she were speaking to a young child. "Next season, we will have our hands full with Blanche's coming out and the new baby. With you married and settled, we will have one less thing to worry about."

So, that's how it was. Dottie was now an inconvenience. And she knew that no matter the argument she raised, she had no suitor in the wings waiting to propose before she met Lord Marshall. Dottie was well and truly trapped.

Chapter Two

THE SOUND OF A wailing child drew Oscar's attention from the book he was half-reading in the orange-gold light of the setting sun. Normally, Oscar Rosewell ignored such distressed children at the seashore because surely there was a nursemaid or mother nearby. But this child seemed quite alone, and it was an unusual time for families with small children to be at the shore.

He frowned as he studied the small creature standing a dozen or so meters away, nearly to the water's edge. He guessed her to be five or six years of age, and she was no urchin. The ribbons and lace on her frock told him as much, along with the blonde ringlets that had likely been carefully curled earlier that day. No more. They were like a golden haystack about her head now.

Oscar sighed and rose from the wooden chair he'd planned to park himself in for the evening while he watched the sunset, enjoyed the emerging glittering stars, and reflected on this day of all days. The tenth anniversary of his parents' deaths. Oscar rarely left his ledgers and business unattended for so long, but this was the one day a year he allowed himself an entire day of reflection—on all that he'd loved, and on all that he'd lost.

Striding across the sand, he approached the crying girl. He glanced about. No one was in close proximity to the child. A man and woman were down the shore a ways, walking together arm in arm, but they were moving away from the child. Others were upon the boardwalk, but no one was paying her mind. Perhaps she'd strayed too far from her parents, and they'd lost sight of her? Or perhaps she'd wandered down from one of the nearby rental cottages overlooking the sea?

Whatever it was, this young thing was nearly hysterical.

"What's the matter?" Oscar stopped near her, keeping some distance. The last thing he needed was an angry matron coming at him with an umbrella.

The young girl barely looked at him. She pointed her small fingers toward the swelling waves of the sea. "M-my hat." The wailing started up again.

Oscar had to shield his eyes from the glowing orange sun to see that, indeed, a straw hat bobbed out in the sea. Quite a ways. Too far to wade. Swimming would be necessary.

"Where are your parents, child?" he asked.

"They're sleeping."

Oscar frowned. *Sleeping?* As in napping? Or perhaps this poor child was an orphan looked after by an elderly aunt and uncle? A quick glance up and down the shoreline told him that no one was in a mad rush to locate this child, and her hat was only bobbing farther away by the moment.

He again assessed the rise and swell of the sea. Oscar wouldn't consider himself a swimmer, but he knew the mechanics of it, so he shrugged out of his vest, then set his hat on top. Next, he peeled off his boots and stockings. He wasn't wearing beachwear, but that couldn't be helped.

"Stay here," Oscar instructed the child. At least she'd stopped her wailing. "Don't follow me into the water, all right?"

The child bit her trembling lip and nodded.

"Very good." He took a deep breath. "I'll be back shortly, and then we'll go find whom you belong to." Oscar strode forward into the water. The cold was a bit of a shock. Many people waded in it, but with the full heat of the sun overhead. Right now, twilight was fast approaching, and the water had cooled dramatically.

By the time he was waist deep, he was shivering. Doing this fast was the only way to go, he determined. He sank lower and pushed his way into the water, inhaling sharply at the cold. The hat seemed to have moved even farther out, and at a very quick pace. He swam, clumsily at first, then it was like his arms remembered the swimming of his youth. The strokes became easier, the water less cold.

At last, he snatched the hat, and then discovered he had another problem. How was he to swim while holding a child's bonnet? Only one thing to be done, and that was to wear it, while keeping his head above water at all times.

He thought he heard voices, but he couldn't be sure. The forms at the shoreline were quite blurry—the salt stinging his eyes didn't help matters. Only a few more meters. As his feet finally found purchase on the seabed, he realized he had an audience.

Quite a large one at that. Someone had joined the child, and upon the boardwalk just beyond were perhaps a dozen people. A few of them were clapping.

He wiped a hand over his face and blinked rapidly, trying to clear the salt and seawater from his eyes. He was quite aware that he was soaked, and his linen shirt and breeches had fared poorly.

"My hat!" a young voice cried in joy.

And deservedly so. He had, indeed, procured the hat. But at what cost?

He had surely created a spectacle public enough that his name might appear in the local gossip pages. Something he'd surely despise. But the only thing wounded would be his pride, and he had plenty of that to spare.

The little girl stood, hand in hand, with a woman. The lady's dark hair and nearly olive skin were in such sharp contrast to the young girl's blonde curls and fair skin that Oscar decided this woman must be the nursemaid. Or not. Her clothing was too nice for a house employee. Perhaps the governess? That was it. And by the high color on her cheeks, she was none too pleased with losing track of her charge.

Or perhaps it was the way his shirt was plastered to his chest.

"That's my hat!" the girl cried again.

"Yes, I believe it is." Oscar took the hat from his head and focused on the young girl again. It was better than noticing much else about the governess. The elegant line of her neck. The way the breeze tugged at the hair beneath her hat. The cherry of her lips...

He crouched. "It was the only one I could find out there. Are you sure it's yours?"

The little girl's smile could have lit up an entire ballroom. "It is! Dottie made it for me!"

"Dottie? Is that—"

"I'm Dottie," the woman said above him. Her tone was schooled, measured. "Officially, Dorothea Atkinson."

"She's my new sister," the young girl said.

Oscar straightened, his gaze shifting to the blue eyes of the woman who was not a governess after all. "Sister?"

"Stepsister," the woman said. "Our parents have recently married. My mother to Alice's father. And you are?"

Oscar reached up to sweep off his hat, then realized he wore no hat.

The woman's cherry lips twitched.

"Oscar Rosewell, at your service, Miss Atkinson." He had no idea if she was a miss, but he suddenly hoped so. She didn't correct him. The name Atkinson was familiar, but he couldn't quite place it. Would it be too forward to ask her parents' names? It seemed her father must be deceased if her mother had remarried.

"Literally at our service, it seems," Miss Atkinson mused.

"Yes, well, your sister seemed to have lost her hat."

Miss Atkinson looked down at the younger girl. "What did I tell you about running off without me?" Her tone managed to be firm yet kind.

Still, the young girl looked up with tears in her eyes. "I'm sorry, Dottie. The wind took my hat, and you were talking to the lady with the purple skirt, and I didn't want Mother to be angry."

Oscar watched as Miss Atkinson bent to meet the girl's eyes. "The hat is not as important as *you,* Alice. I was very worried when I couldn't find you."

Alice's lip was trembling again as giant tears cascaded down her cheeks.

"I am right here," Alice said.

Miss Atkinson nodded. "So you are, and I'm glad for it." She drew the child to her, and as they embraced, Miss Atkinson looked up at Oscar. "Thank you, sir, for your help."

"You are most welcome." Oscar was curious about this pair, which he shouldn't be. They were likely on vacation with the rest of their family. They'd be here for a few weeks, then disappear like all the others. Leaving the seashore empty, the boardwalk quiet, and the town once again peaceful.

"You are in town for a holiday?" he asked, when he probably shouldn't be prolonging this conversation, since he was standing in soaked clothing. At least the onlookers from the boardwalk had moved on.

"Yes," Miss Atkinson said. "It seems my stepfather brings his family here on an annual basis, so here we are."

The faint line between her brows told him she wasn't too happy about this holiday. Which made him curious again. "Do you not care for the sea, Miss Atkinson?"

Her gaze flitted away from him, straying to the horizon beyond. Did she know that her eyes were nearly the color of azure—a color that could only be found by an artist mixing paint on a palette?

"It is beautiful here, I must admit, but . . ." She seemed to catch herself. "There have been many changes to adjust to of late."

Oscar dipped his head. "Yes, I can only imagine."

Her gaze moved across his face, and he wondered what she saw there. "You are on holiday as well, Mr. Rosewell?"

"I am a resident of about ten years," he said. "I found that the quiet suits me."

Miss Atkinson tilted her head, and her eyes seemed to ask questions that she could not speak. "I imagine that it is very quiet here after all the tourists leave."

"Very." Oscar tried to remember the last time he'd had a conversation of any length with a woman. Surely it was before he was snubbed by the elite society. Speaking to his housekeeper wasn't the same as speaking to a young woman whose raven hair gleamed in the deep orange of the setting sun. No, he'd had no significant conversations with a woman in years, and he was well out of practice.

"Did you come from London, then?" he asked. Apparently, he was still wanting to talk to her.

She didn't seem to mind the delay. Her chin lifted just a touch. "Yes, we were there for the season and—"

"Oh my goodness, Alice! You gave us all such a fright." Two young misses came trotting through the sand toward them.

Moonlight Summer

Oscar guessed them to be seventeen or eighteen. Their blonde hair and similar features to Alice made it clear that these were relations by blood.

"Did you say thank you to the nice gentleman?" one of the young women said, her green gaze assessing him.

Well, assessing his attire—soaking wet attire, which left him at a disadvantage here.

"Yes," Alice said. "He swam in the sea to get it for me."

The young woman wasn't paying attention to the girl, though. "You are Mr. Rosewell, are you not?" she continued.

Oscar frowned. He was not a forgetful person, but he could not remember meeting either of these young women before.

"My father introduced us last year," the young woman said. "I'm Blanche Fisher, and this is my sister Nora."

Oscar tried not to hide his surprise. Leave it to the viscount to have an outspoken daughter, just like himself. "So you are," he said. "A pleasure to see you both again. Now, if I may, I'm going to return home to find a change of clothing. I wish you all a good evening." He looked down at Alice, a smile playing on his lips. "And be sure to mind your sisters more carefully. Hats do not belong in the sea."

"Thank you, Mr. Rosewell," Alice said, her own eyes twinkling.

He nodded once at her, then to her sisters. Next, he scooped up his vest and hat, and strode to his wooden beach chair, where he'd retrieve the rest of his things.

He wondered how soon the Fisher girls would find out about his family and their ruin and why Oscar and their father would never share more than a few cordial words if they happened to cross paths.

It wasn't like Oscar regretted fetching the young girl's hat, though. That had been perfectly all right. But a twinge of regret had begun to form over speaking to Miss Atkinson for so long. For letting his curiosity get the better of him. For letting his gaze linger over her lovely features.

Many women were lovely. And some women might even overlook his fallen status.

But not a woman connected to Lord Fisher. Not even a new stepdaughter.

Fisher would never allow it.

And neither would Oscar.

As much as the *ton* had shunned him, Oscar had equally shunned them.

Chapter Three

"HE *WAS* QUITE PLEASANT, don't you agree?" Blanche said as they walked back to the rented house.

Dottie knew better than to show any favor, toward or against, any man. They'd been in the seaside town of St. Johns for three days now, and it was clear Blanche was on the prowl for male attention. Preferably from a wealthy man. Just last night, she'd confided to Dottie that she hoped to marry soon. "If I don't marry before your mother has her baby, then I'll feel like a spinster."

This was ridiculous, of course. Blanche was only eighteen, two years younger than Dottie. "You'll have a season this coming year," Dottie had told her.

"Father is giving all of his time and attention to your mother, and I know once the baby comes, I'll be forgotten. Even if you are my chaperone, we won't be going to London if our parents are occupied with a baby."

Especially if it's a son, Dottie thought, and she was sure that was what Blanche was thinking as well. Dottie then realized that she hadn't been the only one displaced by this family.

"He is so very old," Nora said, her hair nearly in as much disarray as Alice's.

Alice was skipping and humming. She'd already declared that she couldn't wait to tell Mother about the nice man who'd saved her hat.

"That's because you're only sixteen, Nora," Blanche pronounced with an authoritative air. "To me, he is not so old."

"You're only two years older than me," Nora protested as she tugged at one of her ringlets that had nearly straightened.

"He can't yet be thirty," Dottie cut in. "That's an average marrying age for men."

Both of her stepsisters looked at her.

"You should marry him, then," Alice pronounced. "You're the oldest sister."

Dottie laughed, and hurried to change the subject. "Oh, there's our carriage." She didn't want this type of attention upon herself. Mr. Rosewell seemed agreeable enough—handsome too. His auburn hair had a bit of a wave to it, even when wet. He was taller than most men she'd been around, and he had a tan, as if he'd spent plenty of time outdoors. Did that mean he was the sporting type? Mostly, she'd noticed the warmth of his hazel eyes. And his kindness toward Alice.

But with Blanche already proclaiming interest, Dottie would have to put the man clean out of her mind. She'd have to forget how he somehow smelled of pine and leather, even though he'd just been swimming in the ocean. Perhaps it was how all men smelled. But even she knew that wasn't true. She'd been around enough to breathe in various colognes that were cloying to her senses.

Besides, tomorrow, she was to meet Lord Marshall. Her future husband. She ignored the flutter of nerves now blocking out thoughts of the man she'd just met.

The distance to the house was not far, but a carriage still waited for them at the end of the boardwalk. For once, Dottie was grateful they didn't have to walk the rest of the way, although there was still plenty of light from the setting sun, and the air was warm. Alice's disappearance had given her a fright, and right now, the sooner they were secured in the walls of the house, the better. She might be dreading the lecture she was sure to receive about Alice's disappearance, but Dottie would shoulder that responsibility. For she was glad Alice had been found safe. That was all that mattered.

When the carriage came to a stop in front of the house, Dottie felt the weight return—the feeling she had every time she was inside with her mother and stepfather. It was as if time were ticking down the minutes of her fate. At least outside of the house, while visiting shops, strolling the boardwalk, or eating an ice, she could ease her mind and enjoy a better perspective.

Inside the walls of this house, as well as the one in London, life revolved around her mother's wishes and stepfather's expectations.

Alice reached the front door first, and Dottie grasped her hand. "Let us explain to our parents what happened. We don't want you to be in trouble."

This gave Alice pause, and the eagerness of her expression faded somewhat.

"I will tell Father," Blanche declared. "He simply must invite Mr. Rosewell over and thank him properly."

Dottie winced at this suggestion. It wasn't that she didn't want to see the man again, and he should be properly thanked, but already, Blanche was setting Dottie's teeth on edge.

No one argued with Blanche as she headed into the house and asked the butler, "Where is the viscount?"

"In the library, Miss Fisher," he replied. "Supper is in an hour."

"I must speak to him before supper," Blanche said. She

looked back at Dottie and the others. "Come along. We all must face him."

Dottie agreed, although if she hadn't agreed, she would have still accompanied Blanche. Might as well get this over with at the same moment.

The rented house was far less grand than the Fishers' permanent residence in a county outside of London, and less opulent than their London townhouse. But this house was still beautiful in its own way, and although her mother had complained of reduced comforts, Dottie enjoyed the lighter wood, pale-colored carpets, and sumptuous seascape paintings in blues and greens.

Blanche knocked lightly on the closed library door, then entered. "Father, we're here to report on an incident."

Lord Fisher, who was sitting in a large wingback chair with a book on his lap, rose to his feet immediately. He took off the spectacles he used when reading and frowned at his eldest daughter. "What is all this?" His gaze moved from Blanche to the rest of them.

The viscount was a short man, but his presence was commanding all the same. His nose was a bit too large for his face, and thankfully, his daughters seemed to have inherited their mother's features in this regard.

Blanche explained in a rush all that had happened, and by the time she finished, the viscount's gaze had shifted to Dottie. He didn't seem overly concerned that Alice had escaped her sisters, because his one question was, "What did Mr. Rosewell say to you?"

Warmth heated her neck, and she swallowed before she replied. "He merely asked if we were a family on vacation, but it wasn't until Blanche joined us that he realized he was already acquainted with the Fishers."

Lord Fisher's gaze narrowed a touch, and he looked as if

he wanted to probe deeper, but instead he said, "Thank you for bringing the report. I'll have you know that Mr. Rosewell is not welcome in my home, no matter the kind deed he extended toward Alice. Rosewell's father and I have no friendship between us."

"Which kind deed?" their mother said from the doorway. She swept into the room and moved toward her husband. "And what is wrong with this Mr. Rosewell? Do we know him?"

Lord Fisher stiffened. "He is an old acquaintance. No one to concern yourself with. And I'll let the girls tell you about Alice. As for me, I must get back to my studies."

"Ah, you and your studies, husband," her mother said in a fond tone. "You're already a brilliant man. You should be writing these books yourself."

Dottie was impressed with how easily her mother could pump up her husband's ego—not that it needed any pumping.

"Come along," Dottie said, because she sensed Blanche was about to protest, and they didn't need a family argument. Things were still new and precarious between them all. Peacemaking was the best thing that Dottie could do right now.

Alice came readily, followed by Nora, and finally Blanche.

"Why would Father say that about Mr. Rosewell?" Blanche asked as they headed up the stairs to the bedrooms.

"I don't know," Dottie said, "but I am sure your father has his reasons."

Blanche made no secret of feeling put out, and she pursed her lips together.

After Dottie delivered Alice to the nursemaid, she returned to her bedchamber and dressed for dinner. They hadn't brought a full staff with them, and they all shared the same maid. Dottie elected to do her hair in a simple chignon that she could manage herself. So by the time Ginny arrived, Dottie only needed help fastening the buttons at the back of her dress.

Tonight would be the last dinner Dottie would eat in peace. For tomorrow, Lord Marshall would be in attendance—apparently, it would be his first night in St. Johns. Dottie was both curious and dreading the meeting at the same time. What if he was unsuitable? In *her* opinion, of course. He was suitable in Lord Fisher's opinion. Suitable in wealth and standing. But what about the other components that made up a marriage? Common interests? Shared humor? Attraction?

There was still a quarter of an hour before she was to go down to dinner, so she retrieved her sketchbook and sat in the window seat. It was now dark outside, and the moon had yet to fully rise, so she used the candlelight in the room to draw by. Her sketchbook was a diary of sorts. A way to document her days.

Yesterday, she'd drawn the boardwalk, with its lords and ladies strolling with their umbrellas to keep off the sun. Tonight, she sketched young Alice standing at the seashore, holding her hat in hand. In the distance walked a man, returning to his chair, vest and hat in hand. Dottie didn't give him much definition. No, that would seem too intrusive. Besides, what if one of her stepsisters got ahold of her sketchbook?

Still, Dottie spent another moment defining more of the Good Samaritan's wavy hair. By the time she heard her stepsisters heading down for dinner, she'd added quite a bit more detail. Perhaps she'd rip out the page and start over. Later tonight.

She checked her appearance one more time in the mirror,

then walked out of her bedchamber. Alice would be taking dinner in the nursery, like usual, and soon after, she'd go to bed.

So, Dottie stopped at the nursery for a moment, assuring herself once again that the child was safe and sound. A lost hat was nothing to fret over, but the moment that Dottie had realized Alice had disappeared was a moment she never wanted to relive again.

"Dottie!" Alice said, and rushed over to wrap her arms about Dottie's legs. The child lifted her eager face to gaze at her. "You look pretty."

Dottie smiled. Alice seemed to be the only one in the household who noticed the effort she put into her appearance.

"I can't wait until I get to go have supper with the grownups."

"It will be here before you know it." Dottie squeezed her shoulder. "I'll see you tomorrow. Remember to go to bed good for Mary."

Even as Dottie left Alice, she knew that she wouldn't be sleeping well tonight. Tomorrow, she'd meet her fate.

Chapter Four

It wasn't that Oscar was antisocial, or that he didn't have friends, but he chose to spend his weekends catching up on ledgers, reading, or working on one of his oil paintings. He was no master of art—it was more of a hobby—but he enjoyed making improvements upon whatever he'd painted last.

Current subject: the garden section that he'd convinced his gardener to let run wild. Oscar stood at the easel he'd set up this morning at first light. The sun had since climbed the sky, and if it weren't for the lemonade Mrs. Stanley had brought him an hour before, he would have quit already.

This particular garden area was only a small patch, full of briars and wild roses and seeded lavender. But it made for an interesting subject to paint. Not that Oscar was even close to Monet, but he found painting the tedious details relaxing. It took very little thought, yet somehow, it was fulfilling to see his progress.

Unlike other progress in his life.

His shipping company continued to grow, continued to expand, and continued to bring in more money than any decent fellow could spend in a lifetime. And there was the crux. He shouldn't be keeping it all to himself—in investments, that was—and sprinkled among a few charities here and there. He should be starting a family and establishing a legacy. Taking care of a wife and providing for children.

It wasn't that there weren't plenty of women to choose from—most women would be grateful for a nice home, nice things, a congenial husband, and children. But he wanted a woman he could match intellectually. Which meant she needed to be educated. This narrowed the field by half, then half again, since only high society educated its women. And Oscar was avoiding those caliber of people like one would an Egyptian plague.

So that left the women who had fallen from grace, so to speak, like him. Women whose family situations had forced them to become a governess to another woman's children, or a lady's maid to a duchess. Or women whose fathers had gambled away fortunes, then conveniently died, leaving his wife and children destitute and dependent upon relations.

Oscar dipped his brush into the oil paint mixture of two greens that he'd blended. As he dabbed the shape of a rather twisted leaf, his thoughts strayed to Miss Atkinson. She was lovely, to be sure, and although he didn't know who her real father was, her stepfather was high enough in the *ton* that Oscar would likely never cross paths with her again.

Unless Alice happened to lose another hat.

A smile curved his lips. It was nice, he decided, this smiling thing. He should do it more often, but usually there was little occasion for it.

There.

The leaf was done, and if he might say so, quite perfect.

He should really break for sustenance. The weekend wouldn't last forever, and he had planned to pay his solicitor a visit. No, he didn't expect Mr. Baldwin to discuss business on the weekend, but he'd been ill of late, and so Oscar had been doing double-duty. He'd be a good employer who checked on his employee to see how he was faring.

Oscar put away the oils and stuck the brushes in a jar of water and lye mixture. Then he rose. He'd clean up, eat, and then be on his way.

Once he'd changed into more appropriate attire—without his valet, to whom Oscar always gave the weekends off—he headed into the dining room to see the array of food Mrs. Stanley had set out.

"Is everything to your satisfaction, m'lord?" she asked in that no-nonsense tone of hers. She'd worked for his parents, and he'd kept her on so long that he'd seen the change of her dark hair to nearly full grey.

"It is. Thank you." Oscar had long since given up correcting Mrs. Stanley for calling him "my lord." She'd told him in no uncertain terms that she was his employee, and he the master who had a title, whether he liked it or not.

Mrs. Stanley bustled out, but he knew she'd be hovering nearby if he should need anything.

Oscar settled at the rather long and lonely dining table

Lonely dining table?

He'd never thought of it that way, but now, looking down the length of it assured him that yes, the table was quite empty. It could easily sit twelve, yet it was only Oscar's place that occupied the vast space. He began to eat and wondered at his reflective mood today. He'd been alone for ten years and a day now. But why today of all days was he itching over it?

All was as usual in his world.

Summer was on the decline. Final shipping runs of the season were arriving. Distribution had never been more brisk with the rise of more and more mercantile stores about the country. His days were entirely predictable. Yesterday, even though it was an anniversary day, had gone as usual for the most part. Only interrupted by the young girl losing her hat, his unexpected swim, and then meeting Miss Atkinson and her two stepsisters.

In his mind's eye, he pictured Miss Atkinson. Her observant blue eyes. The warm color of her skin that contrasted with the paleness of the other young women. The interest in her voice when she asked him questions.

Lud. Just because it had been a long time since he'd had a conversation with a woman—an unmarried woman—didn't mean he needed to continually dwell on the things that had been said between them. Oscar needed to put a woman such as Miss Atkinson out of his head. If he were truly considering finding a wife, perhaps he could write to his cousin Fredricka, who was in the know about practically everything. She was also the only member of the *ton* who purposefully spoke to him. Or wrote letters, as the case might be, since she was in London, and Oscar refused to budge.

On his way to Mr. Baldwin's, the idea of writing to Fredricka began to grow. She'd see right through his innocent line of questioning, of course, so there'd be no reason for any subterfuge. He'd just come right out and say it. They both knew he was thirty, and they both knew it was time to find a wife.

"Oh, Mr. Rosewell," Mr. Baldwin's wife said in surprise when she opened the cottage door. Hastily, she curtseyed. "What a pleasure to see you."

Oscar nodded. "Are you well, ma'am? And how is your husband?"

"Oh, I am well," Mrs. Baldwin said, her brown eyes crinkling at the corners. "It's so nice of you to ask. And my husband, well, he's much better today. He was just saying that he expects to return to full duties tomorrow."

"Good news on all counts," Oscar said. "Is he up for a visitor?"

Mrs. Baldwin's round face flushed two shades. "Oh, of course. Where are my manners? Come in, come in. I'll make a spot of tea while you visit."

Oscar was about to say, *don't trouble yourself,* but Mrs. Baldwin had already bustled off. The cottage was clean and cozy, and Mr. Baldwin was sitting near a large set of windows, a book in hand.

Before the solicitor could rise to greet him, Oscar said, "Stay seated. How are you feeling?"

"Almost mended." Mr. Baldwin adjusted his spectacles. He was a man of indeterminant age, although Oscar guessed him to be in his fifties since his two children were grown and gone. "Thank you for your visit."

The two men chatted for a few moments about business, and soon, Mrs. Baldwin brought the promised tea. Then, for whatever reason, Oscar shared the story of rescuing the young girl's hat.

Mrs. Baldwin listened, too, hovering in the kitchen doorway.

"The Fishers, did you say?" she said. "Didn't his wife pass away last winter?"

"Indeed." Mr. Baldwin took a swallow of his tea. "But it seems he's remarried."

"So quickly?" Mrs. Baldwin asked.

Now, Oscar didn't care for gossip, but he was intrigued.

"With all those daughters, it's no wonder," Mr. Baldwin said. "Three of them, did you say?"

"There were three at the seashore," Oscar confirmed. "And a stepsister too."

"Ah, so quite a houseful now." Mrs. Baldwin came farther into the room. "All in need of a husband?"

Oscar set his teacup down. "I don't believe so—at least I didn't ask."

Mrs. Baldwin only smiled and headed back into the kitchen.

"I'm sorry about that," Mr. Baldwin said in a hushed tone. "She didn't mean to imply—"

"Of course not," Oscar said, with a flick of his hand. "I haven't interacted with the *ton* in years, and don't plan to now, even if they would accept me back. There's something to be said for getting comfortable where you're planted."

"Sure, sure," Mr. Baldwin said with a nod.

A short time later, Oscar took his leave, his thoughts circling again to Miss Atkinson. He really should find some way to get her out of his mind. Why had he shared the incident with the Baldwins? Now it might come up in a future conversation, which would only keep it at the forefront of his mind.

"Whoa," someone said above him.

Oscar reared back and realized he'd stepped in front of a curricle and horse. His thoughts had been so involved that he hadn't paid attention to where he was walking. He shielded his eyes from the sun, which was just in line with the driver's head. "Sorry about that," he called up to the man.

The sandy-haired fellow nodded, then he leaned forward. "Well, well, Oscar Rosewell. Earl, now, is it?"

It had been a long time since Oscar had been called by his title. He peered at the gentleman, who did look familiar. The sandy hair that nearly touched his collar, the too-long nose, the generous freckles.

"Edgar Marshall," Oscar said. "It's been ages."

"I'll say." Right there in the middle of the road, Edgar hopped down from the curricle. His waistcoat was the brightest orange Oscar had ever seen. He'd always been an unconventional fellow, and it seemed he hadn't changed.

They'd been at school together, way back when they were both at Eton. They weren't exactly friends, but they hadn't been enemies, if that was saying something. Oscar had been several years younger than Edgar, so they didn't exactly move in the same circles.

Edgar's hand clamped down on Oscar's shoulder. "How are you doing, big man? I haven't seen hide nor hair of you. Thought maybe you'd left the continent."

Oscar laughed. "Not exactly. I've been here for years."

"*Here*?" The man's brown eyes widened.

Oscar nodded.

Edgar looked about the quaint street, with its shops and vacationers. "But why?" His gaze swung around to Oscar again. "Surely, this place is as dull as a rock when the summer is over."

"Perhaps a little dull," Oscar agreed. "But it suits me."

Edgar looked like he wanted to argue, but then his eyes narrowed. "Wait a minute . . . did I ever send condolences about your father? And mother, too, right? I was sorry to hear about their passing. How long ago was it now?"

Oscar winced. Nothing good would come of this conversation. "Ten years."

Edgar whistled. "Time sure does pass in the blink of an eye." He paused. "My apologies—"

Oscar waved off the comment. "Like you said, it's been a long time since we've seen each other. I hope you enjoy your vacation—"

"Oh, it's not exactly a vacation," Edgar said. "It's more of an . . . arrangement with a certain lady."

Oscar wasn't sure if he was hearing correctly. There were no houses of ill repute in St. Johns that he knew of.

Just then, Edgar burst out with a laugh. "Penny for your thoughts, Rosewell. Never mind. I don't want to know. The lady in question is to be my future fiancée, should she agree. It's all been arranged with Fisher."

"Fisher?" This caught Oscar's attention, and he thought through the daughters of Lord Fisher. Only the eldest was of marriageable age, he guessed.

"Ah, I know what you're thinking," Edgar said with a chuckle. "They are quite young, but it's not one of his daughters. It's his stepdaughter. Dorothea Atkinson. Fisher is making it more than worth my effort. Seems he wants her out from under his care as soon as possible."

The grin on Edgar's face made Oscar's stomach twist into a knot.

Dorothea Atkinson . . . it had to be the Miss Atkinson he'd met on the beach. He tried to picture the lovely and intriguing woman with a man such as Edgar Marshall.

"Perhaps I'll see you tomorrow night at the concert?" Edgar continued. "I'll introduce you to my fiancée." Another clap on the shoulder, and Edgar was climbing into the curricle.

Sometime later, Oscar was still standing on the edge of the road, looking in the direction that the curricle had disappeared.

Chapter Five

THIS WAS IT, DOTTIE knew, dread mixed with curiosity pooling in her stomach. The moment she'd meet her future, face-to-face. She could already hear the rumblings of the deep male voices. One her stepfather, the other Lord Marshall.

Her mother linked arms with her before they rounded into the drawing room, where the men were waiting.

"This is very thrilling," her mother whispered. "To think that my daughter will finally be married to a wonderful man."

Dottie wanted to argue, but instead, she kept quiet. Her mother hadn't even met Lord Marshall, so how could she say he was wonderful? She drew in a breath and forced her expression into something that would pass for pleasant.

The two men stood by the hearth, which had been lit with a fire, although the heat wasn't needed for the perfectly comfortable room.

They both turned as Dottie and her mother walked into the room.

"Here they are, at last," her stepfather boomed in quite a large voice for a small man.

The man next to him was a few inches taller than Dottie, at least. She knew he was fifteen years older than she, but he looked much older than that. Sandy hair threaded with gray, and his eyes were heavy with lines. His rather long nose would likely be inherited by his children. But her attention was drawn to his rather bright orange waistcoat. An interesting choice. And then he smiled.

The best she could describe it was a toothy smile. Did he have more teeth than the average person?

"Good evening," Lord Marshall said. "You must be Miss Atkinson."

"Y-yes," she croaked out. Where had her voice gone? She tried to clear it silently. "Good evening to you, sir."

Lord Marshall strode forward and took her hand, then pressed a kiss on the back of it. His fingers were cold, as if he hadn't just been standing by the hearth. A shiver trailed along her arm, and not the pleasant kind. "Tell me about yourself, Miss Atkinson. What are your likes and dislikes? For example, what is your favorite dessert?"

He had yet to release her hand. Would it be rude to pull it away? "I am quite f-fond of trifle." She exhaled, hating that her stutter was back. Her mother's gaze upon her told Dottie that it had been noticeable.

But Lord Marshall didn't seem to notice. Instead, he chuckled at her dessert remark, and finally released her hand. Dottie quickly clasped her hands together in case he got other ideas.

"I'll never turn down a well-made trifle either," he said. "Is that it? No other desserts?"

Dottie didn't know what to make about all this dessert talk. She deliberately concentrated on her words to avoid stuttering. "I'm partial to puddings as well."

Another chuckle. "Again, we are in agreement." He looked at her stepfather. "I think we are a match. Dessert will sweeten every marriage. Let's get the contract."

The viscount stuck out his hand and the two men shook.

Wait . . . had they just agreed on the marriage contract? Dottie took a small step forward, her pulse fluttering madly. "I think . . . I think I'd like some time."

Everyone stared at her.

"T-to get to know Lord Marshall." She really needed a drink of something, anything. Her throat was absolutely parched "Before making such an important decision." Smiling was the only way to cover how her heart rate had climbed sky high. She didn't know where her bravado had come from, but apparently it had appeared without any coaxing.

"Very well," Lord Marshall said in a cheerful tone, although his left eye twitched.

Bless him. For now.

Her mother grasped Dottie's arm in a rather tight grip. "Are you sure, Dorothea? There's no reason to delay. Just think, you can be introduced as a betrothed couple right away."

Although Dottie felt her stepfather's eyes burning into her, she focused on her mother. "I'm sure, and I'm grateful for the added time." She turned another sweet smile upon Lord Marshall. "Thank you for your consideration and patience."

He nodded, although his left eye once again twitched.

Dottie wished she could be anywhere but here in this drawing room, with the awkwardness becoming thicker by the moment. What was wrong with asking for more time? Surely, it was a rational request.

"Well, now that we know what we all like for dessert," Lord Marshall said in a smooth voice, "what has your cook stirred up tonight?"

Lord Fisher's brows tugged together. "I believe my wife can enlighten us."

"Oh, yes," her mother said. "It's trifle, in fact. So we will all look forward to it."

Once they were seated at the dining table, it seemed that Lord Marshall had found out all that he needed to know about Dottie, because he didn't ask any more questions. Both Blanche and Nora joined them. Nora's necklace was askew until Blanche pointed it out, and Blanche herself was wearing a fine ruby necklace, making her look older than her years.

Lord Marshall regaled the family with his love for hunting and his cook's excellent dessert-making skills. In fact, he joyfully listed his top three favorite desserts, which were all various trifles. "And that is why I'm looking forward to trying the Fisher trifle."

The viscount chuckled at this. "We will look forward to your opinion."

The dessert was served, and after his first bite, Lord Marshall declared, "This is excellent. My compliments to your cook, Fisher." Then he looked over at Dottie. "Since we are to spend time getting to know each other, I'll pick you up tomorrow night at half past six to attend the musicale at the Jacksons'. I've secured an invitation."

Dottie hadn't been addressed by him recently, so she was momentarily taken aback. She darted a glance at her mother, who spoke up, thankfully.

"She will be accompanying Blanche since I won't be attending, but Dorothea will be happy to meet you there." Her mother nodded to Lord Marshall. "Perhaps you can sit together so that you might converse easily."

Lord Marshall paused as he brought his glass to his mouth. "Ah. It is a plan, then. I shall await the lovely lady's arrival tomorrow night." His smile showed quite a few teeth.

Dottie smiled in return. Maybe she could get used to this—get used to *him*. He seemed to be of good nature, and if his reputation was sound, then who was she to complain? Just because she'd hoped for a small spark of attraction didn't mean she had to be wholly disappointed. Some ideas took getting used to, that was all.

Nonetheless, she was relieved when the men separated and went to the library for their port and cigars.

"Must we reconvene in the drawing room?" Dottie mumbled.

"Dorothea!" her mother said.

Nora and Blanche giggled.

"My apologies," Dottie said. "It's been quite overwhelming tonight, and I could do with some fresh air." She waited as her mother considered this.

"Very well," her mother said in a rare moment of grace. "I will inform Father that you are walking the terrace garden, and that you look forward to seeing Lord Marshall tomorrow night."

"Thank you," Dottie said, rising to her feet. She moved toward her mother and kissed her on the cheek. This reprieve felt heaven-sent, and she grabbed her sketchbook from her bedchamber, then headed out the back door to the terraced gardens.

When they'd first arrived at the house, Dottie was delighted to discover that the garden path led to the seashore below. It wasn't a private beach, but it wasn't all that popular. So on the days that Dottie walked the gardens, she felt like she was in her own private world.

Now, it was dark, and by the light of the moon, she made her way as far along the path as she dared. If Mother should look for her or send for her, she didn't want to be completely out of earshot.

Dottie paused at the top of the path before it sloped sharply to the sand below. The vastness of the undulating sea somehow brought her back to center again. Gave her a better perspective. Tonight, she'd sketch the serene evening scene.

Moonlight Summer

She headed down the path until she reached a boulder she could sit upon. She was close enough to the sea to smell it, but she was out of the main path of wind that came off the water.

Tonight's sketch would be simple. The hovering moon, the place its reflection touched the water, the indiscriminate outcropping of rocks here and there.

As she sketched, she thought of how many women, and men, married for convenience. It was a common thing. Marriages were hard work no matter what instigated them. Dottie had seen her mother living in two of them, and although her real father was a beloved man, he hadn't been perfect.

And Lord Fisher was far from perfect.

But they were both good and honorable men.

Was Lord Marshall?

Perhaps in time, they'd discover they had more in common than favorite desserts. Like their children.

The breeze kicked up, and Dottie pinned the ruffling pages of the sketchbook with her other hand. Her thoughts shifted again to Lord Marshall. He wasn't exactly a handsome man, but he had some charm, or at least entertaining color choices of waistcoats. She didn't know the mysteries that took place between a married couple, but she supposed if women before her could endure, then so could she.

She sighed along with the wind. She should return home now.

As she stood, another gust of wind tugged at the pages, and the sketchbook slipped from her hands.

"Oh no," she muttered as the book slid down the boulder and plopped in the sand below.

Her attention was caught by something moving to her right. Her heart jolted, and she scrambled off the boulder, her pulse pounding in her ears.

"Who's there?" she called out in a shaky voice. Perhaps she should run up the path instead of asking a question.

"My apologies," a male voice said.

Dottie's breathing froze. Her sketchbook could stay in the sand. It was time to head to the house. But could she realistically outrun a man?

She took another step backward as he came into fuller view on the other side of the boulder.

"I didn't mean to startle you," the man said, his voice familiar. "I was sitting over here when you climbed atop the boulder. I didn't make my presence known because I didn't wish to startle you."

Dottie drew in a breath. "So you sat there being silent."

"Yes."

She blinked a couple of times. She knew this man . . . Well, had met him once. Yesterday.

"Mr. Rosewell?"

He dipped his head. "Yes." He moved again, stooping. When he straightened, he had her sketchbook in hand. "I believe this is yours?"

She opened her mouth, then closed it. "Did that land on your head?"

He hesitated. "It did."

"Then it is I who must a-apologize."

"It didn't hurt . . . much."

Her eyes had fully adjusted to the moonlit darkness, so it was now clear he was smiling. Dottie didn't know if she should feel mortified or laugh. "What you must think of me. First my stepsister's hat caused y-you to take an unexpected swim, and now my s-sketchbook has surely given you a bump."

He lifted his other hand and rubbed his forehead. "No bump yet, but I shall keep you informed if you wish."

Her lips twitched, then she laughed. "I should very much

Moonlight Summer

like to know when you've recovered." She'd probably stepped outside of some boundary she wasn't supposed to. "To assure myself that you are still of sound mind."

"I think I'll survive," Mr. Rosewell said.

He really did have a nice smile, and it made him even more handsome in her opinion. Her pulse did a little leap. "Do you live nearby, Mr. Rosewell? Or do you walk miles and miles to sit next to this boulder?"

"I live right there," he said, motioning to the adjacent property. His house couldn't be seen from the viewpoint, but Dottie had seen it from the front through the large gates. She might have wondered who lived there, but no one in the family had mentioned the name of the nearest neighbor to their rented house.

"Ah, so I am intruding on *your* privacy," Dottie said.

"The seashore belongs to no one," Mr. Rosewell said. "Least of all me." He set the sketchbook on the boulder between them, as if he were reluctant to get any closer to her.

Or maybe he was being a gentleman.

Dottie moved to the boulder and picked up the book. "Well, I thank you all the same."

He nodded. "Do you often sketch in the dark?"

"No," she burst out, then stifled a laugh.

He chuckled. "That's good to know. I thought maybe you had nocturnal powers."

She shook her head, still smiling.

"And what is it that you were so fervently sketching tonight?"

"Oh." She hadn't expected that question. "Nothing special, just the moon upon the water. My sketchbook is more of a diary—in images. I sketch my experiences from the day."

Mr. Rosewell didn't laugh. In fact, he looked intrigued. "Perhaps I might see it one day?"

For some reason, this made her feel inordinately pleased. "Perhaps." Was she flirting with this gentleman—someone she hadn't even been properly introduced to? "I should get back to the house before my mother looks for me."

Mr. Rosewell nodded. "It's been a pleasure speaking with you, Miss Atkinson."

She moved toward the path as Mr. Rosewell remained by the boulder. A final time before heading up the incline, she looked over her shoulder. He was still there, but now he was looking out toward the sea, his hands in his pockets.

What an interesting man. Lonely, it seemed. She knew nothing about him, but she at least sensed his solitude. Not even her stepfather would socialize with him. What did it all mean? She was now more curious than ever.

Chapter Six

Oscar had had better nights of sleep. Just not last night.

Usually when he was restless, it was because he was worried over a delayed shipment, or a dishonest captain, or an unruly crew. But last night, his thoughts were nothing like that.

He'd been running over the conversation he'd had with Miss Atkinson. Why? He wasn't quite sure. Their conversation had been frank, but also friendly. The fact that she'd come to the darkened seashore, like he had, to seek quiet and solace was . . . intriguing.

She'd been intriguing. Miss Dorothea Atkinson. Dottie. But he shouldn't think of her that way. Her more formal title was the appropriate way to dwell on the lady in question. Well, he really shouldn't be dwelling on an almost-betrothed woman.

But what were the chances of happening to meet Miss Atkinson one day, and then the very next day running into Edgar Marshall?

Oscar's sigh was rough. He should be focused on the review Mr. Baldwin was giving about the Ferree account. Oscar tuned back in to the conversation with the man sitting on the other side of the desk in the library.

"The price of silk is rumored to be going up," Mr. Baldwin continued. His healthy color was back, and his illness had completely disappeared. "I'd recommend that we start our own price hike now, so once it hits, we are nearer to the mark. A larger price jump will be less pleasing to our vendors, should we wait."

It made sense, and Oscar was grateful to have such an intelligent man of business working for him. "I agree. A small price increase, but we will also give out a few bonus bolts of cloth to each vendor who purchases above the threshold. That way, the sting is less, and they will be accustomed to the new price when we no longer offer the bonus."

Mr. Baldwin tapped a finger against the side of his spectacles. "That might do well, indeed, sir."

Oscar gave a brisk nod. "What else do we need to discuss today?" His tone was more urgent than he intended.

Mr. Baldwin's forehead creased in surprise, but he only said, "That will be all. I've letters to write with this new offer so that the news is not fresh when the deliveries are made."

"Very well." Oscar paused, wondering if he should offer an explanation of his impatience. But there was no explanation. He was simply restless. Last night, and today. "Thank you."

Mr. Baldwin rose and gathered his papers. "Tomorrow, same time?"

"Yes, of course," Oscar said. "Until then." He and Mr. Baldwin had a long-standing meeting time every morning. It worked well for both of them to tie up any loose ends from the day before and to curtail any forthcoming issues.

Once Mr. Baldwin had vacated the library, Oscar crossed to the long windows. He stood before them, hands clasped behind his back, as he gazed over the side garden. It was the area of his untamed garden plot. From here, he could also see the seashore where he'd met Miss Atkinson the night before.

And now she was inside his head again.

This would not do.

He determined to get out, walk the town, breathe in fresh air. Hopefully, he wouldn't encounter Edgar Marshall again. Mind made up, Oscar strode out of the library and snatched his hat from the front hall table.

Mrs. Stanley must have heard his hurried steps because she came out of the dining room and said, "Is there anything you need?"

"No, thank you," Oscar said. "Tell Mr. Topham I'll be out for a few hours." Not that he expected any callers, but occasionally, a tradesman would stop in with a request. The butler's duties had diminished over the years—with so little social interaction on Oscar's part, there was very little need for Mr. Topham to attend to the comings and goings of visitors.

Oscar forewent the idea of a carriage. A long walk would do him good, and the day was pleasant enough.

It just so happened that on the way into town, he passed by Lord Fisher's rented house. It wasn't like Oscar expected to see Fisher's wife and daughters—or stepdaughter—on the front lawn. Reading, or lunching, or chatting . . . But still, he looked.

No one was outside, it seemed.

Perhaps they were in town themselves. Browsing shops. Eating ices. Walking the boardwalk.

This line of thinking was all silly, he very well knew, but his thoughts were rebelling on him. So much so that every woman he saw, he immediately scrutinized to see if she was Miss Atkinson or one of the Fisher ladies. None were, and it wasn't good for his peace of mind to be around the elite anyway. Even if they were minding their own business. Even if there was little chance anyone knew him by name.

He'd head to the seashore, then. Walk above the boardwalk so he wouldn't have to greet passersby. But before he turned toward the boardwalk, he heard a woman say, "Alice, we don't have time. The musicale is tonight, and we have much to prepare for."

The response by the young Alice was lost in a murmur of words, but Oscar knew before he turned whom he would see.

Miss Atkinson was with the Fisher girls. They stood with a couple of other young women, while Alice was tugging on Miss Atkinson's hand. Likely asking to do some other sort of activity.

Oscar took a long look at Miss Atkinson's profile, her graceful neck, her firm chin, her high cheekbones. Her angular features might exclude her from being a diamond of the first water, but her gentle way with Alice, her open and interested features, made her no second-class beauty either.

He marveled as to why a man such as Edgar Marshall had been paired with her. Such a lovely and graceful woman to marry a bumbling . . .

Miss Atkinson turned nearly in his direction, so Oscar quickly moved out of her line of sight. Then he headed toward the seashore, keeping a brisk, businesslike pace.

He nodded to a few people he passed by, but he didn't stop to talk to anyone. It took several moments before his pulse settled down enough for him to also slow his pace. Once he neared the boardwalk, he'd regained most of his faculties. But now he was overheated. He headed to a grouping of trees and stayed close to them as he continued to walk.

Had she seen him?

Had Alice? Or either of the other Fisher sisters?

No one had called to him, but they wouldn't, would they?

Lud.

This would not do. He needed more of a change of

scenery. He continued past the areas where the public gathered on the seashore and headed to the less charming part of town. The docks were a composite of laborers, sea vessels loading and unloading, carts and their horses, and general organized chaos.

"Rosewell," a man said. "Have you come to check on inventory?"

Oscar turned to see Mr. Palmer. The man was burly, eyes squinted from years of working in the sun, but he was as trustworthy as they came. He worked for Oscar as a dock foreman. *Inventory.* What a good distraction. "I have."

Mr. Palmer schooled his surprised expression. Mr. Baldwin usually handled inventory inspections, but occasionally, Oscar paid a visit.

"All right then, come this way," Mr. Palmer said. "There's been a bit of a mishap with a fishing boat that broke some of its crates, so it's best to not get in the middle of that."

Oscar followed the man. The docks were busy this time of day. Everyone trying to load or unload cargo. Boats being cleaned and repaired. Sailors looking for food and rest. Dock workers negotiating their day's wages. It was a perfect distraction.

But two hours later, after he had inspected several crates on one of his boats, then chatted with the captain of another boat, Oscar wasn't any better. He wasn't any less restless.

So he decided to put an end to his restlessness.

If Miss Atkinson went to a musicale tonight, she'd be out late. And if she decided upon her return to take a walk and sketch in the moonlight, then perhaps he could be there waiting. Perhaps they could have a conversation again. He could find out if she was betrothed. Then, he could forget about her.

The sun couldn't set fast enough.

The hours passed far too slowly, and Oscar's internal debate continued. He couldn't expect Miss Atkinson to show up at the boulder a second night in a row, could he? Certainly, he'd scared her off the night before. Besides, at the musicale, she'd be surrounded by friends and new acquaintances, something she'd probably enjoy. Being a member of high society, and all. And what about Edgar Marshall? Were *they* enjoying each other's company? Oscar hadn't asked Miss Atkinson about him, but perhaps by now she was betrothed.

Still, Oscar sat next to the boulder, leaning against it, as he had so many summer nights. It was really the only time he took to himself all day—at night, ironically. He was simply following his usual habits, and it appeared that he was listening for any sound above the sea or wind. Perhaps the sound of a footstep or a feminine sigh.

It was late, though, much later than the previous night when Miss Atkinson had come upon his revery quite suddenly. He'd frozen when he'd heard another person and hadn't moved until that book plopped onto his head. He didn't want her to come around the boulder, searching for it, then be startled out of her wits at seeing him.

She'd been startled anyway.

He was sorry for that, of course, but it couldn't be helped.

Oscar guessed the time to be nearly midnight when he decided to return home. He had an early morning, like usual, since he could never sleep past dawn. The rising sun was like a ticking clock telling his brain to wake up.

He looked down at the sketchpad he'd brought along. The sketch of the moon and sea was nothing to be pleased about. It seemed his hobby should remain with oil painting.

The sounds of scattering pebbles caught his attention. Oscar turned to see that a figure was coming down the path from the Fisher home. The moonlight made no secret that it was a woman, and Oscar hoped it was her. Miss Atkinson.

He didn't move as she neared, waiting for her to see him.

And when she did, he felt her soft smile reach across the space between them and warm his skin.

"You're here," she said simply.

"I'm here."

She was still smiling as she neared the boulder and perched on the edge. He remained on his side of the boulder because it seemed more proper that way. Not that there were any gossiping matrons about, but he didn't want anything below propriety. Besides, tonight Miss Atkinson might tell him she was betrothed, and that would mean this would be their last private conversation.

If she was betrothed, then he absolutely should not be talking to her alone on an empty beach. If she was not, then he also should not be here. Waiting for her.

Chapter Seven

―――~~~~―――

HE WAS HERE.

He'd waited for her.

Dottie knew it with every shallow breath she took—a result from hurrying through the garden and toward the seashore. Or was it because of her growing curiosity about this man?

"I didn't think you'd be here so late," she said.

"I was enjoying the night breeze."

They both knew that wasn't entirely true.

His smile seemed to defy the dark night, and she wondered what in the world this man was doing to her heart rate. He wore a jacket, but no hat, and his cravat was untied. The breeze ruffled his dark hair and stirred his scent of leather and pine in with the salty taste of the air.

Dottie noticed a sketchbook in his hands. "Don't tell me you were sketching the moon?"

His brows lifted. "As a matter of fact, I was."

She couldn't help the next smile that spread across her face. "Can I see?"

"If you let me see *your* sketch."

Dottie brought her sketchbook to her chest. "Never mind, then."

He gave a short laugh. "You are so protective of your work?"

"Remember I told you my sketching is my diary?"

"I remember."

Their gazes continued. The breeze was rather cool tonight, and although Dottie had donned a shawl, she'd been nearly shivering. Right now, though, she was far from cold. Not with this man's gaze on her.

Mr. Rosewell didn't move, didn't press his case; he only gazed at her, openly. It should have been disconcerting to have a gentleman being this candid. But she found she didn't mind it in the least.

"All right," she said in a breathy tone. "If you promise not to turn the page, forward or backward."

"I promise."

And she believed him. So she walked around the boulder as he came up toward her. They both halted when they were only a few feet apart. Then, they made the trade.

Dottie turned Mr. Rosewell's sketch more fully toward the moonlight so she could have a clearer view. It was far from rudimentary; in fact, it was well done. Very well done. He hadn't used long, sleek lines like she did in her sketches. His pen had created short strokes, but as a whole, the shape was obvious. Light playing against dark. He'd also captured tiny details of the water and sand—nuances that most art glossed over. She wondered if he was a man of science and had studied how particles made up the basis of all forms.

"Very nice," she murmured, then looked up because she felt his gaze upon her. She knew his eyes were hazel from their first encounter, although they looked as dark as warm chocolate in the night.

Then her skin heated because her sketchbook was not open to the drawing of the seashore she'd done the night before, but of another sketch from this morning: Alice sitting on the floor of the nursery, playing with her dolls. Dottie felt both relief that the sketch wasn't the one she'd done of him, and self-conscious, since a sketch of a person was much different than a landscape.

"You are very talented, Miss Atkinson," Mr. Rosewell said. "This is an interesting seashore, though."

She smiled, her pulse jumping all over the place. "Wrong page. I'm sorry. Here." She moved closer and turned the page one back to display last night's art attempt.

Mr. Rosewell was taller this close. His shoulders seemed more broad. His eyes darker. His scent... lovely.

"Ah," he murmured.

She didn't move away, nor did he.

"Your talent far outweighs anything I could ever attempt," he said.

His low voice was like a warm rumble, vibrating through her. She tilted her head, trying to see her sketch how he saw it. She considered it ordinary, lifelike, repeating what she saw onto paper. Whereas his sketch was filled with details, emotion, and depth. "I don't agree with you."

He chuckled.

The sound made her smile, and she peered up at him. "Perhaps we can appreciate each other's renditions and leave it at that."

His mouth quirked as he scanned her face. "So we don't need to continue heaping praises upon each other?"

"Precisely."

Mr. Rosewell handed over her sketchbook. "I should give you custody of this again, for I am too tempted to turn more pages."

Dottie was flattered, truly, but she took her own book and returned his. Mr. Rosewell moved closer to the boulder, distancing him a few more feet from her. He leaned against it and gazed out over the water.

His casual, unaffected stance gave her courage where she didn't know she had it. "I did not see you at the musicale tonight."

He didn't respond for a moment, but his shoulders stiffened.

Was the statement rude? Presumptuous?

"No, you would not see me at such events."

This surprised her. "You don't like music?"

He looked over at her then, his brows furrowed as if he didn't understand her question. "I am a lover of music."

He offered nothing else, so she said, "Then you don't care for dancing?"

Mr. Rosewell turned slightly, his gaze still on her. "Dancing is perfectly enjoyable." His tone was soft, and his gaze seemed to twinkle like the stars above, and it was as if he were egging her on.

Dottie moved closer to her own side of the boulder and rested a hand upon the cool rock. "It must be the crowds, then. You prefer the solitude of a dark night on the seashore to bustle and chatter?"

One edge of his mouth lifted. "I wouldn't say I love crowds, but I don't hate them either."

The breeze swirled around them both, and Dottie smoothed back an escaped strand of her hair. "It is the finery, then. You prefer untied cravats, or dropped vests in the sand, to being starched and trussed."

The other edge of his mouth lifted, and the breeze tugged at his hair. "I'll admit that casual clothing is more comfortable, but I have nothing specifically against fashion."

She almost laughed. "Can it be the *food*? Certain foods make you ill—everything but water and bread—and you've tired of explaining yourself to hosts and hostesses."

Mr. Rosewell chuckled. "If only it were so. But let it be known that I would have no problem relaying to my host or hostess my specific dietary needs, were I to have any."

A grin threatened. "Well, I quite give up, Mr. Rosewell," she said. "I can no longer stand the suspense."

He regarded her for a moment, and then his demeanor changed from humorous to somber. "Might I ask you a question first, Miss Atkinson, before I reveal my most personal reason for not attending the musicale tonight, or any other event like it?"

The back of Dottie's neck prickled with something like a warning. She hadn't felt uncomfortable at all around Mr. Rosewell, but did she really know him? The answer was no. She shifted so she was another step apart from him. "What is your question?"

"Are you betrothed to Lord Marshall?"

Any other question couldn't have surprised her more. "I—I am not."

His shoulders visibly relaxed.

It was none of his business, or perhaps it was entirely his business. He'd waited for her tonight. And Dottie had *hoped* he'd be waiting . . . "How do you know him, and how do you know that we are . . ." She swallowed back more questions.

"I ran into him on the road the other day," Mr. Rosewell said in a stiff tone. "We are acquaintances from school, and he informed me of his intentions."

Oh.

Dottie drew in a breath. Mr. Rosewell and Lord Marshall knew each other. Were they friends? The edge to Mr. Rosewell's voice told her they might not be. "Lord Marshall has not exactly proposed in the manner you are suggesting, but there is an understanding between him and my stepfather. The only missing component is my acceptance."

She had Mr. Rosewell's full attention, and his eyes, murky in color, seemed to bore into her.

"Will you accept his proposal?" Mr. Rosewell's voice was not much louder than the sighs of the sea.

Dottie averted her gaze. How could she *not* accept Lord Marshall's proposal? Yet, she continued to delay. "A woman in my position has very few options."

Mr. Rosewell waited a few beats before replying, "You may have more options than you think."

"Pray tell? Turning down Lord Marshall will incite my parents' displeasure, that is certain," she said. "And it will affect any future interest or proposal. Or if I refuse to marry at all . . . Well, that would mean I'd be under the roof of my stepfather's house for the unforeseeable future. Something I could not abide."

"Your predicament is grave indeed."

The breeze caught her hair again, and she felt Mr. Rosewell's gaze upon her as she fixed it.

"I'll tell you why I wasn't at the musicale tonight," he said after a long moment.

Dottie lowered her hands, then folded her arms. She was suddenly feeling cold.

"Ten years ago, my parents were in a carriage accident that took their lives."

She inhaled. "I am so sorry."

He only nodded; his gaze had returned to the sea. "My parents were grieving . . . the loss of my older brother, who'd died the month before from a short illness. My mother was a ghost of herself. Hardly saying a word to anyone. Spending day and night in her bedchamber. But my father . . ."

Mr. Rosewell's shoulders were stiff again.

"My father," he began again, his voice hoarse, "took to gambling and drinking. Numbing the pain and disbelief. It wasn't long before he boasted his way into some of the top card games. Lost more than he could pay outright. He was distressed that night of the accident, embarrassed over an argument with another gentleman. He'd come home in a fury—although I think he was just scared—and told Mother that she needed to move house and he was driving her that night."

Dottie couldn't move, couldn't reply. This story was horrible, tragic. Mr. Rosewell had lost his older brother and parents in such a short time.

"No one knows exactly what happened with the carriage," Mr. Rosewell said quietly. "They were found the next morning. Carriage overturned. Horses injured. My parents . . . both deceased."

"Mr. Rosewell . . ." Dottie blinked back hot tears. "I am so sorry."

He held up a hand. "I do not mean to distress you or bring pity to my situation. But, that was not the worst of it. My father's name was blighted, even after I paid his debt, which wasn't so great as it was simply embarrassing. Rumors circulated, each one more exaggerated than the last, until my father's name was no better than mud. My mother's too. I might have been able to overcome the *ton* speaking ill of my father, but not of my mother. She was an angel on earth."

Dottie's throat went tight and stung with grief. She understood loss and grief all too well—she'd experienced it with her own father. But her reputation had never been lost. Her honor was still intact.

"So, to answer your question, Miss Atkinson, I was not at the musicale tonight because some things can't be forgiven."

She nodded slowly. "I am sorry for your pain, Mr. Rosewell. I don't know why anyone would relish in another's misfortune, but you've borne the brunt of many tragedies."

He gazed at her for a moment, then straightened from where he was leaning against the boulder. "I have spent the past ten years on the fringes of society," he said. "And I've never been tempted to re-enter . . . until now."

Nothing else he could have said could have surprised her more.

Mr. Rosewell retrieved his sketchbook, then took a few steps back. "Have a good evening, Miss Atkinson."

She opened her mouth to reply, but she had no idea what to say. Instead, she watched him walk away beneath the moonlight. He turned onto a path she hadn't noticed before, and soon he was out of sight.

Chapter Eight

OSCAR SHOULD HAVE SAID nothing. He shouldn't have poured out his whole, tragic story to the unsuspecting Miss Atkinson. Sure, Mr. Baldwin knew it, and Mrs. Stanley. And many of the older members of the *ton* who remembered his parents. But Miss Atkinson was a fresh-faced young woman who didn't need to be burdened with his broken past and isolated present.

Not even the rising sun this morning had dispelled Oscar's bothersome regrets.

Perhaps he could send her a note . . . No, that would not do.

He could meet her a final time at the boulder tonight—assuming she'd appear—and apologize for the weight of the information he'd dumped on her. Tell her he'd been too presumptuous and that it was better they no longer had their clandestine meetings.

Speaking of meetings, the morning's events had concluded, and now Oscar was planning his next business trip as the library clock ticked away the time. He'd meet with several vendors, shake hands, discuss price increases, and keep a good relationship with those he worked with.

Oscar had never intended to be in trade. His father's fall

from grace had shoved aside any plans Oscar might have had of running his father's estates and maintaining social obligations that came with that. To fully separate from the *ton*, Oscar had sold several holdings, but kept the seaside estate, another smaller home in London, and the family estate, which was currently maintained by a manager. Then he'd bought boats and cargo and hired men to work for him.

Mr. Baldwin had been godsent. The man had worked in shipping for decades, and now he wanted to live a quieter life, so working with Oscar fulfilled that wish. His gaze shifted from the tall windows to the rows of books. His brother Harry had been a great student. Destined to take over the family name and estates, Harry was well-read and meticulous, and would have had no problem standing up for their father in his gambling debacle.

But Oscar . . . he always felt a step behind, even with his brother and father gone these ten years. No one was looking over his shoulder. And by any measure, Oscar's business turned a healthy profit. His investments had grown and built, and Oscar should really do something with them. Either buy up more boats, expand . . . or turn away from his bachelor days.

But what society woman would want a secluded life such as his?

Even a woman as gentle and lovely as Miss Atkinson would surely go batty if she were cut off from society because of being married to him.

Oscar straightened and rose from his chair.

Here he was, jumping ahead, and positioning a woman—specifically Miss Atkinson—in a role she'd never play. Not in this life or the next.

He shook away thoughts of her; his mind was foggy. Perhaps getting out of this seaside town for a few days, or a few weeks even, would be good. By the time he returned, Miss Atkinson would be betrothed, and quite possibly heading back to London for a wedding.

Oscar paced to the windows, then back to the desk. He could leave this afternoon, in fact. It would take shuffling a few things so Mr. Baldwin wouldn't be left in too big of a lurch, but it was possible.

Or... Oscar's gaze strayed to the line of small portraits of his mother, his father, Harry, and himself. The portraits were completed two years before they were gone from this life. Oscar hadn't even been twenty yet. In death, his family's name was marred. He was the only one left—the only who could rectify their reputation.

So... he could attend a society function. See how he was received. See if there was a chance to return to the elite.

No. He didn't want to be in their whirlwind circles. He didn't want to be back in the good ole boys' club where deals were made and favors passed on. Did he? Yet, he wouldn't want his wife to suffer outside of them. He could be detached and only attend events as necessary, and his wife could be involved to her heart's desire.

Not that he had a wife or someone in mind.

It appeared that Miss Atkinson was spoken for.

The thought made his neck itch, and Oscar rubbed it, then ran his hand through his hair. *Blast.* Edgar Marshall was a lucky man. Nonetheless, Oscar had to be grateful for his chance encounter with Miss Atkinson. She had made him realize that time was not exactly on his side, and if someone like Edgar Marshall could find a lovely woman to settle down with, perhaps Oscar could make it a priority as well.

Instead of leaving town today, tonight he'd attend a society event. Come hell or high water. But first, he had to find out where one was taking place and how to secure an invitation.

Moonlight Summer

Mind made up, Oscar stopped his pacing and fetched his hat from the front hallway. Mrs. Stanley came out of the kitchen, her hearing sharper than a hunting dog's.

"I'll be out for an hour or two," he said. "And let Mr. Topham know I'll be needing him to act as valet tonight. He might set to dusting off a few of my nicer items of clothing."

Mrs. Stanley's brown eyes widened, and she nearly sputtered when she said, "Yes, my lord. Right away, my lord."

Oscar sighed and strode out of the house.

He'd forgo a carriage again, but he'd need a horse. Once he entered the stables, he had nearly saddled Max, one of the more spirited stallions, when the head groom, Mr. Connolly, came in.

"Let me help you with that, sir," Mr. Connolly said.

The two finished preparing the saddle, and within moments, Oscar was riding off his property. He headed along the path that avoided the center of town. The place he was going was on the far side of the seaside town. It was also one of the oldest established estates and owned by his mother's sister.

Aunt Beatrice.

It had been ninety-five days since he'd seen his aunt. Why did he know this? She expected him to visit her three times a year. On the dot, to the day.

That meant this visit would be unexpected and unwelcomed.

It wasn't that Oscar didn't care for his aunt—as a relative. But even in life, Aunt Beatrice and his mother were at odds. Last year, Oscar had learned the truth, the whole truth. Aunt Beatrice had hoped for Oscar's father to propose to her. Instead, he proposed to Oscar's mother—the younger sister.

Aunt Beatrice's estate was grand and immaculate. Oscar had once estimated that over forty people worked for his aunt.

He reined in his horse at the massive gates, and a guard he recognized from previous visits stepped forward with a nod, then opened the gates.

Oscar continued at a trotting pace up the long drive, and by the time he neared the stately home, a groomsman had already appeared.

"Lord Rosewell, welcome."

"Thank you," Oscar said, trying not to bristle at his title. Correcting the groomsman would be peevish. Besides, if his plan went as he hoped, he'd be called Lord Rosewell plenty of times before the night was through.

By the time he stepped up to the front door, the butler had swung it open. He eyed Oscar for a moment, clearly surprised to see him. "Is Lady Pierce expecting you, my lord?"

"She is not, unless she has a looking glass."

The joke fell short.

"I will inform her of your arrival," the butler said, his back stiffer than his clothing.

Oscar was left alone in the grand hallways. From floor to ceiling, everything was extravagant and elegant, with marble columns, ornate rugs, and gilt-framed paintings. His aunt might have married into money, but she was still disgruntled over her lost beau.

Footsteps clipped along at a rapid pace, drawing Oscar's attention. The butler had returned. "This way, my lord. She will receive you in the music room."

Oscar followed the butler along the marble floors, and then was ushered into a room of pink and gold.

"Lord Rosewell, my lady," the butler intoned.

His aunt was seated at the pianoforte, her back straight, her fingers paused over the keys. Oscar always earned a painful jolt when he saw Aunt Beatrice, for she looked a lot like his own mother. There were differences, of course, but the woman's hazel eyes and fine features were certainly familiar. Aunt Beatrice always dressed as if she were expecting company, and today was no different, with her peach organza dress and plethora of pearls.

"I thought I was having one of my bad dreams," Aunt Beatrice pronounced as her gaze landed upon him.

Thankfully, the butler had bowed his way out of the room, because Oscar wasn't sure how to take his aunt's comment.

"Dear aunt," he said, walking forward, then bowing. "You look lovely."

She sighed and lifted one of her hands, which he grasped and kissed.

"I have a feeling I am going to regret letting you inside my home." She folded her hands in her lap but made no move to find a more comfortable chair.

Oscar crossed to the hearth, which had a low fire in it, even though the room was plenty warm on this summer day. He didn't want to sit either. "I've decided to attend a society event. Tonight."

This captured his aunt's attention, and she rose to her feet. "Really?"

He nodded.

She exhaled, but he couldn't tell if she was intrigued or bothered. "I suppose you want *me* to secure you an invitation?"

He met her steady gaze with his own. "It's been ten years."

They were no longer talking about social events and invitations.

"It has." Aunt Beatrice moved toward the hearth. Her expression was less stoic now, more . . . tender?

No, that wasn't the word.

"Perhaps it's time," Oscar said in a quiet voice, "to let them rest in peace."

Aunt Beatrice swallowed and looked away. The ticking of the clock could be heard across the room. Outside the room was only silence, as if all house activity had paused. When she next looked at Oscar, she had tears in her eyes. "I'm sorry, nephew, for all of it. And you're right. It's time to honor your parents and brother's memory by doing what they loved."

Which meant socializing, attending events, forging friendships. His mother always had a full social calendar, and his father was a congenial partner in everything. Harry was never one to lack a friend or turn down an adventure.

"I'd need only one invitation," Oscar said over the nerves climbing his throat. "From there, I can manage on my own."

"Nonsense," Aunt Beatrice said in a tremulous tone. "Consider your social calendar now full. And it starts tonight with Lady James's evening garden party, so be ready at half past seven. We will do this in style, dear nephew. I'll be picking you up in my carriage."

Oscar opened his mouth to say that he could very well take his own carriage, and that his aunt needn't trouble herself. But she leaned forward and kissed his cheek, then patted his shoulder, leaving him quite speechless.

"And don't keep me waiting," she said, her soft eyes belying her stern words. She turned, and without another pause, walked out of the room, her organza skirt swishing in the silence.

Oscar waited a few heartbeats, wondering if what had just happened had really happened. At what his aunt agreed to, his mouth went dry and his senses muddled.

It took a great deal of effort to move his feet, one in front of the other, and walk out of the drawing room. He had a lot to prepare for, and there was no turning back now.

Chapter Nine

~~~~~~~~

THE GARDEN PARTY WOULD have been more lovely and enjoyable if time weren't running out. At least according to Dottie's mother. Lord Marshall hadn't called upon Dottie that day, and her mother was worried he'd slighted her. This led to her mother requesting an audience with Dottie a short time before they were due to leave for an evening garden party.

"You can't keep a man such as him waiting much longer," her mother had said, sitting in front of her dressing table. "What if he's already put off? Father won't stand for you slighting the man, and neither will I. You had better not embarrass our family."

If Dottie hadn't been looking directly at her mother, she would have wondered if the woman speaking was indeed the same woman who'd raised her. "I don't plan to embarrass the family," Dottie said, a hot lump growing in her throat. "Perhaps he was busy today. And it's not like I even know the man. I'd like to at least know a man's character before I consent to be his wife."

"Oh, pish," her mother had said with a wave of one hand as the other hand fluttered to her belly. She hadn't started showing her pregnancy yet, but she was already acting as if she were close to confinement. In fact, she'd said she'd only stay at the garden party for a short time, so they'd taken two carriages.

Now, Dottie was regretting coming in the first place.

"There he is now," her mother said.

Dottie snapped back to the present to look to where her mother had gestured. Sure enough, Lord Marshall was standing in a group of gentlemen, who all had drinks in hand. Their conversation seemed quite lively, and there was laughing by all, Lord Marshall showing many teeth. On the other side of the group of men, a lawn bowling game had been set up. Torches lit the grassy space, and couples had formed teams.

"Make your way closer to him," her mother said. "He'll notice you soon enough, and then he'll have to speak to you. We can't let him think you've snubbed him, Dorothea. We want him to continue his interest. Pray that he hasn't already erased you out of his mind."

Would that be a bad thing? Dottie hid a sigh. Of course, it would. She needed to be more grateful, more logical. Marriage to a man who could provide for her would be a good thing.

Dottie wished Blanche, or even Nora, had been allowed to attend tonight. At least they would be someone else to talk to. But her mother had said that there would be no more social events for Blanche until Dottie was betrothed. She didn't want any distractions.

That pronouncement didn't earn Dottie any favors from her stepsisters, and the pressure was even greater than before.

"Walk with me," Dottie said. It wasn't ideal, but it was better than walking alone through the crowd, or hovering by the refreshment tables.

"I am overheated." Her mother began to fan herself as if

to prove it. The evening air was plenty cool, but Dottie wasn't going to argue the temperature.

"Bring me a glass of lemonade, my dear."

Her mother's request was the perfect excuse to move into Lord Marshall's proximity. Would he talk to her? Did she want him to? She knew she was being peevish, and how could she not be? Especially after hearing Mr. Rosewell's tragic story. Not only about the loss of his parents and older brother, but because of the way he was treated, even after paying off his father's debts.

Dottie wasn't privy to the conversations and dealings between men, but she did know that the *ton's* response seemed overly harsh. She rose from her chair, reluctant. Her mother had already started talking to another woman, so Dottie was truly on her own.

She moved through the crowd, speaking briefly to those who stopped and spoke to her. She couldn't remember everyone's names, even though she'd met most of these people more than once. The nearer Dottie grew to Lord Marshall, the more hot she felt. And not in a comfortable way. Maybe she'd get two lemonades. Even though she was walking plenty slow, she never caught his eye. She continued past, then stopped at the refreshment table. From here, she could see her stepfather with the usual cronies he conversed with at social functions.

He had seen her. Lord Fisher didn't seem to miss much, and he certainly didn't miss her lingering at the refreshment table. She picked up two glasses, and managed to thread her way back through the crowd without spilling a drop.

"You should not have returned so soon," her mother said, a crease between her eyes. "You didn't give Lord Marshall enough time to notice you."

Dottie pursed her lips as her mother drank from her lemonade.

"Go to the lawn bowling game and join in," her mother suggested. "Let him see you enjoying yourself and acting carefree. Give him something to smile about. You can't spend your entire marriage talking about your favorite desserts."

Dottie's neck went hot. "*He's* the one who asked me that question, then turned it into something of significant importance."

Even worse, her stepfather was now striding straight toward them, and his expression was quite severe. Whatever he had to say to Dottie certainly couldn't be pleasant.

"Dorothea, you are a full-grown woman," her mother said under her breath before Lord Fisher reached them. "You have an opportunity to secure your future. Now, go and do it."

Her mother might as well have shouted the last phrase, since it pounded straight into Dottie's chest. Marrying Lord Marshall would certainly get her out of the household that had become a topsy turvy existence, but would Dottie be trading one misery for another?

"Enjoying your lemonade, dear?" Lord Fisher said, placing a hand on his wife's shoulder.

She beamed up at him. "Very much. It's a lovely party, don't you think?"

His gaze down at her was brief. "I do, indeed." Then his gaze lifted to bore into Dottie. "I'm surprised to see you sitting with your mother. Don't you have someone you should be speaking to?"

By "someone," they all knew he meant Lord Marshall.

"Yes," Dottie managed to say without stuttering. "Mother and I were just talking about joining in with the lawn bowling. Perhaps Lord Marshall could be my partner."

"Excellent idea," the viscount said. He held out his hand to her, and she had no choice but to take it and rise to her feet.

"Do you want your lemonade?" her mother trilled with a smile.

"I am quite f-finished," Dottie said. Without another look at her mother, Dottie headed toward the lawn bowling game. She'd played many times, of course, and found it fun in general. She'd never done so under the guise of trying to attract a man's attention.

Again, Lord Marshall didn't seem to notice when she passed close enough for him to see her.

As she stepped up to the grassy area, it looked as if a new game was about to begin. She asked one of the women, "Is there room for another?"

The woman turned, her blue eyes sparkling, her cheeks flushed bright. "Of course, sweetie. Here. Take my spot. I am quite parched." Her laughter spilled out, and Dottie guessed that whatever the woman had been drinking, it wasn't lemonade.

The lawn ball was heavier than Dottie remembered playing with. No matter. She walked to the line where everyone was gathering. Once she took her place next to one of the women, the others noticed.

"We have a newcomer," a woman who looked to be in her thirties announced. Her green dress was embellished with extensive embroidery. "Aren't you Lord Fisher's new daughter?"

"I am," Dottie said. "Dorothea Atkinson."

The woman's smile was friendly. "I'm Lillian Wormwood, and I hope you won't take offense when I win the game."

Dottie wasn't sure if she should laugh. "I assure you, I won't."

Lillian gave her an appraising look. "Very well. Now, we need to find you a partner. We are playing in teams of two. Did you bring a gentleman with you to play?"

"I-I am here alone." Should she mention Lord Marshall? At this moment, she didn't spot him nearby.

"We don't have much time before the next round starts," Lillian said, her gaze searching the surrounding spectators.

Dottie turned to look as well. She couldn't invite someone she'd never met, could she?

"Sir," Lillian said suddenly. "Will you be this lovely lady's partner in a game?"

Dottie looked over at the man Lillian had just invited. Everything inside of Dottie seemed to still.

Mr. Rosewell was here. At a social function. The type of function he said he no longer frequented... His words from last night suddenly returned: *And I've never been tempted to re-enter... until now.*

Had he come because of... her?

He was dressed in elegant evening attire that made him look older and more sophisticated than she remembered. His auburn hair was smooth, his cravat perfectly tied, his jacket tailored to his shoulders, and his jaw clean-shaven. It was most definitely the man from the seashore, *her* Mr. Rosewell, yet tonight, he seemed to be someone else entirely.

"I would be happy to," Mr. Rosewell said in reply to Lillian's invitation.

At the sound of his voice, the one Dottie was well familiar with, a bud of warmth began in her stomach, growing as he walked toward her.

"If I knew your name, I could make introductions," Lillian said in a light tone.

"Oscar Rosewell," he said, then gave a short bow.

Lillian trilled a laugh. "I'm Miss Lillian Wormwood, and this is Miss Dorothea Atkinson."

"A pleasure to meet you both." Mr. Rosewell bowed to Dottie and gave her the briefest wink.

The warmth in her stomach moved into her chest. So, he wasn't going to admit their acquaintance.

Moonlight Summer

Lillian was apparently finished with introductions, and she turned to the others in the game. "Let us begin."

As the first couple stepped forward to take their turn, Dottie felt Mr. Rosewell's gaze upon her.

"You're at a social event," she said in a quiet tone.

"I am."

"How is it going?" She lifted her gaze to meet his. In the light of the multitude of torches, his eyes gleamed a tawny gold.

"Rather terrible. Only the buffoons have spoken to me." The edge of his mouth quirked. "At least until someone invited me to bowl with a beautiful lady."

She heard the teasing in his tone and held back a laugh. "Was that earlier this evening?"

His gaze searched hers for a moment. "If you count a handful of seconds earlier, then yes."

Dottie could smell his scent—reminding her of when she'd stood near him on the seashore. Sea breeze mixed with leather and pine. "I'm glad you agreed to be my partner. I didn't know what to expect coming over here, except for obeying orders."

His brows rose at that. She really should watch the game. Gazing at Mr. Rosewell would certainly draw notice—the unwelcome kind by her mother.

Dottie shifted her gaze to the next couple, who were getting ready to take their turn. The young woman of the pair looked to be no more than seventeen, and she was as delicate as a flower. She tossed the lawn ball onto the ground, then giggled as it rolled only a handful of feet.

Her partner, a tall man with a shock of gray hair, was certainly gallant. His toss was much better.

The surrounding spectators clapped politely.

"I hope you are better than her," Mr. Rosewell said in a quiet tone.

"I hope you are better than him," Dottie replied.

Mr. Rosewell's chuckle was quiet. "I'm out of practice, but I think I can manage."

Dottie kept her gaze forward, but she could practically feel his smile.

Soon, it was their turn. Mr. Rosewell handed Dottie the lawn bowl, and she hefted the weight of it. Then, taking a step, she tossed it. The ball rolled swiftly, then slowed at precisely the right time so as to not overtake its mark.

"Bravo," Mr. Rosewell said, then he strode forward to fetch the ball.

When his turn came, his toss was smooth, but didn't stop quite as perfectly as Dottie's had. Still, they made a good team.

"Rosewell!" a voice said from behind them. "Is that really you?"

Mr. Rosewell stiffened next to her before he turned.

Dottie turned as well.

The overset man with his small eyes studied Mr. Rosewell. "I never thought I'd see you again. What hole have you been hiding in, Lord Rosewell?"

Dottie stared at the rude man. Who was he, and why was he calling Mr. Rosewell by "lord"? Was Mr. Rosewell titled?

"What are you bellowing about at a nice garden party?" another man said, joining the first.

Dottie suspected these men had already had too much punch.

The second man sported a mustache, and his mouth gaped as if he were imitating a fish. "You *are* alive. Well, well. Are you still an earl, or did you abdicate that title after your father—"

"I've abdicated nothing, Lord Darrell and Lord Williams," Mr. Rosewell said in a cold tone. "I see you're still around too."

Dottie's chest froze. Mr. Rosewell was an *earl*? A titled man who was higher in the *ton* chain than her stepfather?

The first man, Lord Darrell, narrowed his already small eyes. "We'll always be around. What did you do? Spend the rest of your father's money, and now you're going to worm your way into a card game?"

"Does it look like I'm playing cards?"

The second man, Lord Williams, chuckled. "You always were witty." His gaze slid to Dottie. "This your wife?"

She was about to reply when Mr. Rosewell—*Lord* Rosewell— took a step forward. "Don't speak to her. If you have more to say to me, we can reconvene someplace else."

Lord Darrell took his own step forward, but Lord Rosewell easily towered over him. The two men gazed at each other for a tense moment. Others in close proximity had stopped their conversations to watch.

"You're a fool to show up after all these years," Lord Darrell said in a low tone.

"Am I?" Lord Rosewell matched his tone. "Why?"

Dottie wanted to tell all the men to stop being foolish. Lord Rosewell—an *earl*—had every right to be here. It was only a garden party, and if the host had allowed him to come, then that should be fine with everyone else.

Lord Darrell seemed taken aback by Lord Rosewell's question.

And Dottie noticed that Lord Rosewell had curled his hands into fists, so no matter how calm his words were, inside, he was far from calm.

The other man—Lord Williams—scoffed. "Some things are unforgivable, Rosewell. No matter how much money you have."

"Some things *are* unforgiveable," Lord Rosewell echoed. "But my father's debts are paid with his life. There is no greater penance than that."

It seemed neither of the men could argue with that. Something in Lord Darrell's eyes shifted, and Dottie wasn't sure if the man was more angry, or less.

"Dorothea," a sharp whisper sounded behind her.

Dottie turned to see her mother, the color in her cheeks a deep pink—something that only happened when she was angry.

"Come with me, immediately." Mother's words weren't loud, but surely plenty of the spectators heard them.

Next to Dottie, Lord Rosewell looked over at her mother. So, he'd heard too. Her mother's face went from flushed to nearly white.

Something like dread twisted in Dottie's stomach. She shouldn't have partnered with Lord Rosewell simply on the principle of knowing that her stepfather had refused to invite him to the house. Did Mother know this too? Apparently she did, because of her mother's sudden, firm grip on Dottie's wrist.

She wanted to say goodbye to Lord Rosewell, but her mother was already tugging her away.

Chapter Ten

OSCAR SHOULDN'T HAVE COME to the garden party, but he had, and now he must deal with the consequences. Whatever they might be. He'd seen the shock in Miss Atkinson's eyes about his status among the *ton*. Blast Darrell and Williams.

The only thing that was keeping him from not slugging both men in the mouth right now was the fact that he'd come with Aunt Beatrice, and he didn't want to embarrass her.

So, with every ounce of calm he could muster, he bit back each retort and argument that had been ten years in the making. He had to turn this tide of animosity, and fast.

"Would you gentlemen care to join in a game of bowling?" Oscar could practically hear the intake of breath from the spying *ton* around him.

Lord Darrell looked toward the lawn, then back to Oscar. "Lord Williams and I have important business to attend to over our card game tonight." He paused. "Business that you'll not ever need to trouble yourself over."

"Best wishes, then," Oscar said with a short bow, hoping the men would leave. Hoping that others wouldn't be so openly disdainful. He didn't know where Miss Atkinson had gone, but the crux of it was that her mother looked very familiar. And when the color in her face had drained, Oscar knew the former Lady Atkinson had recognized him as well.

What was the connection? Something with his mother? His father?

When he returned home, he'd comb through every single paper of his father's in order to discover his family's connection to the Atkinsons.

Meanwhile, Lord Darrell and Lord Williams seemed to have delivered all of their barbs, for they took their leave. Without giving him the cut direct.

Progress, indeed.

Until they disappeared through the crowd, Oscar didn't realize how tense he'd been. He wouldn't be surprised if his neck and shoulder muscles were sore tomorrow, as if he'd been in a curricle race instead of conversing with unpleasant people. He turned to Miss Wormwood. "I'm afraid I find myself without a partner, so I will have to bow out of the game."

"Nonsense." Miss Wormwood said. "I am sure *an earl* would have no problem finding a new partner."

"My daughter can be your partner," a woman said, practically shoving her daughter a step toward Oscar.

The poor young woman was blushing red, and Oscar guessed she was barely eighteen. Ah. Society and the mothers who were searching for matches for their daughters. It wasn't like he'd forgotten, or that he wasn't due for a wife, but to be faced with a blushing girl and her formidable mother made it all the more real.

"Certainly," Oscar said.

"This is Miss Vivian White, and I am Lady White," the matron continued.

Oscar bowed over Lady White's proffered hand. "Lord Rosewell. At your service, Lady White and Miss White." He

Moonlight Summer

almost choked on giving his title. But it couldn't be helped now. In for a penny, in for a pound.

It seemed not everyone in society knew of his parents' fallen reputation.

The next hour crawled as Oscar politely played the game with Miss White. He'd come for this reason, he tried to tell himself. To rejoin society, no matter how painful it might be. He was doing it for his future wife, who'd most certainly not be Miss White. But if he could get through this first social event, as awkward as it might be, the next one would only run smoother. Correct?

Even so, Oscar's skin prickled at the knowing gazes sent in his direction, and the whispered conversations that he was sure were going on.

Aunt Beatrice was in her group of cronies, gossiping surely, but *she* was on his side. So she would only speak words of support about him. Still, he felt that every moment since Miss Atkinson's departure was pointless. And the mystery of her Atkinson name was still plaguing him. Relief jolted through him when the bowling game concluded, and Oscar thanked Miss White, then left her in the care of her mother as soon as he could.

He couldn't even remember what they'd talked about. All he knew was that she blushed furiously through every sentence she spoke.

Perhaps he'd obtain refreshment, then see if his aunt was ready to depart. But he'd only made it halfway to the refreshment table when someone stepped in front of him.

"Rosewell!" Lord Marshall boomed. "I didn't quite believe my eyes when I saw you in the lawn bowl. What a surprise."

"Excellent to see you, Marshall," Oscar said, hoping his tone sounded sincere when all he wanted to do was brush past the man.

Marshall smirked. He wore a ridiculously bright purple waistcoat. "Are you sure about that? I saw you bowling with Miss Atkinson. An interesting choice, especially after what I shared with you."

Oscar's cravat was tied much too tight. "Are you betrothed, then? She did not say."

The smirk left the man's face. "Not officially," he said. "But as far as you're concerned, you need to be more careful about the women you pick to dally with."

This man deserved an uppercut to his jaw.

"I will keep that in mind," Oscar said, his tone stiff.

Marshall moved closer. "You've held back on me, Rosewell. My acquaintances have filled me in on your family situation."

Oscar's breath stalled. He didn't like this turn of conversation. Again. "Ten years is sufficient time for bygones to be forgotten."

Marshall's forehead pinched. "I guess it would depend."

"Upon what?"

"If you are like your father."

Oscar knew he should just let the challenge die. He should excuse himself. Make acquaintances with those whom his family had no previous association with. Instead, he gazed at Marshall. "My father lost his oldest son, and in his grief, he made a grievous error. He paid for it with his life. Then I paid off all of his debt to his cold-hearted friends. You did not know him at all, Marshall, and so you have no right to judge my own character. But I can assure you, no one will find it lacking as you are so implying. Perhaps you should look in the mirror yourself."

Oscar had gone too far, and he knew it. But he no longer cared. Coming had been a mistake. This had all been a mistake.

Marshall's gaze had darkened. "You'd do better to go back into hiding, Rosewell. No one wants you here."

"Are you the spokesperson for the entire *ton*, then?" Oscar looked about them, his eyes catching that of several onlookers. Some, he didn't know; others, he'd have to search his memory for their exact names.

When his gaze shifted again to Marshall, Oscar said, "No one seems to feel the same as you. They are silent. Which says more anyway." He took a step back and gave a solicitous bow. "Have a nice evening, sir."

Oscar strode past the man. The crowd parted like water encountering a rock in the middle of a stream. No one else spoke to him as he walked to the refreshment table. Still feeling multiple gazes upon him, he drank down a glass of punch.

The rest of the evening, he stood near the bowling lawn, watching other couples play, but not participating himself. Two other mothers brought their daughters over for an introduction. Oscar was polite but didn't prolong the conversations.

When Aunt Beatrice was finally ready to go, Oscar accompanied her to her carriage.

"Only a handful of run-ins is impressive, indeed," she said when they were settled inside the carriage.

"I suppose."

"Well, next time will be better," she said. "And before you tell me you've given up, remember that you made me promise not to let you give up."

Oscar sighed and looked out the window. There wasn't much to see—the homes they were passing were dark, and within moments, they'd be at his home anyway.

"She must be a special lady," Aunt Beatrice murmured.

Oscar lifted his chin. "There is no lady."

Aunt Beatrice harrumphed.

There was nothing to do but keep quiet. He didn't want to make confessions that he wasn't ready to make. Besides, he had a mission tonight. When the carriage stopped before his house, and before he could escape his aunt's scrutiny, she said, "Don't forget, in two nights' time, we are going to the Lady Ashton's ball. Her daughter has just come out, and I think the two of you might suit."

Oscar tried to hide his surprise. Aunt Beatrice only chuckled. "I'll pick you up in my carriage, so you better not bow out."

With a sigh, Oscar said, "I won't. Thank you for being my patron."

"It's only temporary," she said. "Until you can convince the buffoons that you are more than worth your salt."

It was a compliment of sorts, Oscar decided. He thanked his aunt again, then climbed out of the carriage. The night had cooled and the breeze tugged at his clothing, but he stood in his driveway for a long while after her carriage had disappeared from sight. He wasn't looking forward to going into his house, because then he knew his search would begin. And he was worried about what it might turn up.

The night deepened, and Oscar knew he couldn't put off this search any longer. He headed into the house and lit several candles in the library. He started through the paperwork from his father's estate, scanning for the name of Atkinson. Finding nothing after an hour of searching, Oscar next turned to the ledgers. The ones from ten years back were kept in the stacked boxes in one corner of the room.

Oscar had never thrown them out, nor had he shelved them. Opening the ledgers and seeing his father's handwriting caused a pang in Oscar's chest. Memories of his father flooded back. He and Harry were similar in personality and temperament. Always surrounded by friends, always engaged in one activity or another, always generous.

Oscar was more quiet like his mother. Thinking of her sweet nature only made the pang in his chest intensify. He dragged a box over to the desk, where he dug out the ledgers and stacked them on top of the desk. First, he leafed through the one that was kept during the last year of his father's life.

Oscar had been over this ledger before. It helped him determine his father's financial state before he got into heavy gambling. His father had started to sell off furniture to procure more money, and those transactions were painstakingly recorded.

When the name of Atkinson jumped out at Oscar, he froze. Then he reread the entry.

Two thoroughbreds. Purchased from Joseph Atkinson. Hired a trainer.

Another line on the next page read:

Horse races. Thoroughbred lost against Joseph Atkinson's horse.

Another line later on:

Horse races. Lost against Joseph Atkinson's horse again.

Oscar skimmed through more entries until he reached one that read:

Bought another thoroughbred to race against Atkinson.

That was the final entry with anything about Atkinson or horses. But Oscar already knew his father hadn't won any races with the expensive thoroughbreds he'd bought. So . . . Joseph Atkinson had bred horses, which were sold to Oscar's father *and* raced against him. It sounded suspect. As if Atkinson was purposely selling the thoroughbreds that were beatable.

Did his wife know about it? Did his daughter? If the man let others believe he'd given them fair deals, then that was just as criminal as his father not paying his gambling debts. Whatever had happened, Atkinson had been involved with

Oscar's family, and it was clear his former wife didn't want any association with Oscar. Which told him that she knew her husband was guilty of . . . something.

Chapter Eleven

DOTTIE WAS STILL FURIOUS by the time she reached home with her mother. Her stepfather hadn't joined them, and that was for the better. She hated how those men had treated Mr. Rosewell. No, *Lord* Rosewell, an earl. She'd had no idea of his elevated status in the peerage, and she wasn't sure if he'd assumed she knew or if he'd deliberately withheld that bit of information.

But now, who knew if Dottie would ever be able to ask him for herself?

"Come up to my chamber when you have changed for the night," her mother said in a clipped tone. This was the only conversation they'd had since the silent carriage ride home.

Once in her bedchamber, Dottie undressed herself. She didn't want to call one of the maids since she didn't want any conversation. Dottie slipped on her night rail, then drew on a robe. She crossed to the window of her room and looked out on the moonlit night. It would take her mother longer to change, so Dottie had a few moments to compose her tumultuous thoughts into a sketch.

She picked up her sketchbook and made bold, harsh lines, drawing a semblance of the lawn bowling game, the spectators and their garish expressions, then a tall man in the midst of them—standing strong and speaking the truth. She didn't bother drawing the two men who'd confronted Lord Rosewell. Dottie didn't want their renditions in her sketchbook.

Lord Rosewell had not exaggerated in the least. There was real animosity between his family and the *ton*. Mostly toward his father, it seemed, but that certainly extended to Lord Rosewell. Dottie had sensed the pain and uncomfortableness that he must have felt at the garden party. Yet, he'd come. He'd endured. He'd stood up for his family.

It couldn't have been easy. Dottie was proud of him.

But her mother's reaction had been unseemly, and Dottie was going to find out why.

She picked up one of the candles she'd lit and left her room. On her way to her mother's chambers, Dottie paused at the door of the nursery. She'd made it a habit to look in on Alice. Quietly, she opened the nursery door and stepped into the bedroom portion of the suite.

Alice was sound asleep, curled on her side like usual. Her expression in slumber was so peaceful that Dottie was envious. How would it be to sleep and dream with no worried thoughts plaguing one's mind?

When Alice stirred, a small smile flitted across her face. Dottie's heart melted at the sight. She committed the sweet scene to memory, so that she could draw the sleeping Alice later.

Dottie left the nursery and continued to her mother's chambers, dread growing with each step.

She didn't want to hear about how she must accept Lord Marshall right away. She didn't want to hear about how Lord Rosewell's family reputation also made him someone she couldn't speak to or play an innocent lawn bowl game with.

Moonlight Summer

Her mother was sitting at her dressing table, her hair uncoiled, and wearing a heavy satin robe. The fire in the hearth had been lit, and the orange glow should have made the room cheery and cozy, but Dottie didn't feel warm at all.

"That will be all, Jenny," her mother said to the lady's maid who was smoothing out the dress her mother had worn that evening.

Jenny bobbed, then headed out of the room, leaving Dottie alone with her mother.

"Sit, Dorothea," her mother said, her tone far less sweet now. "We must discuss something, and you need to listen very carefully."

Dottie felt like she'd swallowed a rock as she sat in a chair close to the dressing table.

Her mother eyed her for a moment, then said, "First, Father spoke to Lord Marshall earlier this evening. He will be paying a morning call, but we'll discuss that in a moment."

When her mother looked down at her hands in her lap, Dottie sat up straighter. It was a rare moment for her mother to act hesitant.

"Your own father . . . He and Lord Rosewell's father had some business disagreements."

Her mother looked up, and Dottie was taken aback by the sorrow there, reminding her of the first few weeks after her father's death. Her parents had loved each other, and that had always been a comfort as a child, but it also meant her mother had truly grieved.

"The night before the former earl died, he visited our home," her mother said in a quiet voice.

Nothing could have shocked Dottie more.

"He had bought horses from your father, you see, and it seemed that he wasn't pleased with their health or something." Her mother brought a hand to her chest. "I heard most of their conversation through the library door. I'm not exactly proud of eavesdropping, but I had to know what was going on in my home so late at night. Besides, I was truly fearful for your father's safety. The earl was quite belligerent."

"Was it true?" Dottie asked in a careful voice. "Did Father cheat him?"

When her mother didn't answer right away, Dottie's heart sank. Her father doing a bad business deal was just as bad as Oscar's father not paying gambling debts, if not worse.

Her mother reached for a handkerchief. "Your father told me the entire story after the old earl left our home. Father . . . didn't exactly confess to his misdeed, but I could tell the transactions were taking advantage of the man's eagerness to be a respected thoroughbred racing owner."

Dottie felt the air rush out of her. "Did Father make it up to him?" Perhaps this story had a decent ending, at least on her family's side.

"He didn't have a chance to," her mother said. "News of the earl's death reached us a couple of days later, and his numerous gambling debts were public by then. It seemed he'd been spending all hours at the card tables. Hadn't paid his debts, and he had more than one *ton* member upset. Your father was . . . I hate to say it . . . relieved. And I knew that it was because the earl's threats wouldn't come to light. No one would have the chance to take sides or think ill of your father."

Dottie didn't move, didn't reply. This was a lot to take in. She imagined the scene. An older version of Oscar pounding on her parents' door late at night, demanding audience with her father. Confronting him. An argument must have taken place. The earl went away, knowing that he'd been duped, but not having any recourse. Knowing the man who'd cheated him might not make things right—combined with his increasing gambling debts—likely the earl was distraught beyond reason.

Moonlight Summer

What had Lord Rosewell said? His parents had died in a carriage accident rushing somewhere in the middle of the night?

Dottie's stomach hurt and her head pounded. Would things have been different if her father had confessed his errors? Paid the difference? Would the earl still be alive?

"I thought you should know," her mother continued, as if she hadn't noticed Dottie's distress. "I don't want you associating with Lord Rosewell in any way. Father would agree. He doesn't even know the whole of it like we do now, and I don't want him to. Your own father deserves to rest in peace. What's done is done."

Dottie's eyes burned with tears now. "Just because the two men involved are now dead, doesn't mean that wrongs can't be made right."

Her mother's eyes narrowed. "The past will stay in the past, Dorothea. Your father doesn't need his name dragged through the mud, and that's final." She rose from her dressing table, the fire in her eyes returned. "Now, tomorrow, when Lord Marshall visits, I expect you to treat him like gold. And if he proposes, you need to be the strong young woman I raised you to be and do the right thing. You're no longer a child, Dorothea, and you cannot shirk your duties as a woman and future wife and mother."

Dottie shivered as her mind raced. Her mother's bedchamber had been almost too warm, but now all she felt was a deep chill. Almost to her bones. She stood as well, since her mother had risen. "Lord Rosewell should know the truth."

Her mother's cheeks reddened. "Do you want our reputation to be lost? Is that what you want for me? For your three new sisters? For your new father? You know how ruthless the *ton* can be."

Dottie stiffened, but she didn't look away. "Of course, I

don't want our reputations to be damaged, but Father made a terrible error, and that should be corrected."

Her mother barked out a short laugh. "*How,* pray tell? What would fix an error ten years in the past?"

"The money should be repaid." Dottie lifted her chin. "Take it from my dowry that Father set aside for me. I don't care. And if the money left over isn't enough for Lord Marshall to extend a proposal of marriage, then so be it."

"That's ridiculous," her mother spat out.

"This needs to be made right to the Rosewells," Dottie said in an even tone. "Unless you have a better idea, this is what needs to be done." Then, for the first time in her life, Dottie walked out on her mother.

She returned to her bedroom and grabbed her sketchbook, but didn't stay. She couldn't be inside four walls right now. Picking her way through the darkened house, she left through the terrace door at the back of the house. Her stepfather wasn't home yet, and it was just as well. She didn't want to run into anyone. She needed to be alone.

But she wouldn't go to the boulder at the edge of the property, because she couldn't face *him.* If he was there, waiting, how could she keep this news from him? He had every right to know. But once he did, what would he think of her? Of her family? Her own father had contributed to his father's demise. How did one rise above that?

Lord Rosewell had become a friend of sorts, even a confidante, and now . . .

That was all over.

Dottie sketched by moonlight while sitting on a bench in the garden. She could see the glowing light from the candles in her mother's bedchamber. So, she was still awake.

Dottie returned her attention to her sketchpad. Most of what she drew was likely nonsensical, but she filled page after page. Her mother sitting at her dressing table. A carriage traveling through a dark night. Miss Wormwood, who'd been friendly to her at the lawn bowling game. The rented house silhouetted in the moonlight. And then, finally, she drew Lord Rosewell at the boulder. Perhaps waiting for her. Perhaps not. His expression was one of earnestness and curiosity. An expression he might have before he knew the truth about her father, of course.

Only when her hand ached, and the candles had been extinguished in her mother's bedchamber, did Dottie finally stop drawing. She had nothing left inside of her. The emotions had all poured out onto the pages of her sketchbook. Yet, she still felt unsettled. *Tomorrow,* her mind whispered; *tomorrow,* she was supposed to accept a proposal from Lord Marshall.

Tomorrow, she'd be an engaged woman, and there was nothing she could do about it unless she wanted to hurt her mother and their new family. Any negative action on her part would also impact her stepsisters. And the thought of little Alice enduring anything she didn't deserve was unthinkable. Even Blanche and Nora. As spoiled as the two young ladies were, they were innocents in all of this.

Yet, there was something that was in her power to do. Make the situation with the Rosewell family right. But how?

She couldn't visit their solicitor herself. She'd have to have her mother or her stepfather with her, and she doubted her stepfather would give permission to have her dowry split up anyway. And her mother would be mortified if the viscount discovered their deep family secret.

Dottie gazed at the placid moon, wishing she had the answers to this dilemma. Wishing that no matter what move she made, it wouldn't bring pain. The pain would be different with each choice, but it would be pain all the same.

Chapter Twelve

OSCAR HAD BEEN THROUGH hard things in his life, but two nights ago when he discovered the connection between his father and the Atkinsons had been one of the hardest realizations he'd ever come to. He'd wanted to visit the boulder by the seashore, but he hadn't. And the next night, he'd refrained as well. Would Miss Atkinson be there, waiting to see him?

Perhaps she wanted to talk about what happened at the garden party. Perhaps she pitied the way he'd been treated by the gentlemen of the *ton*. Well, he didn't want her pity. And now that he knew the connection between their families, he couldn't very well continue their acquaintance with such a big matter between them. Whether she knew about her father's misdeeds or not.

That wasn't the issue.

Oscar knew, and that was enough. Miss Atkinson's mother would never allow Oscar to have any sort of friendship with her daughter, let alone something more. For her reaction to him at the garden party made it clear to him that she knew about the deceit of her first husband.

She was protecting her own reputation, her first

husband's, her current family's, and most importantly, her daughter's.

So be it.

Again, Oscar had been through hard things in life, so this was just one more.

The sharp rap on the front door told Oscar that his aunt was here with her carriage to pick him up. Mr. Topham had already opened the door by the time Oscar strode out of the drawing room where he'd been waiting. "Thank you, Topham," Oscar said, then nodded to the footman who'd knocked.

Oscar joined his aunt in the carriage and settled into the plush velvet seat across from her. She smiled a greeting as the carriage jolted into motion. She wore a blue gown and enough diamonds to rival royalty.

"You look lovely, as always," he said. And she did. She also looked like his mother.

Aunt Beatrice waved a hand. "I'm not looking for compliments at my age. Now. Tell me if the rumors are true."

"What rumors?"

Aunt Beatrice fixed him with her stern gaze, which was quite searing, even from across the carriage. "Is Miss Atkinson engaged?"

"How does that concern me?" He'd heard the news from Mrs. Stanley. It shouldn't have surprised him, though it had. But what did he expect? For her to put off a man such as Lord Marshall? Even if she'd wanted to, like she'd claimed during one of their late-night talks, he knew her mother and the viscount wouldn't stand for her turning down such a proposal.

"I'm no fool, Oscar." Aunt Beatrice heaved a breath. "I could see you were gone on her at the garden party."

He didn't deign to reply.

His aunt continued, unperturbed. "By the way, did you reply to Lord Darrell and Lord Williams?"

Oscar gave a curt nod. "I did."

"Very good," she said. "I know pride is a hard thing to overcome."

He narrowed his eyes. "Are you calling me prideful?" He should never be surprised at his aunt's words, no matter how caustic they were.

"All men are prideful, especially the wounded." Her tone softened, and she fiddled with straightening one of her gloves. "And you've been wounded, Oscar, there's no doubt about that. But now we can put it all behind us. Move forward. Find you a wife."

Oscar had to smile at that. "You're not wasting much time, especially since you think I was mooning over Miss Atkinson."

Aunt Beatrice arched a brow. "Weren't you?"

"I knew from the moment I talked to Lord Marshall after he almost ran me over with his curricle that he intended to propose to Miss Atkinson. Perhaps . . . I was intrigued by her, but I've quite put her out of my mind."

"Ah, perhaps I should amend my letter to Fredricka, then."

"You didn't," Oscar deadpanned. His cousin may or may not keep a confidence. It was hard to know with her. Thankfully, she was in London.

His aunt only smirked, as if she wasn't considering amending anything.

Tonight, there was a fair chance Miss Atkinson would be in attendance at the ball with her new fiancé. It wasn't going to bother Oscar in the least. He wished the woman every happiness. In fact, he hoped she never discovered the true character of her own father. The woman could live the remainder of her life in peace, for all Oscar was concerned. He would do nothing to interfere.

Oscar was now reinstated to the *ton*. Lord Darrell and Lord Williams had both written to him with apologies. Oscar had his own ideas of how those apologies came about—suspecting his aunt's involvement somehow. With Lord Marshall engaged to Miss Atkinson, there was nothing to argue over with that man either.

Regardless, Oscar's pulse thrummed fast as the carriage came to a stop in front of the Ashtons' large estate home. London might have a season, but this seaside town had its own entertainments that rivaled the best out there.

Light blazed and music soared from the open doors of the house. The night air was still warm, and the terraces on the sides of the house were also occupied with guests. Oscar climbed out of the carriage, then handed his aunt down from it. With her clinging to his arm, he led her up the stairs to the massive front doors. They were greeted by the butler first, then just inside the threshold, the Ashtons both welcomed them.

Lord Ashton clapped Oscar on the shoulder. "We'll see you in the library when you're tired of dancing. The card game and cigars will keep you entertained while the women gossip."

Everyone laughed.

It was all said as if Oscar had always been part of the *ton*. As if he hadn't been absent for ten years. As if his parents hadn't died. Oscar swallowed against the thickening of his throat. "I will be there shortly, then."

Lord Ashton chuckled. "Very well." Then he turned to greet the next people coming up the stairs.

Oscar escorted his aunt into the large ballroom and led her to her usual group of friends. They all smiled and fussed over him, so much so that Oscar was feeling like a poked pig.

"Now, go dance with some of the wallflowers," his aunt said, much to the delight of her friends, who tittered their approval.

So, he did. Now that Oscar was re-entered into the good graces of the *ton*, there was no reason for him to put off dancing with young ladies in an effort of getting to know one of them.

He asked a woman whose red hair rivaled that of Aunt Beatrice's velvet carriage seats. Miss Wenton had a high-pitched laugh, and it seemed that everything he said was quite hilarious. As long as she wasn't laughing at his dancing errors. It had been a while...

While dancing the quadrille, Oscar caught sight of Miss Atkinson. Her dark hair was arranged in an elaborate updo, and the rose color of her dress set off those pretty lips of hers. But it was the deep blue of her eyes sparkling back at him that made it hard to look away. Even with Miss Wenton as his dancing partner. He shifted his gaze, but against his will, it returned again and again. Of course, she was dancing with Lord Marshall.

Seeing the two of them together should have solidified in Oscar's mind that the pair were well and truly engaged. She was another man's betrothed now, and Oscar should let all things rest in peace. Yet, his eyes continued to wander toward her until he caught himself, and he refocused on Miss Wenton.

"I am parched," Miss Wenton said with a giggle after their final bows of the dance. "Can I trouble you to fetch me some punch?"

"My pleasure," Oscar said.

Miss Wenton giggled again, of course.

He strode from the woman, wishing he could instead detour outside and absorb some of the cooler air. And to stop

Moonlight Summer

himself from openly staring at Miss Atkinson. When he reached the punch table, he was so caught up in his thoughts of how to sneak his way outside after delivering the promised punch that he didn't notice the woman who came up beside him to fetch her own.

"Lord Rosewell."

Her tone was soft, almost a whisper, but he recognized it immediately.

For an instant, he didn't know how to react. She'd called him *Lord* Rosewell. Then he remembered his manners. "Miss Atkinson. How are you?"

"You have not come to the boulder," she said.

"No." His chest felt heavy yet light at the same time, and he didn't dare look at her, but instead, he reached for one of the punch glasses.

"I need to speak to you."

He glanced over at her then. She was standing perhaps two feet away, a glass of punch in hand. "Do you think it wise?" he asked.

"I don't care about wise," she said, her blue eyes somehow holding him captive. "It's a necessity. Meet me in an hour. In the sculpture garden."

Then she was gone. Turned and disappeared into the crowd with her glass of punch.

She hadn't even given him a chance to turn her down, to tell her that whatever she had to say couldn't change the past. This must be about her family and his family—it was all he could assume. Her mother must have told her what had transpired. And a conversation between him and Miss Atkinson in a secluded garden at a ball would not do.

If anyone saw them alone together, the scandal would be unrecoverable.

So as the hour passed, and Oscar danced with more

young ladies, he knew what he needed to do. There was no way to get a message to Miss Atkinson without arousing interest, so he hoped she'd forgive him in the end. No matter how her father treated his father, Oscar couldn't bring any condemnation to Miss Atkinson.

Instead, Oscar headed to the card room, which was really the library, set up for the gentlemen to wile the hours away, gambling and smoking. Sounded like the perfect way to forget a dark-haired beauty waiting for him in the sculpture garden. Would she be disappointed? Angry?

"Rosewell!" one of the men said as Oscar strolled into the hazy room. Whiskey and laughter abounded, and Oscar found himself seated between the host, Lord Ashton, and Lord Williams. Who would have thought?

"Now, tell us what you've been up to all these years," Ashton said, as if it was something to be discussed in public in front of a room full of men.

Oscar took a sip from the whiskey in front of him for a little liquid courage, then said, "I own Rosewell Shipping & Goods. Our main operations are here in St. Johns, but we've expanded to most of England as far as distributions go."

The room was absolutely silent as a dozen pairs of eyes surveyed him.

Perhaps Oscar should have taken more than a sip of the whiskey.

No one spoke, and it was as if he'd told them he'd sailed the world in a hot air balloon. "Have you heard of my company?"

Ashton leaned forward, his gaze intense. "Heard of it? Rosewell Shipping & Goods owns half this town."

Oscar couldn't disagree there.

Lord Ashton clapped a hand on Oscar's shoulder. "That means, my man, that you own half of us." He chuckled.

The gazes that were focused on his eased somewhat.

"Good thing you're our friend," Williams said.

"Hear, hear," someone else said, and with that, everyone raised their glasses and toasted.

"To Oscar Rosewell, Earl of Rosewell," Ashton said. "May he always prosper, and may we always stay in his good graces."

Everyone chuckled now, and as the games and smoking and drinking resumed, the atmosphere was energetic. Time and time again, Oscar was interrupted by someone introducing himself, then mentioning a piece of business they were involved in. And might Oscar be an interested investor?

Oscar deferred everyone to arranging a meeting through Mr. Baldwin first. Something that his man of business might not find so amusing. He was busy already, and now, it seemed half the town wanted an audience with Oscar.

The evening continued thus, and Oscar almost forgot about the young woman he'd abandoned. Almost.

Chapter Thirteen

LORD ROSEWELL MUST HAVE had his reasons, Dottie decided, for not meeting her in the sculpture garden. After the first few dances, she hadn't seen hide nor hair of him. Although her mind concluded that his reason was perfectly logical, and probably unavoidable, her heart said something else.

He'd learned the truth, and now he wanted nothing to do with her.

Plus, she was an engaged woman. Or had been an hour ago.

Dottie wasn't proud of all of her actions tonight, but the final action, she was standing behind.

And no one could blame her. Not even Mother or her stepfather.

When the evening had approached the supper hour, Dottie was waiting for Lord Marshall to come and claim her for the supper dance. He was late, and then he was later. She didn't want to worry, but she did. In fact, she was distraught enough to begin looking for him, and heaven forbid, asking after him.

Her mother, Blanche, and two of her mother's friends walked with her down the long hallway toward the library where the men were at their card games. Dottie was fine with Lord Marshall playing cards during the ball—they didn't need to be together all the while—but the dance was nearly over, and who would escort her into supper?

Dottie and her group of ladies didn't get as far as the library, though.

No, they were all stopped in their tracks when they heard a soft moan coming from a side hallway, darkened from lack of candlelight.

"Is someone hurt?" Blanche had said, her green eyes as wide as a teacup. "Maybe a lady has twisted her ankle, or—"

A gasp sounded next, and in the dimness, something moved. A young woman in a gray dress moved away from the wall, along with a man, whom Dottie recognized upon sight.

Lord Marshall had been in a shadowed hallway with another woman, kissing her. Dottie didn't know her name, but what did that matter? Her coifed hair sagged, and one of her sleeves was pulled so low that it exposed much of her bosom. She frantically tried to right her dress.

Lord Marshall stepped in front of the disheveled woman, as a courtesy possibly, but it only emphasized their guilt.

"Sir," her mother said. "You have quite compromised that young lady."

"Miss Bernice?" one of her mother's friends said. "What is happening here?"

"And you are engaged to my daughter," her mother continued, her tone cold.

Lord Marshall lifted his chin. "You have misunderstood. This lady is . . . my cousin—"

The woman stepped into full view, her dress righted and her hair fixed. "I am not your cousin, Edgar!" She slapped his arm, then stormed past the onlookers.

Lord Marshall's face darkened to nearly purple.

Dottie might have laughed if her stomach hadn't plummeted to the floor.

Her mother took a step forward, her finger pointing directly at Lord Marshall. "I do not want you near any of my daughters again, y-you rotten rake!" Then she grasped both Dottie's and Blanche's hands. "It's time to leave, girls. We'll have supper at home tonight."

The carriage ride home was silent. No one dared speak to Mother when her expression was thunderous. A polite supper in the dining room was out of the question, and her mother ordered trays to be sent to everyone's rooms.

Once Dottie received her tray, she could hear her mother's crying from down the hall. That, mixed with the viscount's soothing voice trying to calm her. For this, Dottie was grateful to the man.

Dottie ate little, then moved to the window seat. She wasn't even in the mood to sketch anything. The house had quieted; at least, the sound of her crying mother had stopped. When a knock sounded at the door, she nearly jumped.

"Come in," Dottie called.

Blanche poked her head inside. "Father wants to speak to you in the library."

Dottie was expecting this, but not tonight. She swallowed, then nodded. "All right. Thank you."

Blanche paused, her expression wary. "Are you all right?"

Dottie took a careful breath. "I will be."

"It's not as if you loved him," Blanche observed, her voice gaining strength.

"That's true," Dottie said. "And I'm grateful we discovered his character sooner than later." She set her sketchbook aside, then rose. Bypassing Blanche, she headed down the stairs and found her stepfather in the library.

He turned from his desk when she entered the room, his

expression grim. She stopped near one of the chairs, but didn't take a seat yet.

"Your mother told me everything," Lord Fisher said in a steely tone.

Dottie nodded. For some reason, only now were her emotions catching up to her, and she felt like crying.

"She told me about discovering Lord Marshall and that woman," he spat out. "She told me what he said."

Dottie's eyes burned with tears, and she nodded again.

"Then she told me about your father and his deceit toward the older Earl of Rosewell."

This, she hadn't expected. "She d-did?"

Lord Fisher gave a curt nod. "I have made a grievous error. I should have properly thanked Rosewell when he helped Alice at the seashore, and now it seems I owe him money on behalf of my wife's first husband."

"It can be taken from my dowry," Dottie hastened to say, wiping at her cheeks.

Her stepfather's demeanor went from stony to soft. "Your mother told me about your offer, but it won't be necessary. This is a business dealing between men. I'll send a note of apology first thing in the morning and invite Lord Rosewell to our home for supper. The financial arrangements will be made later."

Perhaps Dottie had fallen asleep at her window seat and was dreaming. But no, the room was too drafty and her stepfather's voice too loud for a dream.

"Thank you," she said in a choked tone.

He nodded, and the silence stretched between them. "I regret bringing such a man into our family's lives, especially yours. If I had only known, then we could have been spared this incident."

Something had shifted in their relationship. Dottie saw

the viscount in a different light now, as a protector, as someone who might care for her after all, as a man who loved her mother. New tears started—these ones of gratitude. "You are not to blame for his actions," she said in a quiet voice.

"Thank you for that," he said. "I'm glad you don't hold me accountable, but I am sorry all the same." He approached her and laid a tentative hand on her shoulder. "I am sorry for what you had to see tonight. And I hope you know that I consider you my true daughter and under my protection. Lord Marshall will pay for what he's done, and your reputation will remain intact."

Dottie nodded and wiped away more tears.

When her stepfather excused her, she returned to her room. She changed into her night clothes, but ended up pacing her room. Things were too silent; her thoughts too loud.

She had to move, had to think, and had to reconsider her future. Drawing on a robe, she headed to the garden terrace, where the moon was high and mellow. The breeze moved with her as she paced the gardens, thinking of how she'd finally consented to be Lord Marshall's wife, finally reconciled herself to making it a good marriage with him, and then . . .

All of her expectations for the future had been snuffed out. She would be starting over, completely. If there was one blessing in all of this, she'd rest easy knowing that Lord Rosewell would be made whole. Not completely, of course, but as much as possible. He was out in society again, and perhaps they'd cross paths from time to time, and she would be grateful in the knowledge that his life was less lonely.

Dottie eyed the bench that she'd sat upon the night before when she wanted some time with her thoughts away from the house. Tonight, she didn't want to sit—she wanted to push through the energy consuming her. She'd walk to the boulder and back, and then perhaps her mind would settle. She wasn't doing so in hopes of seeing Lord Rosewell there. His absence earlier that evening in the sculpture garden at the Ashton ball had made his position loud and clear.

The transaction would be between the men, after all. She wasn't to be included.

Dottie made her way to the path leading to the seashore. Just the sound of the sea at night was soothing already and, with each step, her heart lifted a little more. The breeze was stiffer than previous nights, and she drew her robe tighter about her. Her night clothes proved to be weak barriers this close to the sea.

She saw him before he saw her.

It could only be Lord Rosewell who was leaning against the boulder, *their* boulder, and gazing out to sea.

She paused and held her breath. She should turn around, right now, before he saw her. Wearing her night rail and robe was hardly appropriate in mixed company, and at night, alone, was even worse. Perhaps she wasn't in a shadowed hallway embracing another like Lord Marshall had—nonetheless, the hot thrum of guilt pulsed through her.

She turned away from the man in the moonlight. Before she could take two steps, she heard her name.

"Miss Atkinson, please wait."

She didn't move, didn't turn. "I'm not dressed for company. I didn't expect anyone to be here."

"I'll keep my eyes on the sea," he said. "Please, don't go. I need to explain why I couldn't meet you earlier. I'm sorry if you waited, but I could not risk your reputation should someone discover us."

Dottie slowly turned. True to his word, Lord Rosewell's back was to her, his eyes upon the sea.

"You are right, of course," she said. "I was foolish to

suggest it, but I wanted to tell you something, and I didn't want to wait."

"You can tell me now." His voice sounded hopeful and warm.

She drew in a breath. It would not be easy no matter how she framed it. So she started from the beginning, with what her mother told her after the garden party the other night. As she spoke, Lord Rosewell didn't move, didn't shift his gaze, didn't react at all. She walked closer to the boulder as she talked, and still he kept his gaze averted.

When she told him how she'd offered to pay the difference from her own dowry, only then he reacted.

"You cannot possibly do that, Miss Atkinson," Lord Rosewell said. "It is a generous offer, and I am quite humbled by it."

"I believe it's the right thing," Dottie said. "You've endured enough tragedy, and the fact that my father had a role in your father's distress has torn my heart."

There was a long pause before Rosewell replied. "Has it really?" he asked in a quiet voice.

"I don't know how else to apologize for my father's treatment of yours," Dottie said. "Tell me what to do, and I'll do it."

She wished she could see his expression right now, but his face was turned away from her.

"Your apology is enough," he said, his tone a rasp. "When your mother fetched you at the garden party, and I saw the expression on her face, I knew there was some sort of connection. I returned home and searched my father's ledgers. There was enough recorded to understand the connection between our fathers." He paused for a moment. "Truthfully, I didn't think there was any possibility of reconciling the past."

She looked over at him. He'd turned his head more, so now she could see his profile. She didn't like the sorrow and heaviness in his expression. "Whatever will help correct my father's actions, I am willing to help."

"By offering part of your dowry," Lord Rosewell mused, his tone lighter now.

"Yes."

A faint smile stole across his face. "And did your mother and the viscount approve?"

"Well, no," Dottie said, her own smile appearing. "But my stepfather said he's going to write to you in the morning with an apology, for both not formally thanking you for helping out Alice, and to make the business deal right."

Lord Rosewell's eyebrows shot up, and he glanced at her, then quickly away. "This is . . . unexpected. I don't want him to be obligated—"

"It's already settled, if you agree." She moved closer to him. The breeze had died down for a moment, and she breathed in his scent of leather and pine. "I think you should agree. It's the right thing for everyone, and it will let us all move on from the mistakes of the past."

Lord Rosewell lowered his head, his gaze now on the boulder before him, his hands braced on the rock. "The offer is coming from a man who had no part in it."

"Lord Rosewell," Dottie said in a soft tone. She was so close to him, yet he was still not looking at her, just as she'd requested. "You deserve generosity."

He was so silent that she could hear her own breathing above the sea.

She wondered what was going through this man's mind. He'd been through so much, and now someone in the *ton* was extending an olive branch in a most specific way.

Finally, when he spoke, his voice was gravelly. "And what about you, Miss Atkinson? Will your dowry stay intact, and Lord Marshall won't need any explanation?"

He didn't know. Of course, he didn't know. If he'd left the ball before the stir, then he'd be oblivious.

"Lord Marshall will never hear another word from me, about anything," she said, gazing at his profile. "We are quite finished."

Lord Rosewell's brows tugged together. "What are you saying?"

She might as well tell him—it would be all over town tomorrow anyway. "My mother and I caught him in a compromising situation with another woman. I didn't have to say a word—my mother took care of that for me. There is no longer an engagement between me and Lord Marshall."

Lord Rosewell exhaled. "Are you heartbroken?"

The question was so unexpected that Dottie laughed. "Heavens, no. I mean, it's a strange position to be in—finding myself without the expectation of marrying the man. But I did not love him . . . if that's what you mean."

He gave a brief nod, keeping his eyes to the moving sea beyond. "Might I call on you tomorrow, Miss Atkinson? Properly? In the daylight? At your home?"

For the second time that night, Dottie felt as if she were in a dream. But the breeze was cool, the sounds of the sea rhythmic, and the man next to her living and breathing. "Yes, I'd like that."

Chapter Fourteen

PERHAPS OSCAR HAD KEPT Miss Atkinson talking too late last night, and he could only hope that she'd had a good night's rest after all that they had said. Which had been a lot. After they worked through the fact that Miss Atkinson didn't need to feel obligated for her father's choices, and she didn't need to carry any guilt for Oscar's father's demise, they talked about art. And music. And places they'd been as a child. He told her about his brother, Harry. She told him about what it was like to suddenly have three younger sisters.

All of this conversation with his gaze on the sea, and only her profile in his peripheral vision.

And now, in another moment, he'd be walking into her home.

Oscar had elected to walk over to their house—it wasn't so far, after all. So many thoughts had passed through his mind since last night's conversation with her, and then upon receiving the invitation from Lord Fisher.

Oscar rapped on the double front door, and moments later, it swung open, answered by a butler.

"Lord Rosewell, welcome," the butler said. "Lord Fisher is expecting you in the library."

"Thank you," Oscar said.

There was no sign of activity as he followed the butler through the grand entrance, then down a wide hallway. Soon, the butler tapped on a door that was halfway open, and announced Oscar.

"Welcome," Lord Fisher said, moving out from behind his desk. The shorter man extended his hand, and Oscar shook it.

"I appreciate you coming on short notice when I'm sure you have plenty of business to attend to," the viscount said, appraising Oscar. "Quite a stir was caused last night when the gentlemen of St. Johns learned that you are behind Rosewell Shipping."

Oscar nodded. "I'm afraid that my solicitor might be out of sorts with all the inquires this morning. Most of the gentlemen of the *ton* don't associate with shipping companies, so I was able to stay anonymous until now."

Fisher chuckled. "There's no going back now. Now, have a seat."

Oscar had well-guessed how this conversation would go, and he'd already prepared his answer. After Fisher explained how he came about learning of Lord Atkinson's betrayal, he then offered to pay the amount owed, plus interest.

At this point, Oscar lifted his hand. "You both honor and flatter me with your offer, but I must decline. This in no way is a manifestation of my pride, but because I intend to ask something else of you. And if you're amenable to it, then I would not, could not, feel good about settling a debt that's ten years in the past."

At this, Fisher's heavy brows raised. "Speak, sir. I'm all ears."

"With your permission, I'd like to court your stepdaughter, Miss Atkinson."

Fisher blinked. Blinked again. Then he chuckled. "Well... she is available, I suppose. Nothing can be kept secret for long."

"I suppose not."

Fisher leaned back in his chair and folded his hands across his vest. "I will give my permission, if you think she'll be amenable?"

"I believe so," Oscar said, hiding a smile. "I've encountered her a few times, and we seem to be in accord, at least in conversation."

Fisher chuckled again. "Well, then. Let's see what she has to say."

Before Oscar could get over his surprise, Fisher reached for a bell on the corner of the desk and rang it. The butler appeared at the doorway immediately, as if he'd been hovering, waiting for the sound of the bell.

"Please inform Miss Atkinson that she is needed in the library."

"Yes, my lord," the butler said, then disappeared as swiftly as he'd appeared.

"While we're waiting, I also wanted to invite you for supper tonight," Fisher said. "Alice has been asking about the man who saved her hat, and I'd love to tell her that he's still around. Saving things."

Oscar didn't know whether to laugh or frown, but he said, "I'd love to come to supper." Another chance to see Miss Atkinson would never be turned down. That was, of course, if she was accepting of his offer of courting.

"Did you ask for me?" Miss Atkinson said, coming into the room.

For a brief moment, Oscar observed her before she noticed him. She wore a simple day dress, much different than the ballgown of the night before, and of course, the night clothing after that. Her hair was down, reaching to the middle of her back, and he couldn't decide which Miss Atkinson he liked better. There was no doubt she was a beautiful woman in all ways, and she'd completely captured his attention.

But that still left the question of what she thought of *him*.

"Come in, Dorothea," Fisher said. "Lord Rosewell is here at my request, and it appears he has turned down my financial offer, but he has a request of his own."

Miss Atkinson's blue gaze had shifted to him, and by the flush on her cheeks, he knew she wasn't expecting this encounter. Or perhaps she was, and nonetheless she was pleased with it.

"Well, Rosewell, are you mute now?"

Oscar hadn't realized he was taking over the conversation. So be it. He stepped forward and cleared his throat. It wasn't like he was nervous or hesitant . . . all right, so he was nervous. "Miss Atkinson, I spoke to your stepfather and asked for permission to court you. He is amenable if you are."

Her eyes searched his face as her cheeks pinked further. "I . . . It . . ." She exhaled. "I am a-amenable."

Oscar had heard her slight hiccup on words before, but in this case, at this moment, it was the most lovely thing she could have expressed. A smile pushed its way onto Oscar's face, matched by Miss Atkinson's own smile.

"Well, you two, the day will get away from us soon enough," Fisher said. "Take a walk through the garden before the sun sets."

Oscar chuckled; Miss Atkinson's cheeks flushed.

"And don't forget about supper tonight," Fisher said as Oscar walked out of the library with Miss Atkinson.

She led the way along the hallway until she reached the terrace doors that led to a set of gardens. The sea was visible beyond the gardens.

"Dottie!" a young voice called.

She paused on the terrace. "Alice, are you out here by yourself?"

"Mary said I could pick some flowers and come right back." Alice noticed Oscar, and she beamed at him. "You're that man! The one who saved my hat."

"That's right," Oscar said.

"Say hello to Lord Rosewell, Alice," Miss Atkinson said.

"Hello," Alice said in a formal tone, which only made Oscar chuckle.

"Hello," he repeated. "Those are beautiful flowers."

"They need water!" Alice exclaimed.

"You'd better get them to Mary so she can help you," Miss Atkinson said, and Alice scurried into the house.

Miss Atkinson began to walk deeper into the garden, Oscar walking alongside her, his hands behind his back.

"Well," Miss Atkinson said, "I'm not sure I like that she was out here by herself. You know a bit of her personality."

"You're a good sister to her," Oscar said.

She slowed to a stop. Her blue eyes found his, and it seemed that things went still between them. "Are you sure you want to court me?" he asked.

Her smile reappeared, the one that he'd grown very fond of. "I'm sure." She tilted her head as she studied him. "You know that I'd be happy in a quiet life. I don't need all the fuss of society if you are against it."

"Now you tell me."

The look on her face told him she took him seriously.

"I'm teasing, Miss Atkinson," Oscar said. "Yes, meeting you might have propelled me to take action, but the time was due." He stepped closer to her, and asked again, "Are you sure you want me to court you?"

The flush of her cheeks warmed his heart.

"I am sure."

He held back a grin. "Care to give me a tour of the gardens?"

She nodded, and he extended his arm. When she fitted her hand around his forearm, he decided he liked the weight of it, very much indeed.

They walked, arm in arm, through the gardens, with Miss Atkinson pointing out her favorite plants. "I've drawn a few of them, you know."

"I'm not surprised," he said, looking down at her. How was it that her eyelashes were so dark? And were the light freckles dotting her nose new? "Do you prefer being called Dorothea or Dottie?"

She bit her lip. "Dottie, I think. My mother calls me Dorothea when she's upset, so Dottie is more friendly."

"Hmm."

"And you? Do you have a nickname?"

"For Oscar, no." He winked at her and smiled as he drew her to a stop beneath a shady tree. "So what should I call you?"

She smiled back. "Dottie."

"Very well, Dottie, shall we walk to a particular boulder that I'm fond of?"

She laughed, and the merry sound wrapped itself around his heart, tight and secure.

"Certainly," she said, "but maybe we should enjoy this bit of shade a little longer."

Oscar looked up at the overhanging branches above them. The day was proving to be warm, and this shady spot was refreshing. Then he looked down at Miss Atkinson—Dottie—and in her eyes he saw promise, and anticipation, and a future he hoped would be a part of his.

Her smile was slow, warm, and it reached into his heart, making it thump. Somehow, it gave him courage. "Dottie, might I be bold and ask you something personal?"

Her brows lifted into a perfect arc. "What is it?"

"Since we're officially courting, might I kiss you?"

The blush on her cheeks was instant, but she didn't draw away. In fact, she took a step closer, and whispered, "I think that would be wise."

Since Oscar wasn't one to waste much time, he drew her against him, then lowered his head. Brushing his mouth against hers, he could swear that every chattering bird and buzzing bee paused as they kissed. He could only hear the thud of his heart and the soft sigh of the woman kissing him back.

When her arms looped around his neck, and she pressed against him, he was pretty sure he entered into an elevated state of existence. He kept the kissing light, though, considering they were not entirely alone and this was only their first day of courting.

It was a good day—possibly the best day Oscar could ever recall.

"Dottie," he whispered against her lips. "You are beautiful in every way, but now I must release you, or I'll completely lose my wits."

Her lips curved into a smile, then she exhaled and stepped away. "I suppose we'll go visit that boulder, then. I wouldn't want to be courting a witless man."

Oscar secured her hand about his arm, then bent close and kissed a spot below her ear. "I am at your command, Dottie. Whatever you want, you shall have."

She settled her other hand around his arm, bringing them closer. "I already have what I want."

Oscar couldn't agree more, and courting Dottie Atkinson was just the beginning.

Heather B. Moore is a *USA Today* bestselling author of more than seventy publications. Her historical novels and thrillers are written under pen name H.B. Moore. She writes women's fiction, romance, and inspirational non-fiction under Heather B. Moore. This can all be confusing, so her kids just call her Mom. Heather attended Cairo American College in Egypt, the Anglican School of Jerusalem in Israel, and earned a Bachelor of Science degree from Brigham Young University. Heather is represented by Dystel, Goderich, and Bourret.

For book updates, sign up for Heather's email list: hbmoore.com/contact
Website: HBMoore.com
Facebook: Fans of Heather B. Moore
Blog: MyWritersLair.blogspot.com
Instagram: @authorhbmoore
Twitter: @HeatherBMoore

www.ingramcontent.com/pod-product-compliance
Lightning Source LLC
LaVergne TN
LVHW021800060526
838201LV00058B/3177